Family Business

FAMILY BUSINESS

Mark Eklid

HI CAROL

HOPE THIS IS A DIVERSION FROM LOOKING TO FIND JOBS FOR YOUR NEW LIVE-IN HOUSEHUSBAND

Copyright © 2020 Mark Eklid

All rights reserved.

Independently published

ISBN: 9798648417045

To my partner, Sue

Prologue

They were probably dead. I knew that as soon as I arrived at the scene. You develop an instinct when you've been doing this for as long as I have.

The call from Control said there were reports of fatalities and, naturally, you suspect the worst when you hear those words but as soon as you respond to say you're on your way you're already thinking about the best route to get you there as quickly as you can. The sooner you can get there, the better. You never just assume the worst. You should never assume anything in this job because it's rarely straightforward and often surprises you – sometimes in a good way.

I reckoned I was only about five minutes away when the call came through that night and, because it was so late, there was hardly any traffic around, so I got there no problem. I was the first on the scene.

I started to slow down when I saw the hazard lights of a car parked on the left of the road. There was nobody else around, so I reckoned these had to be the people who had called the accident through. It was the end of a fairly long straight stretch at that point, just before the road turned to the right, and there was no street lighting, so you could see the intermittent blinks of amber light for quite a while in the full beam. I killed the sirens and slowed down.

It's a bit of a relief, actually, when you see that the witnesses have stayed and waited for you to get there because they don't always. Sometimes they'll drive off when they see the police car arriving. Maybe they think they've done their bit or maybe there's a reason why they don't want to talk to the police at that time, I don't know, but you have to make sure you get a clear look at them on the camera as you drive up, just in case, so that you've recorded their number plate. This time they stayed, which is good. It means you can get a statement from them without having to go through the hassle of having to track them down later.

I pulled up a bit of a way behind the car because I could see in my headlights a gap in the hedge to my left and the steam rising from another vehicle where it had come to a very sudden halt against a very large tree. The other car was a bit further down the road. I positioned my car on an angle, pointing towards the crash scene so that it was illuminated by my headlights, and left the blues going. If anyone was to come down the road from either direction, you want them to see there had been an incident and, hopefully, they work out that they're not meant to try to continue along the road. You can set up proper road blocks when other units arrive, but you have to do all you can as soon as you get there because it's important to preserve the scene for the Serious Collision Investigation team to do their jobs properly.

I radioed through to Control.

'This is Mike Foxtrot Three.'

'Receiving, Mike Foxtrot Three.'

'I'm on the scene now. There appears to be only one vehicle involved and I'm just about to go to have a look. I'll update shortly.'

'Got that. There are three units on the way and Fire and Ambulance should be with you very soon.'

'OK. Can you divert a couple of those units to close off the road from both directions please, approaching from Upper Whiston and Morthen?'

'On to it, Mike Foxtrot Three.'

'Thank you.'

When I got out of the car, that's when I knew, really, that there was very little chance of getting them out alive because it was too quiet. When you get to a crash scene, if you're the first there, you sometimes have to prioritise and when you have people who are screaming and shouting you want to help them, of course you do, but it's the ones who are quiet and not moving that you have to be most worried about. They're the ones you should check on first but sometimes, of course, there's nothing you can do for them.

There was no noise at all that night. It was a lovely, still, late summer night with no wind. It was almost respectfully quiet. I do remember hearing a burst of a horn from what sounded like a heavy lorry on the motorway in the near distance and the sound sort of lingered mournfully in the air for a while but it was only later, when I knew more, that the sound felt like it carried extra significance.

I could see the tyre skid marks in the light of the headlights, snaking first to the right and then sharply left towards where the vehicle had come to a halt through the hedge. My first thoughts were that they might have been trying to avoid hitting an animal in the road. There were fields on either side of the road, so that's always possible. It's surprising how many accidents are caused by people trying to avoid running over a fox or a badger.

The doors of the other car opened when the people inside saw me walking towards them and I gestured to them to stay by their car. A woman in her twenties got out of the driver's seat and a man, about the same age, got out from the passenger side.

'Are you OK? Are you the ones who called through to 999?'

The woman nodded.

'It must have only just happened when we got here. The horn was going off and the lights were still on when we pulled up.' She spoke quickly, almost tripping over her words she was so keen to pass on the information.

'Callum went over to see if there was, you know, anything we could do but he said it looks like they're both dead.'

I glanced over to the lad. He looked really shaken and was staring towards the crash scene with narrowed eyes, like he was both repelled and irresistibly drawn to the horror of it, unable to take it all in. He said nothing.

Poor kid. It's tough to deal with, no matter how many times you see it. I do sometimes get affected by it myself but usually only later, when you finally get to sit down and have a bit of time to yourself. There's so much you have to do that you can't think about it at the time. You go into what I call 'police mode'. It sounds cold to say but you only have a brief interaction with the victim in a fatal, so it doesn't affect you that much. It's a different matter if the victims are young though – especially babies and small children. That really gets to you.

'Thank you for your patience but can I ask you to stay in your car for a bit longer until either myself or another officer can get a few details from you. I appreciate it's very late.'

'No, no, that's OK,' said the woman. 'We understand.'

She turned and climbed back into the car. It took the man a few seconds more before he could break the thrall the crash scene held over him and he was able to tentatively back away to join her.

I unclipped the Maglite off my belt and took a deep breath as I followed the trail of the skid marks. I could see the car was a right mess. It was a little red MG convertible. An absolute classic. Must have been somebody's pride and joy but it didn't offer very much protection to the poor buggers inside when it hit a bloody big tree at what must have been a fair speed. I picked my way through the gap in the hedge and shone the torch over to the front of the car, which had been crumpled by the impact. The force of it had bent the car at a 30 degree angle.

It was a two-seater and I could already tell, from the angle the car had come to a rest against the tree, that both seats were occupied. I approached from the driver's side and took a pair of disposable gloves from my jacket pocket.

It can be difficult to get to the occupants sometimes in a crash like that but there wasn't an issue this time because the roof was down. I pressed my fingers against the driver's neck to see if there was a pulse but, of course, there wasn't. The steering wheel had practically embedded itself in his chest. He must have died instantly.

I had to go round the other side of the tree to get to the passenger and I shone my light around the immediate area in case anyone or anything had been thrown clear of the car but I couldn't see anything.

The windscreen appeared to have taken an impact blow from inside the car and I was able to confirm that when I reached the passenger. Her body had recoiled from the collision to slump lifelessly back in the seat after her head had hit the glass. She was turned towards me with fixed, blank, open eyes staring through a mask of blood and matted hair across her face. I checked. No pulse.

I stepped back through the gap in the hedge and could hear another police car approaching. I radioed through to Control with an update.

'Mike Foxtrot Three.'

'Receiving, Mike Foxtrot Three.'

'I have two occupants who both appear to be deceased. We have one male driver and a female passenger, both of them look like they are in their mid-fifties. The vehicle is a red MG convertible sports car, registration number...'

I shone the torch on the back plate.

'... yankee one hotel juliet lima.'

'10-4 that, thank you.'

The second police car had pulled up on the far side from the witnesses' car, blocking the road from the opposite direction. I recognised it was Dave Wood as he climbed out and put his cap on. I walked over towards him to have a word but, in the glare of his headlights, I could see what looked like another fresh single tyre skid mark. This was on the left side of the road as I walked towards it, which then curved towards my right. I dropped to my haunches and had a closer look under the torch light.

'Hey, Sarge.'

'Now then, Woody,' I said. 'Does this look pretty recent to you?'

He dropped down beside me.

'Could be. What are you thinking?'

'Judging by these marks, I'd say there was a motorbike heading from your direction which has drifted to the wrong side of the road coming round the bend and he's been forced to brake heavily and swerved when he's seen the car coming towards him. There are skid marks from the crashed car just about 50 yards from here, heading from the opposite direction, and they go to the right first before they swerve off to the left towards the tree. I thought at first it might be an animal in the road that he was trying to avoid, but I wonder if the driver saw the bike on the wrong side of the road heading straight towards him, veered right to try to avoid a collision and then he's seen the bike trying to get back on to the correct side of the road, so he's veered left and lost control.'

Woody nodded. 'What's the situation with the car?'

'Both dead.'

He nodded again.

'You'd better have a good look over to the right there, in case a bike has gone off the road and we've got another victim here. I don't think there's another car involved – did you see anything on the way down?'

He shook his head.

'Have a search further up the road just in case there's anything we've missed. I'll have a word with the witnesses to see if they can tell me anything about a bike.'

'Righto, Sarge.'

We both stood up and headed our separate ways.

I tapped on the window of the car. The driver looked like she was trying her best to comfort her bloke, who had his head in his hands and visibly jumped when he heard the tapping noise. The driver buzzed open the window.

'Sorry to keep you. I will get an officer to you very soon if you'd be good enough to give us a statement but, in the meantime, could you tell me if you noticed a motorcycle at all as you drove here?'

'Yes we did!' Her face lit up at the recollection. 'There was a bike. It was coming in the opposite direction and it wasn't half moving, wasn't it, Callum?'

She turned to him but he barely acknowledged the prompt.

'It whizzed past us about half a mile up the road before we got to the crash.'

I took my pocket notebook out of my jacket.

'Do you have a dash cam at all?' I had a quick look. I couldn't see one.

'No, we haven't. Sorry.' She looked disappointed, as if she fully expected me to censure her for being a bad witness, which was kind of sweet of her.

'No bother. I wonder if you could tell me anything else about the bike. Do either of you know much about them?'

Occasionally, you can get very useful detailed information when you're dealing with bike enthusiasts.

'Not really. Sorry.'

'That's OK. What sort of bike do you think it was – a big powerful one or a little moped?'

'Definitely a big one. It was quite loud as it went past us.'

'Single headlamp? Double headlamp?'

'Err, single.'

'One person aboard or two?'

'One. I think. Yes, one.'

'Did you see the colour of the bike or the colour of the

clothing the rider was wearing? What about the colour of the helmet?'

'It was very dark,' she said, apologetically.

'I appreciate that. Anything you can tell us will be helpful.'

'I think the bike was dark-coloured and I think he was wearing proper leathers, you know, but I do remember seeing a flash of red from his helmet.'

I wrote it all down. It wasn't a great deal to go on, but it was a start. You don't know at the time if the information has any relevance but, as I said, you never assume anything in this job. So I thanked them for their co-operation again and called the information through to Control, just in case any of the other cars had spotted a motorcyclist still on the road matching the description or if they come across an abandoned bike. You never know.

There were more officers on the scene by then and the ambulance had rolled up as well. I could see Woody giving them a bit of a briefing, probably just to confirm to them they didn't need to hurry. I went back to the car to get an incident pad so I could start the log. I'd already decided I was going to pull rank and turn it over to Woody after I'd done my bit. I knew he wouldn't thank me for that.

I looked at my watch. It was just after one. There's never much chance you can get away from the scene until the end of your shift when you're dealing with that sort of incident but that's the way it goes.

1

'Excuse me.'

The old man peered over the counter to where a thinning crown of greying hair bobbed to the noise of rummaging.

The sound of plastic against plastic was interrupted momentarily by a few indecipherable muttered words of frustration before what was clearly an, as yet, unresolved search continued.

The old man rocked back on his heels and peered over again. He was starting to get the feeling he had not been heard, so he cleared his throat and spoke again.

'Excuse me.'

The activity stopped. The bobbing head rose to reveal the face, beneath the lightly perspiring forehead, of a flustered man in his mid-fifties.

'Oh, I'm sorry, sir, I didn't realise you were there. I'll be with you in a few secs. I just need to find this... I know it's in here somewhere because I...'

The process of moving plastic around carried on.

'You can never put your hands on the flaming thing when you need...'

The old man cleared his throat again.

'Is this the family history place?'

The search would have to wait. The customer comes first. The man strained to ease himself off his creaking knees and rose to his full height.

He was not especially tall, a bit above average maybe, and had the slight physique of one who made no effort to stay in shape because he had no cause to. He wore metal-rimmed glasses and a dark shirt and had a city council name badge on a lanyard about his neck. It settled against his chest, the right way forward, to show the old man, if he had cared to look, that he was talking to Graham.

Graham drew a deep breath, put on his best 'you now have my full attention' smile and said: 'The Local Studies Library, that's right, sir. How can I help you?'

The old man stared blankly for a few seconds, as if he had forgotten why he was there in the first place, his mouth slightly agape, waiting for the words to come.

'Aye, well, I've been watching that programme on the telly, you know the one with the famous people – well, I say famous, I've never bloody heard of half of them – anyway, the one where they find out about their ancestors and that. Are You What, Where Do You – oh, I can never remember what they call the bloody thing.'

'*Who Do You Think You Are?*' He had allowed the floundering to go on for long enough.

'What?' The old man was taken aback, not sure if the bloke on the other side of the counter had suddenly become confrontational, before the realisation dawned.

'Aye, that's the one. Have you ever seen it?'

If he had a pound for every time someone had asked him that question – when dealing with customers or when he told people for the first time where he worked – Graham reckoned he would now be spending his days in his own villa in the Canaries instead of fetching and carrying dusty volumes for dusty customers in a run-down Local Studies Library. He sighed.

'Yes, I've seen it.'

'Bloody good programme. It gets a bit irritating when they start blubbing over somebody who died 150 years ago, but bloody good programme. Anyhow, I was watching it the other day and I decided I'd like to do my family history. Make sure the stories can be passed down when I've, you know, gone.'

Graham smiled.

'Good idea. A lot of people come here for exactly the same reason. Can I ask you, Mr…'

'Smith.'

'Mr Smith.' Not a promising start. 'Have you ever done any work on your family tree before or has anybody else in your family had a go?'

'I haven't. I don't think anybody else has. Not as far as I'm aware anyway.'

'OK, no bother. We've got access to the two major family history research websites at the library and either myself or one of the other members of staff here can show you how to get started. Those are our computer terminals over there.'

He gestured to a row of six screens on a raised dais to his right. A man and a woman, both well into their sixties, were at chairs in front of two of them, concentrating hard on the information on the screens. The woman scribbled a note on a pad beside her.

'Computers!' Alarm filled the face of the old man, as if a ghastly fate had just been revealed to him. 'I'm no good at computers.'

That could make it tricky.

'I'm afraid everything is done through the computers. There'll usually be somebody at hand to help you when you get stuck, but you'll have to do most of it on your own.'

'Can't you sit and do it with me?'

The question carried the air of a plea. It was easy to forget that not everyone was hooked to the internet for substantial chunks of their life.

'I'm afraid we're not allowed to do that. We're here to direct you but that's it.'

The old man looked lost.

'Perhaps there is someone you know, a younger relative maybe, who would be able to help you on the computer side of things?'

'Aye, maybe. There's my niece. She's always playing about on her phone, you know, like they all do these days. She'll know.'

Graham's attention was caught by an interaction on the other side of the central counter.

'Excuse me a second, Mr Smith.'

He called to where another member of staff was fielding a question from another customer.

'Nadeen!'

The colleague and the customer both looked towards him.

'Is this about box five?'

Graham recognised the man in the baggy blue sweater as the person he had fielded a query from earlier and had told he would retrieve the documents he wanted within a half-hour because he was dealing with a request from another customer first. That was about ten minutes ago.

'Yes, that's right,' said the baggy blue sweater.

'I will bring it up for you, sir, very shortly. I haven't been able to see to it yet.'

'Oh, that's OK. No hurry.' With a wave of a baggy blue sleeve, the man returned to pawing over the day's newspapers.

'Sorry about that, Mr Smith.' His attention was back with the old man, who still appeared to be wrestling with the concern that he had got himself into something far more onerous than he had envisaged.

'The advice we give to people like yourself who are looking to build their family tree from scratch is to start with what you do know. Put together a list of names of people from the previous generation, like your parents and their brothers and sisters, and then see if you can add names for their parents as well – your grandparents and their siblings. It's also a really good idea that you talk to other older members of your extended family, like cousins, and ask them if they have any stories about your shared ancestors. If anybody has any documents – birth certificates, marriage certificates, that sort of thing – they can be a big help as well. Do you know much about your parents and where they came from?'

The old man pondered.

'My dad's family were all from around here, I think, but my mum's family were Welsh. I'm sure she was born in Wales.'

'Oh, yes? Do you recall her maiden name?'

'Jones.'

Ah!

'What about old family stories? Do you know of any of those? People who fought in the World Wars? Unusual family legends?'

'Well,' the old man's thoughts were drifting to the darkest recesses of his memory. 'I remember my mum telling me about her Uncle Gareth. He was a miner in Wales and a great big bloke. You know, huge.'

He held out his hands to give an estimated width of an unspecified part of great-uncle Gareth's considerable anatomy.

'She said there was this one time when a little boy got into bother in the hills because he'd slipped and fallen over the edge and had come to rest on a narrow ledge 20 feet down with a sheer drop below him.'

'Oh dear!'

'Anyway, the men were sent for and came up from the valleys to rescue him and it was my mum's Uncle Gareth who volunteered to be lowered by a rope around his waist to the ledge with, you know, the other men at the top holding on.'

'Very brave.'

'Aye, it was. He reached the ledge and tied the rope around the boy for the others to pull the lad to safety. They'd just got him clear when the ledge gave way under Uncle Gareth's weight and he fell all the way down the side of the cliff – and do you know what?'

The old man raised his finger, poised to deliver the denouement to this thrilling family tale of great heroism.

'I bet you're going to tell me he survived the fall with barely a scratch and was back at work down the mines the next day.'

'What?' The old man's expression changed to bemused disbelief.

'Don't be daft. He was killed stone dead. Broke every

bone in his body, I should think.'

Graham realised it was time he got on with something more pressing.

'Lovely talking to you, Mr Smith, and, as I said, chat to as many people as you can to put together some background information and then I'm sure you'll be able to find out a lot more about your ancestors like Uncle Gareth. I must warn you that starting out with surnames like Smith and Jones means you might not find it as straightforward as some folks with more, shall we say, distinctive surnames, but I'm sure we can still get you there.'

'Oh, I see.' Mr Smith appeared unwilling to take the hint and close the conversation.

'Have you done your family tree then?'

Graham sighed internally and smiled.

'I have. I've been able to trace my family back to the 17th century so far.'

'What's your second name then?'

Here we go. Graham braced himself.

'Hasselhoff.'

The information rattled around the old man's brain for a second or two. He appeared pained as he wrestled to reconcile it with the big bell of recognition it had rung.

'You mean like that actor fella? Are you related?'

If he had a pound for every time someone had asked him that question, Graham reckoned he would be able to afford to line the swimming pool at his theoretical villa in the Canaries with real gold.

'No. No relation at all.'

'Oh!' The old man still appeared reluctant to end the discourse. Years of working at the library had more than adequately prepared Graham for dealing with people who had far too much spare time on their hands and had lost all sense of recognition that other people had jobs to get on with. He had natural depths of patience but it was tempting sometimes to want to tell customers to shut up and go away. He never had.

'Funny surname, though. Where's that from?'

'It's German but my family on my dad's side came from a small town on the Netherlands side of the German border, so they were all Dutch.'

'Very exotic.'

Graham gave him a tolerant smile. 'They weren't really. All I've found is generation after generation of peasant farmers who grew up, farmed and died within a few miles of the same small town. They were even largely unaffected by two World Wars. It wasn't until my dad moved to England in the 1950s that anybody really did anything different. My mum's family were mostly miners and, going a bit further back, farm labourers, so they were a pretty dull bunch as well.'

The old man stared blankly back. 'Aye, well, I can't stand around here chatting all day, I've got things to do. I'll do what you said about making a list and talking to folk and I'll see you soon.'

With that, he turned and walked towards the exit.

'I'll look forward to that,' Graham called after him, without too much irony in his tone.

He shook his head. Where was I? Box five.

He was intercepted on his way to the file storage room by his colleague, Nadeen.

She often bore the demeanour of one who was carrying the problems of the world on her shoulders and now was no exception.

'Have you heard anything?' she asked in the hushed tones of a conspirator who did not want to arouse undue suspicion as she pulled her cardigan tightly around her slim waist.

There had been rumours of redundancies. Again. More council funding cuts.

'I haven't heard anything. Have you?'

She shook her head, anxiously.

'As I said, I can't see them cutting anybody else here. We're already down to the bare minimum. If they lost another job here, the library wouldn't be able to run properly and who would see to all these customers? That has to count for something, surely?'

Nadeen did not look reassured. She had not been sleeping very well since the latest rumours began circulating. How could she keep up the rent on the flat and take care of the cats if she didn't have her job?

'Try not to worry. They're only rumours.'

She nodded but not convincingly. Graham touched her upper arm and she moved away, still clutching on to herself through her cardigan pockets.

He watched her walk busily away. He knew how she felt. All the talk was very unsettling and he didn't believe for a minute that the library service was untouchable. The council needed to save more money and something had to give. They were a soft option.

He attempted to dismiss the thought again. What was I doing?

A man in a baggy blue sweater rose expectantly.

Box five.

2

He crouched behind the cover of a large pine tree and watched as the security guard completed a rudimentary check of the open yard then lowered himself wearily back behind the wheel of his patrol van.

The April night cold had long since seeped through his layers of dark clothing to stiffen his joints as he tried to stay low to the damp ground in the only spot where it was possible to keep out of sight and yet still be able to overlook the whole yard from beyond the perimeter fence. It was crucial to make sure nobody was still around when it was time to make his move. He wanted to be sure it was done without detection. Clinical. Like a commando. Quick strike and go. For that, he had to stay patient and wait until the time was right.

The van did not move. The guard was clearly in no hurry to get to the next place on his list.

It had been a relief to see the van turn up so early. You could never be sure what their timings would be. It had to be random or it would be too easy to beat the system. The only way to do this was to get in place as soon as it turned dark and wait. Stay patient. A few more minutes won't hurt.

Finally, he heard the sound of the engine fire. He withdrew a little further into the shadows as the red rear lights pierced the pale white of the yard arc lamps and the van moved slowly, reluctantly, towards the exit gates. He watched until the luminous yellow flashes on the side of the van could no longer be seen and listened until the sound of the engine, shifting through the gears, could no longer be heard. Then he waited a little more.

It was time.

He knew where it was easiest to get over the fence, out of view of the cameras, and picked up the grey plastic jerry can by his side, then pulled down the black balaclava to cover his face, leaving only his dark eyes exposed. He eased down the grass bank, still careful not to make an unnecessary sound. Just in case. He moved deliberately, rigidly, towards the metal security fence, trying to ease the chill from his joints for the next part of the exercise.

The tree was at the bottom of the slope and he gazed up towards the sturdy overhanging branch he had identified on one of his reconnaissance missions, then looked across to the top of the rusting shipping container on the other side of the fence. A gap of about a metre and a half. Slightly higher on the tree side. He fancied he could cover the distance in one leap without snaring himself on the jagged tops of the fence posts but it wouldn't be easy.

He stretched out the muscles of his legs and hips to dispel the chill from the parts the adrenaline had not yet reached and, gripping the jerry can in his left hand, took a firm grip on one of the lower branches with his right to begin to haul his burly frame up the tree, using whatever purchase he could find from his robust boots to scale higher until he was able to swing his feet on to the overhanging branch where it met the trunk of the tree.

He checked the yard to make sure there was still no-one around and then surveyed the gap to the shipping container. It appeared further than it did from the ground but it was still achievable, as long as he got his leap right. Find a solid base for your feet and jump with conviction. Trust your athleticism.

The branch felt solid but he squatted and raised himself rapidly, several times, until the whole tree shook, to reassure himself it was able to bear the stress of his leap. If it gave way, he could be hurt and the mission would fail. Best to make sure. The branch passed the test.

One more check of the yard. Clear. Go for it. He gripped the trunk of the tree with his right hand and the jerry can in his left, focused on his landing area and rocked forward one, two, three before propelling himself off his right foot into the night air, flying momentarily like a heavy black shadow until he landed with a dull thud on top of the shipping container.

He crouched, unmoving and silent, to be certain no-one had heard the noise and had been alerted by it. All was quiet. All was still. Good.

There was room between the shipping container and the fence for him to lower his frame to the ground. Three wooden pallets had been dumped there. He spotted them and piled two of them next to the container, then propped up the third against it, on top of the others. That would help him climb back up after he had done the job. Do the job, climb back up, jump over the fence on to the soft ground beside the tree and disappear into the night before the alarm was raised.

Peering from the side of the container, he surveyed the yard again and gazed towards his target. A pile of pallets stacked a metre high, four pallets long and three deep, holding a load of thick plastic sheeting ready to be loaded by the forklifts for shipping out early in the morning. They must do the same run just about every day because the plastic sheets had been left in the same place every night, ready for the morning, every time he had checked. Ready for loading on to the lorry.

Not this load.

Stealthily, keeping low, he quickly covered the short distance between the container and the pallets. Taking a knife from his pocket, he ripped at the thin clear film which protected the load from the weather and then opened the jerry can, trying not to spill any of the petrol on his gloves or his clothes as he poured its contents, liberally and evenly, over the exposed wooden frames and their cargo.

He retracted the blade and put the knife back in his pocket, taking out a green plastic disposable lighter. The flame danced in the gentle breeze of the night. He kept his thumb against the wheel of the lighter until the flame touched the petrol-soaked wood and caught hold. The fire spread quickly across the surface and then seeped deep into the pile of pallets. He backed off to watch until he was sure the job was done properly and then scampered back towards the shipping container.

The damage would not be great but that was not the intention. This was just a warning. They would do well to heed it.

Stick to your business. Don't try to move in on our ground. We are not to be messed with. Next time, the damage will be a lot worse.

****

'Excuse me.'

The fat middle-aged man loomed over the kneeling frame and folded his arms. The person beneath him carried on with what he was doing, his thinning crown of greying hair bobbing as he replenished the stock of chrome-effect round internal door knobs on the bottom shelf and occasionally picked out an aluminium-effect round internal door knob which had been put back in the wrong space by a careless customer, then relocated it to where it should be.

The fat man glared impatiently.

'I said "excuse me".'

This time the rummaging stopped. The flustered man in his mid-fifties strained to ease himself off his creaking knees and rose to his full height, pushing the frame of his glasses back up the bridge of his nose. He wore a black polo shirt and black trousers which gave stark contrast to a bright yellow apron, upon which was pinned a black name badge with yellow lettering which said 'Graham'.

'I'm sorry, sir, I didn't realise you were there. How can I help?'

He arched his back, relishing the simple joy of being able to stand up straight again.

There was no joy in the face of the fat man.

'How come I can never find one of your lot every time I come to this place? Nothing's ever where it should be and you can never find anybody who actually works here to help you. Where do you all hide?'

Graham tried not to allow his shoulders to sag. He didn't

think he had encountered as many rude and fractious customers in the whole of the rest of his working life as he had in the last five months.

'Sorry about that. There are always members of staff around but it is a very large depot.'

The shelves of aisle 31: Door Knobs and Handles rose high above them and, higher still, the echoing white noise words of a smooth-talking company DJ were drifting indecipherably, bouncing back off the metal roof. It was a vast, soulless, purely functional building and Graham hated it. It sapped his spirit every time he stepped through its doors.

'What can I help you with today?'

'I need a white 13-amp single pole switched double socket.' The arms remained folded. The words were delivered more like a challenge than a request.

Electrical. Aisle 33: Switches, Dimmers and Sockets. He was beginning to know the place like the back of his hand. Hardware, then Electrical, Tools and the Building Yard.

'They would be on aisle 33, sir. I'll show you.'

Graham walked briskly off and the fat man followed, still bristling with disdain.

'I've just walked up and down that aisle. They're not there.'

Ignoring the comment, Graham strode around a third of the way up the aisle and his hand hovered over the range of plug sockets until he spotted and snatched at the right one, on one of the middle shelves.

'Here we go. White 13-amp single pole switched double socket. Is that the one?'

He tried not to sound too triumphant, but these were the moments he lived for in this job. There wasn't very much else going for it.

'Oh!' The fat man took the packet and stared at it, incredulously. 'That's it. I can't have seen it. They should be labelled more clearly.'

Graham glanced back at the white label which read 'White Switched Double Socket £4.97' and at the half a dozen pale blue boxes on the shelf just above the label, each of which had the words '13-amp single pole switched double socket' printed in black on it.

No. I think that's pretty clearly labelled.

'Is there anything else I can help you with?'

The fat man was still staring at the packet in his hands.

'No, that's all I wanted.' Still without attempting eye contact, he then uttered a grudging 'Thanks.'

Graham smiled.

'Not a problem. Hope you enjoy the rest of your day.'

He knelt again in front of the chrome-effect round internal door knobs. In the short time it had taken him to walk down to Electrical and back, another customer had put an aluminium knob amongst the chrome ones.

He looked down at his watch. Still more than three and a half hours until the end of the shift.

3

The first raindrops dotted the windows of the bus just before it got to his stop. By the time he had pressed the button to request the driver to pull in and stood, ready to disembark, he could see the rain practically bouncing off the road ahead of them.

It had been a miserable summer so far. Was it really almost July?

Not only was he greeted by pounding rain as he stepped off the bus into the premature gloom of early evening, it was whipped into his face by a chilly wind. It felt more like October.

Graham hadn't far to walk from the stop to his home but it seemed a lot further than usual as he zipped up his inadequately thin jacket and tilted his head into the face of the wind, the rain plastering his hair to his scalp and swimming over his glasses as it ran to form droplets on the end of his nose.

By the time he turned off the main road and on to Seathwaite Street, the rain was easing off. It was only a squall and he cursed the bad timing which had brought him a damp, yet fitting, end to another spirit-sapping work day.

He felt soaked, cold and disconsolate. All he wanted was to cover the remaining 300 yards of his walk quickly and get home so he could close the day away behind him. Then he would get changed out of his wet work clothes and try not to sound doleful when Janet asked him how his day had been.

Oh, you know, the usual, he would reply. That seemed to cover it. How was yours?

What else are you meant to say? It was mind-numbingly dull. It's a mind-numbingly dull job. It was mind-numbingly dull today, it was mind-numbingly dull yesterday and it will be mind-numbingly dull tomorrow. There would be no point talking like that. It wouldn't change anything.

Janet usually got home from work three-quarters of an hour earlier than he did. She took the car because her place was harder to get to by bus. That's how they worked it when Graham was still at the library, which was in the centre of town, and that was fine. There was no way they could afford to run two cars.

He could make out the shape of the red hatchback on the drive in front of their neat little semi-detached as he moved briskly closer and felt comforted by what lay just ahead. A change of clothes and a cup of tea. Right now that was all he needed. He swung his sodden backpack off his shoulder and began unzipping the front pocket of it to retrieve his house key but stopped when he heard the sound of a voice behind him.

'Hello. Hello. Is it Graham?'

A man holding a black umbrella was moving in a half-run towards him from the other side of the street. Graham could not make him out properly because his glasses were still spattered with raindrops but he did not think he recognised him. He certainly could not place the voice. He faced the advancing figure warily, half-expecting something unwanted.

The man slowed as he reached the other side of the street and stopped at the edge of the drive.

'Sorry, are you Graham?'

Graham unzipped his jacket and took off his glasses to wipe them dry, as best he could, against his black polo shirt. He wanted to see this person properly.

They were of similar height but the stranger was plumper and considerably smarter dressed, in a suit and tie. He was quite a bit younger, maybe thirtyish, and his round, tanned face was clean-shaven. His fixed gaze bore into Graham's eyes so intently that the scrutiny made him uncomfortable.

But reassured that the person opposite was far too well turned-out and nowhere near stealthy enough to be a mugger, Graham felt it safe to respond.

'I am.'

The man took tentative steps forward, as if hoping not to frighten away a small animal he wanted to try to pet, and slowly raised an outstretched right hand, edging forward until he was little more than that arm's length away.

'My name's Andreas, Andreas Johnson.'

Graham leaned forward to accept the handshake. His hand was gripped firmly and the stranger held tight for so long that Graham began to feel it a bit awkward and wanted to pull his hand free.

'You have no idea how glad I am that I've managed to track you down.'

Track me down?

'I'm sorry, should I know you?'

The stranger became suddenly aware that he had held the handshake for too long and released his grip.

Graham could still feel the pressure of it as he withdrew his arm to his side. Who was this guy and why is he making this odd approach on my driveway? He no longer felt threatened, just utterly confused. This was not normal. He could not think what to do, what to say. He could make no sense of it but then he looked properly into the face of the man opposite him for the first time and their eyes met, locking on each other like the opposite ends of two magnets brought close enough to fix to each other.

There was something in those eyes. Something.

'We've never met, but...' The rest of the sentence stalled in the throat of the stranger. He seemed as if he was on the verge of being overcome by his emotions.

'Look,' he said. 'I have something really important I need to tell you. Can we just sit for a minute and talk – in my car, if you like, if you don't feel comfortable letting me into your home.

'And that's OK, by the way,' he added hastily. 'I understand.'

Graham was disarmed. Intrigued now rather than suspicious.

'Sure,' he said.

The younger man began to edge away and then turned back, remembering his manners and offering the shared shelter of his umbrella. The rain had just about stopped but Graham accepted the gesture with a grateful smile.

They walked silently together across the street. As they neared it, Graham heard the click of car doors unlocking on a long silver Jaguar parked a few doors up on the opposite side. The car's hazard lights blinked three times, welcomingly, and the stranger steered them towards it.

Whoever this guy is, he appears to be doing well for himself.

'Please, get in. It's open.' The stranger held the umbrella over Graham until he gripped the door handle and pulled it open before sinking into the passenger seat, feeling self-conscious of his wet and bedraggled state and it's potentially detrimental effects on the soft leather seats.

The stranger opened the back door to toss his dampened umbrella into the foot-well and then climbed in through the front door behind the steering wheel. He looked at Graham and smiled, warmly.

'Sorry, Andreas, but what is this all about?'

The man paused for a second, making sure he delivered his words right.

'Do you remember the name Lena Christopoulos?'

Lena Christopoulos.

A name like that will stick in the mind. The mention of it immediately evoked youthful feelings of shame and missed opportunity in Graham's.

They were on the same history course at the University of Leeds between 1980 and 1983. They were in the same tutor group occasionally, too. She was a quiet girl. Half-Greek, as he recalled, with dark Mediterranean skin and dark eyes, which qualified her as quite exotic at a time when there were not as many overseas students as there seemed to be these days. He did not consider her especially attractive, to be brutally honest, in either looks or personality but she was nice enough. They talked a few times but not very often. Just chat. Course stuff, mainly.

They never mixed in the same social groups outside the lecture theatre or the tutorial room.

Then there was the party.

It was the night before the final year results were posted on the faculty notice board and in an environment where the flimsiest of excuses was seized upon as a cause for a piss-up, that was an unmissable reason for everybody to drink away what little flexibility still remained in their overdrafts. They were about to find out the reward for their hard work over three years or, as in Graham's case, to be reminded that they really should have worked harder. In a few days, the course would officially be over and they would all go their separate ways to hit the real world.

That night, though, Graham and his mates hit the pubs and had already lost count of how many pints of Tetley's were swilling around in their systems before they got to the party, which was in one of the halls of residence blocks.

They took with them two four-packs of Stones' bitter as a token contribution to the general party booze stock but it was not tinned beer that Graham had his eye on as they swayed into the dimmed light and stale air of the common room area. On a grey metal-framed table which appeared in danger of sagging under its weight sat a large punch bowl, astonishingly vulnerable to displacement from any one of the many erratic drunken students who crowded the room but, for now, two thirds full of a sloshing orangey liquid with chunky pieces of fruit floating on top.

For reasons unknown, the sight was instantly appealing to Graham. As his mates took their four-packs to the designated bar area and began to sift through the selection for something better to drink than the cheap stuff they had brought, Graham felt compelled to take a white plastic cup from the stack and dip it into the bowl.

A few drops dribbled down the side of the cup and dripped onto his fraying Green Flash trainers as he took his first swig. Not bad. Maybe the Tetley's had numbed his taste buds but he made the swift assessment that it wasn't much more than orange squash with a bit of a kick to it. He swigged down the rest of the cupful and, just to be sure, dipped in for a refill.

It was all right. Tasted worse.

'What do you think of our punch?'

There was Lena, holding a can of Skol. The details are a bit hazy now but Graham noticed she was wearing a skirt and that was strange because she only ever seemed to wear jeans. In the half-light of a room shaking to the sound of Simple Minds and with the best part of double-figure pints on board, he thought she looked good. What's more, she was smiling at him and talking to him, which not many girls were prepared to do at parties, in his experience.

'It's OK but it's a bit weak. What's in it?' He had to lean towards her to be heard above the noise made by a ghetto blaster turned up to top volume.

He turned his head for her to yell her reply into his ear.

'Wine, vodka, whisky, Pernod – anything we could get hold of really.'

Graham looked quizzically at the orange liquid and swigged down the rest of the cupful. He ruckled his nose and filled his cup again, sinking the contents down in one and giving Lena the same unconvinced expression of suspicion. For whatever reason, his tasting session had quickly escalated into a chest-thumping game of machismo.

'Are you sure?' he mouthed.

Lena hunched her shoulders, as if now doubting the

evidence of her own memory.

He dipped in the cup again and took another gulp.

'I don't feel like I'm getting drunk at all.'

Without hesitation, she leaned towards him again and he turned his ear towards her.

'I've got a bottle of Cinzano in my room, if you'd like.'

Graham could not recall being taken aback at the suggestion in the invitation or unduly elated at the opportunities it might bring. Nor could he have claimed he was trying to play it cool but, in his inebriated naivety, he simply said 'OK', set down the remainder of the cup of punch on the table and followed her up the stairs to the second floor.

Two along on the left of a row of brown doors down a long corridor, Lena stopped and took a key out of her shoulder bag. The room was as compact as a cell, with a single bed down one side and a desk on the other. Above the desk was a shelf of text books and beyond the bed was a large poster of a Salvador Dali painting and a smaller one advertising a gig at the students' union which must have been well enjoyed and was fondly remembered. At the foot of the bed was a built-in unit with a sink and a mirror on one side, a shallow wardrobe on the other and cupboards for storage space above.

Lena tugged at the stiff single window to open it a couple of inches at the top and then dragged closed the brown curtain. For the first time, Graham realised this was beginning to look a bit promising.

She opened a drawer next to the desk and took out a bottle of Cinzano Bianco, then picked up two half-pint glasses which looked suspiciously as if they had been lifted from a pub and took them to the sink to give them a bit of a clean. Without speaking and without asking, she opened the bottle and half-filled the dampened but still murky glasses.

'Here you go.' She handed one to Graham and sat down on the bed. He sat beside her and took a sip of the drink. Despite his newly discovered taste for indiscriminate drinking, it struck him as pretty nasty but he tried not to show it and put the glass down on the floor beside him.

They must have talked for a while but he had no recollection of what they said. Almost certainly, that was because his accumulated and rapidly accelerated intake of alcohol swiftly took its toll on Graham's ability to recall normally and the rest of the night swam in front of his memory in a sea of kissing and fumbling before giving way, inevitably, to unconsciousness.

What he did remember was waking up in the morning.

His right eye was the first to bravely allow the intrusive shaft of bright sunshine to stir his still barely functioning brain and his left eye reluctantly followed seconds later. The sun was on the rise but high enough to sit fully above the three-storey halls building opposite them and it peeked through the gap between curtain and wall directly on to his face as if his was the visage of the blessed one. He lay on his right side and raised a hand to shield his sensitive awakening pupils from the glare, then turned slowly to face Lena, who was pressed between him and the wall on what little remained of the small single bed.

She was still asleep and still, as far as he could tell from what the thin blanket covering her to just above her waist allowed him to see, fully dressed.

Graham remained oblivious to any recollection of what, exactly, had gone on but he knew one thing. He had pulled. He was in bed with an actual girl and that was such an unusual experience for him that it had far from lost its novelty value.

He eased slowly back to his right side, trying as hard as he could not to wake Lena so that he could savour the moment of his conquest. Raising himself on his elbow, he pulled the curtain back a little further and looked out to the clear blue sky of a beautiful June morning, saw the shadows cast on the maze of footpaths and dewy lawns by the buildings of the campus and listened as a single small bird, unchallenged by the silence around it, chirped its melodic greeting for a glorious day to herald a future filled with new possibilities.

Here, in the heart of the Leeds suburbs, he had found paradise and he absorbed it all. It was magnificent. In a few short hours, he would have confirmation of his grade and be entitled to write the letters BA (Hons) after his name, would be clear to complete the formalities on the job offer he had already received from Bradford Council and would soon be bringing in a wage. Earning money!

He had a girl by his side and the world at his feet and in the very moment he bathed in the shimmering light of his exaltation a realisation dawned, rising higher than the rest of his thoughts and bestriding them like a Colossus.

I am going to be sick.

That was unmistakably the case. The only course of action open to him was to act quickly.

Graham attempted to roll off the edge of the bed without making a jolt or a noise which might disturb Lena and rose to his feet as sturdily as a new-born calf, bringing down his socked foot on a wet patch of Cinzano beside an overturned glass at the end of the bed.

Where are my jeans?

Once his eyes had readjusted to the dark of the room, he saw them on the floor near the waste bin and leaned against the wall as he pulled them on to reduce the possibility of falling in a heap in the act. He then attempted to wiggle into his still-tied trainers as he moved towards the door, conscious that every second counted, and eased down the door handle as quickly as he dared, glancing back for a moment towards the bed.

She hadn't heard him. Good.

He cushioned the door closed again and increased his pace. Where are the loos? There must be one on each floor, surely.

Dashing down the corridor, his eyes darted to either side looking for the vital sign as the curdling sensation in his stomach increased to crisis proportions. He was going to have to find a toilet soon or the consequences were going to be very messy.

Almost at the end of the corridor was a door with no number and no sign on it. In desperation he began to run towards it, his hand over his mouth as the first heave of his guts filled his throat with foul-tasting regurgitated liquid, some of which seeped between his fingers.

This has to be it.

He yanked open the door. Groping desperately on the inside wall, he located a light switch and turned it on. It was a store cupboard.

There was no more time. He felt the growing imminence of another violent contraction in his mid-section and saw it; his one chance to avoid spray-painting the whole room. A metal bucket with a mop. He grabbed the mop and threw it aside, then dropped to his knees and hurled what felt like the full contents of his and several other people's stomachs splashing into the pail.

When the fifth wave had overwhelmed and drained him, leaving only remorse and a furious pounding in his head, Graham attempted to spit the noxious taste out of his mouth and crouched helplessly, barely daring to move for at least three minutes. When he felt he could, he raised himself to kneel and unsteadily got to his feet.

The bucket had caught most of the malodorous liquid, but by no means all of it. It was a horrible mess. Looking down, Graham noticed the tell-tale patches of warm orange puke down the front of his shirt and on his jeans.

What could he do? He knew he should at least attempt to clean up the cupboard, but could not face it. He certainly could not go back in to Lena. So he turned off the light, closed the door behind him and skulked off into the glorious summer morning.

'Yes, I remember Lena. We were at uni together, on the same course. Why do you ask?'

Andreas's expression became grave. His eyes dropped to linger with unseeing sadness over the gear lever between them.

'She was my mother. She passed away 10 months ago.'

Graham's heart sank. Though they had not seen each other since that end-of-term party and had made no attempt to get back in touch, he felt the sorrow in those words.

'I am sorry to hear that, Andreas. She was a nice person. Please accept my condolences.'

'It was a car accident,' the younger man continued without lifting his gaze or acknowledging the offer of sympathy.

'She and my pappa were returning from a meal with

friends when their car left the road, apparently without reason, and hit a tree. They were both killed instantly.'

Graham was struggling to find any response which could fit the gravity of the added detail. He shook his head sombrely and said meekly: 'That's awful.'

A heavy silence settled over the car interior for what felt like an age until Graham could find the courage to speak again.

'I'm so sad for you, Andreas. I'm sure you must have been through so much, but could I ask - why did you...? I mean, why did you feel you needed to find me to tell me your news? I mean, Lena and I barely knew each other really and I haven't seen or heard from her since the day we finished uni. It just seems...'

'My mama was a very open and honest woman,' Andreas added. 'She told me everything. Trusted me. She was even prepared to confide in me the truth that I was conceived out of wedlock. You see, I was not truly my pappa's son.'

Andreas raised his head and stared piercingly into the eyes of the man beside him.

'You are my real father.'

4

The red tail lights of the silver Jaguar glowed brighter with a touch on the brakes as the car paused momentarily at the end of Seathwaite Street and turned left, disappearing from view behind the line of houses.

Graham stood on the path outside his home and watched it go. He stared up the road even after it had eased out of sight like an imagined spirit.

The numbness which had enveloped him when Andreas revealed the reason for his unexpected visit had not yet eased. They stayed in the car, together, for a few minutes more after the revelation. Five minutes? Ten minutes? It was mostly Andreas talking. Graham didn't say much. He couldn't think what to say. Andreas told him a few more things but he couldn't remember the details. Graham muttered an 'I see' and a 'yeah, OK' but quite what that was in response to was impossible to recall.

Maybe the last expression was after Andreas had offered him the business card he now clutched in his left hand. Just after it was handed over, Graham said something about needing to go because he was already late home and had fumbled to locate the handle to open the car door. He had to get out of there. Did they even say goodbye? Must have. Probably shook hands as well.

He glanced at the card.

Andreas Johnson
Managing Director
Harry Johnson Global Logistics Ltd

He had a telephone number and an email address now. Did he give Andreas his number in exchange? Must have.

Graham flipped the card over to look at the back, as if expecting that side to offer some reflection of the magnitude of the news he had just been given but all it had was a colour picture of a large and gleaming lorry in red and yellow livery with the name of the company emblazoned down the side of the trailer.

He turned it back and read it again.

My son?

It was far too much to take in. How could such a thing even be possible? It must all be a big mistake.

Then his heart skipped a beat and he turned his head sharply to look at his home, as if startled by a noise from within it.

What the hell am I going to tell Janet?

She was in the kitchen with the radio playing, preparing their evening meal, and was singing to some half-remembered pop song from the 1980s which would really have been best completely forgotten. She had changed out of her work clothes into jeans and a loose top, as she usually did when she first arrived home, and had her back to him, cutting vegetables and moving her hips slightly to the music.

He stood in the doorway watching her and, just for a second or two, could see her as she was when they first met 30 years ago, only a couple of weeks after he moved to Derby to start a new job in the libraries service.

It was a blind date. Graham's mate from Leeds University, Pete, had alerted him that there was a job going and suggested he apply for it. He said it would be great to work together and pick up on their social life again. Graham had worked for three years for the council at Preston, following the best part of three years in Bradford. He didn't enjoy either job and had found it difficult to make good friends, so he thought that might be a good idea. Why not?

Anyway, he got the job and Pete took it upon himself to make it one of his first tasks to fix Graham up with a girlfriend. His lack of success with women seemed more of a concern to Pete than it was to him, though he was happy enough to go along with the plan.

So Pete convinced his girlfriend at the time – what was her name? Caroline? Catherine? Something like that. Anyway, he convinced her to talk one of her friends into coming along on a double date. She was a secretary too.

They met up at The Dolphin. Graham's nervousness translated into a huge feeling of awkwardness at the whole situation and, on first impressions, Janet appeared to feel exactly the same. They barely exchanged a word in the pub and could hardly hold eye contact with each other beyond a glance but, after a couple of drinks, they all went across the road to the American diner place on the corner of Queen Street and the two of them began to relax.

By the end of the night, they were getting along like a house on fire and had already arranged to see each other again. She was two years younger than him and a Derby girl. He liked that she was quietly spoken and shy and could see there was no falseness in her. Getting her to talk about herself was a challenge to the point of being difficult, but he got the feeling that was not because she was reluctant to open up but because she considered there was not much to tell. Graham decided there was plenty about this petite, unassuming, charmingly wary young woman that he wanted to get to know.

Two years later, they were married.

Pete was his best man. It seemed appropriate. He was happy to take full credit for the union in his speech. He had a different girlfriend by then and Caroline/Catherine had lost touch with Janet after moving jobs. Pete also moved on shortly after the wedding. They only ever made contact through social media now.

But he and Janet were in it for life. They were made for each other in every way but one. They had never been able to have children together.

She sang the chorus one last time as the song reached an end, getting the lyric slightly wrong, as she often did, and turned in rhythm to retrieve something else from the fridge. She was a little more rounded than she was when they first met and her hair had been drained of much of its natural blonde, but she was every bit as beautiful now as she ever was, in his eyes. Possibly even a touch more beautiful now than usual.

She started when she realised he was watching her from the door frame.

'Oh hello, duckie. I didn't hear you come in.'

She stretched to the tip of her toes to kiss him on the lips.

'You're a bit later than usual. Get held up?'

Before he could answer, she touched his jacket with her fingertips and pulled a motherly, concerned face.

'Look at you! You're soaked! Go and get yourself out of those wet things before you catch your death. Dinner will be ready in about 15.'

He smiled and turned to do as instructed, happy for the extra time to think how he might break his news. He had to tell her. It was a matter of trying to work out how.

They decided they would try to start a family four years after they married, when they were both in their thirties. At first, it was fun, spicing up their sex life liked a shared naughty secret, but month after month passed and the real thrill they wished for never came. The excitement waned and concern began.

They read up. They changed their diets. They stopped drinking. They tried to work out the optimum time for conception. Still nothing.

After a year of trying, they went to see the GP. The GP told them there was not much more they could do to increase their chances of a successful pregnancy. Tried to reassure them. Let nature take its course, he said. Told them that of the couples who don't conceive in the first year, about half do so in the second. Said that they should come back in another six months to a year if there was still no news and they could talk about further measures.

They left it eight months. The GP referred them to the fertility clinic at the hospital. The doctor at the clinic was very nice, which helped them deal with all the uncomfortably personal questions. She took blood from them both to try to establish the source of the problem and sent Graham into a room by himself to ejaculate into a tiny pot, which he found acutely embarrassing.

When the results of the tests came back, they were told Janet wasn't ovulating properly. Quite a common problem, the doctor said. She was prescribed medication to try to redress her hormonal inbalance and they were relieved. It sounded like a pretty straightforward potential solution and was certainly much less invasive than some of the procedures they had read about.

They had hope again.

Three months into the course of treatment, Janet was pregnant. She had bought four testing kits and used them all before she felt safe breaking the news to Graham. Before she dared believe it herself.

No matter how much they urged themselves and reminded each other to remain cautious at such an early stage, the brakes were off. Their imaginations raced into the future to favourite names and nursery plans and pram walks and first steps and those were, in so many ways, the happiest days they had ever shared. They were going to be parents.

A few days later, Janet miscarried.

As they were stacking the plates in the dishwasher following their meal, Janet placed her hand on his arm.

'Are you all right tonight, Gray? You seem a bit off it.'

He thought he had done a pretty good job of acting as if everything was as normal, in the circumstances. He had given all the appropriate responses to all the details of her sister Linda's latest bust-up with her husband, who always came out of these tales sounding like a bit of a cock but never struck him as being that bad a bloke really. He thought he had shown sufficient enthusiasm at the suggestion of inviting her parents around for lunch the next Sunday. Clearly, the performance was not good enough. He could never hide anything from Janet.

He pulled a pained expression. There was no point putting it off.

'Not really,' he said. 'Let's have a sit down. There's something I have to tell you.'

He took her by the hand and led her to the sofa. He kept hold of her hand. She looked concerned.

'It's nothing serious. Well, it is serious but it's nothing...'

Not a good start. Her sense of dread deepened. He thought he could see her face pale.

Out with it.

'As I was walking from the bus stop tonight, just about as I was on our drive, actually, a man called out my name and came across the road to me. He introduced himself and we went to sit in his car for a bit and he told me...'

He drew a deep breath.

'He told me he was my son. He told me he was the product of a one-night stand between me and this girl who was on my course at university. I knew nothing about this, obviously, until he said that and I was a bit, like, you know, taken aback by this, as you can guess, but anyway he said that I was his father and that his mother had told him about me and that she and her husband had been killed in a car crash about a year ago, I think, sometime last year anyway, and that he felt he needed to find me to talk to me and tell me that he was, you know, my ....son.'

The quietness of the room was suddenly deafening. Her gaze had been fixed on his face throughout as he stared at his knees. He looked up now to meet her eyes, hardly daring to learn what her reaction would be.

She was expressionless. Stunned, as if a firework had exploded within feet of her and had clouded her eyes with bursts of bright light. She needed a few moments to readjust to the world in its more familiar tones.

'What does he want from you? I mean, we haven't got much,' she said, finally.

'I don't think he *wants* anything. He drove off in a great big shiny Jag and the card he gave me...' He felt in his pockets for the card but realised he had pushed it into the pocket of his jacket when he came inside. '...said he owns a haulage company. I don't think he *wants* anything apart from to finally meet his real, you know, father. At least, that's what I think he wants.'

She nodded, reassured to an extent.

'And is it true? Do you remember this girl and having sex with her?'

He smiled, which did nothing to make her feel easier about the situation.

'I remember her. She was called Lena. We were in the same tutorial groups sometimes. I remember the night it must have happened but, to be honest, I never knew for sure if we went all the way.'

He told her the story. The punch. The room. The morning. The bucket.

'Charming.' She listened with an air of distaste rather than ribald amusement. He knew she didn't approve of behaviour like that, which was why he had never been tempted to tell her the story before. Actually, he had never told anyone.

'It wasn't my finest hour.'

'And you just ran off and left the poor girl to wake up to find you'd not even had the decency to say goodbye? It's no wonder she didn't want anything else to do with you.'

'I was embarrassed.' He needed to attempt mitigation. This was not going down well.

'I had sick all down my front and I felt like shit and I was embarrassed. I couldn't go back to her room like that. I just wanted to get out of there and that was the last day of the course. I didn't see her when I went to collect my final grades and I meant to catch up with her and apologise on graduation day but she didn't go.'

A realisation dawned. 'I know why now, of course. I had no idea where she lived and I didn't have a telephone number. It's not as if you could track somebody down on social media, like you can today, so I decided it was perhaps best to just ...forget about it. Of course, if I'd known...'

If I'd known – what? What would I have done? I was 21. We barely knew each other. What would I have done? What would *we* have done? My whole life could have taken a completely different course.

Janet's expression softened. She knew he would have done the right thing. She knew he wasn't the type to take advantage of a girl and then run away. She could sympathise with his embarrassment.

But she could not stop this from hurting.

'I'm so sorry I couldn't give you a child,' she said finally, sadly.

Graham shuffled closer to her and gripped her in an embrace, pulling her tight.

'No, no, no, no, no – don't say that. You can't even think that. We agreed to never go down that route. No blame, no regrets, remember?'

No regrets. That wasn't entirely true. He had plenty. He wished he had been able to cope with the loss of that early pregnancy much better than he had, for one.

And if anyone was to blame for them remaining childless, it was him.

Graham had been haunted by the powerlessness that ripped at his heart as he watched her doubled by the agony of cramps and saw her become drained, physically and emotionally, while her body gave up the pregnancy that had already come to mean so much to them. When the blood test confirmed that her body had completed its dreadful task efficiently enough for the doctor to decide no further intervention was necessary, it was the most scant of consolations.

After the tears – and there were lots of tears – Graham felt angry.

He felt angry when people were sympathetic and felt angry when people tip-toed around them because they didn't know what to say. He felt angry when he saw strangers with pregnant bumps and he felt angry when adverts came on TV for baby products. Then he felt angry with Janet because she appeared better at coping with their grief than he did and he didn't understand why that should make him angry at all, so that made him feel angry with himself.

Not once did Janet confront him for being incapable of giving her the solace she needed. When he began to understand the benefit of the professional help she suggested they seek together and as the veil of anger began to lift, only then did he realise how recklessly he had been endangering the security of their marriage. That really scared him.

It scared him so much so that he could not face the possibility of going through it all again. They talked about the possibility of IVF but he had to confess to her that his fear of further grief had become greater than his desire to be a father. It took a lot for Janet to accept that but she did and even though she clung on to the thought that he might have a change of heart one day, she knew really that their dreams of having a family were over.

He understood the sacrifice she made. Without it, he knew a wedge could have been driven between them. They might never have been as close again.

Her strength, her sacrifice, had saved their relationship.

Now he had opened the old wounds with all this.

And she felt the need to apologise to him?

'I'm so sorry to put you through this again,' he said. 'You know I wouldn't do anything to hurt you, not for the world. I love you very much.'

As the words left his mouth it pained him to realise that he did not say them often enough these days.

She lifted her head from his chest. Though she smiled, she still looked wounded. 'I love you too, Gray, and you're right. I wouldn't change a thing really. I'm all right. It's just been a bit of a shock.'

'For you and me alike, love.'

Janet nestled back into his chest and they both drifted into their own thoughts. The silence between them was a healing force now. They could cope with anything as long as they could share moments like this.

'So what was she like then, this girl?' she said softly, not wanting to challenge the bond between them.

'Lena? She was nice enough, I think. I didn't really have

that much to do with her, to be honest, until ...well, you know. She always struck me as nice but I never fancied her or anything like that.'

'Was it a regular occurrence then, this ending up in bed with girls you hardly knew?' She was teasing him now. He knew it.

'I wish! I've told you before, I only had one proper girlfriend in the whole of the three years at uni and I managed to make a right mess of that relationship as well.'

'Tell me again.'

'She was called Sarah and we saw each other for quite a few weeks, in the first year. I quite liked her and we got along really well but the group of blokes I used to hang around with at the time never really accepted her and used to take the piss. I don't know why they didn't like her but they always made her feel awkward, like an outsider, when she tried to join in, even when she was with me. I should've taken that as a sign that it was time to get some new friends, but I let them get to me and I went all cool with Sarah until we stopped seeing each other altogether. I was a real prick then but it wasn't because I was nasty or anything. I guess I just decided it was more important to me to try to be accepted by that bunch of mates than it was for me to have Sarah as a girlfriend. I know that's stupid now, but it made sense then. Anyway, she dropped out, so it probably wouldn't have worked out anyway.'

'And you didn't get another girlfriend until the last day of the third year?'

'I know!' He shook his head. 'I was useless with women. I never had the confidence to do all that chatting up. It's a good job you were desperate.'

She pounded her fist into his chest, playfully.

'Cheeky sod! I had loads of blokes asking me out. I just felt sorry for you.'

'Fair enough.' He chuckled. 'I'm glad you did.'

They allowed the silence to take over again, relishing their closeness, until Janet spoke.

'So what do you think you'll do about this guy? What's he called?'

Graham sighed.

'Andreas. I honestly don't know. I mean, I'm not thinking that I never want to see him again or anything like that, but I don't know if it's really ...I don't know. I've got his number. I'll have to think about it and maybe give him a ring so I can talk to him when I've had the chance to take it all in. I wasn't really in any fit state to listen tonight. We'll see.'

She put her arm around him and gave him a reassuring squeeze. He moved his hand from her shoulder to stroke the back of her neck beneath her hair.

Whatever change this might bring to their lives, they would cope with it. Together. Just like they always had before.

5

The coffee was almost certainly too cold to still be palatable. The chocolate powder had congealed to a crusty film on top of the froth and was defiantly unlikely to seep through to the chilled liquid beneath. He thought about asking someone if they could warm it up for him in the microwave but didn't want to take a chance on the timing being wrong.

It was his own fault. Arriving 25 minutes early was ridiculously cautious, especially when the starting point of your journey is only 10 minutes' walk away. Daft, really. But he had been nervous about coming all afternoon and didn't want to risk being late. Having made that commitment to be so early, he decided not to start drinking the coffee straight away so that when Andreas did arrive it would look as if he had been there only a couple of minutes, rather than 30.

Graham looked at his watch again. Nearer 35, actually. Andreas was late but, then again, he was driving up from the south – a business meeting, he said – and the traffic on the A38 could be heavy at this time of the evening.

He heard someone coming upstairs and glanced over to

see if it was him but it was only the young girl, in her green apron and with her tray under her arm, who had already done a sweep of the room twice to collect empties and would surely notice that the anxious-looking bloke at the table in the corner had still not taken so much as a sip of his drink. So he picked up the cup and pretended to be poised to take a mouthful.

Where is he?

It was three days ago when Andreas called (they must have exchanged numbers, after all) and said he would be driving back past Derby and asked if they could meet up again for a chat. Over coffee. Graham had not been able to muster the courage to make the call himself over the previous two days, so he was glad to have the initiative taken from him.

But the closer it came to the time to meet up again, the more apprehensive he grew. He was still far from certain how to process this whole situation. Part of him was still unsure he believed it to be true – but then why would someone who was apparently far more comfortably placed in life want to make something like this up? In the end, his overwhelming curiosity made it inconceivable that he would cancel or avoid the meeting.

He looked at his watch again.

There was another noise on the stairway. Heavier footsteps this time. The source of them came into view. It was him.

Graham shot to his feet a little too keenly, nudging the table with his legs and sending some of the cold coffee sloshing into the saucer. He raised a hand to signal his position, in the sparsely populated room, but the noise of the chair legs scraping across the floor and the chink of the spoon as it fell from the saucer on to the table had already done that job.

Andreas smiled towards the waving figure in the corner, unable to return the acknowledgement more demonstrably because of the large cup he carried in one hand and the plate in the other.

It had been a warm June day, warm enough to leave the jacket in the car. Warm enough, too, for rolled-up shirt sleeves and an unfastened top button beneath the pulled-open blue tie, but he looked far from over-heated at the end of a long car journey. That was one of the benefits of driving a big posh car, no doubt. His substantial overhanging belly added to the impression that here was a man who enjoyed the good things in life and could afford to indulge in them but his demeanour, not least the way he walked, marked him as someone probably more comfortable on the shop floor than in the boardroom.

He put the cup and the plate down on the table before wiping his right hand on the back of his trousers, as if to make sure it was clean, and then offering it to be shaken by Graham.

'Sorry I'm a bit late. The A38 was a bitch coming towards Burton.'

The handshake was accepted.

'That's OK. I've not been here long myself.'

Graham lowered himself back into his chair and picked up his cup, blowing gently at the cold froth to extend the pretence.

Andreas sat opposite and eased forward, cupping his hands, grinning broadly at the figure across the table.

'I'm so glad you wanted to see me again. I thought I might have scared you off, accosting you in the street like I did.'

'No, no, I...'

'Honestly, you looked like you thought I was going to kill you, you were in such a hurry to get out of the car.'

Graham could see in the expression that the words were a ham-fisted attempt to break the ice, but he was ill-prepared to deal with such full-on playfulness so early in their conversation.

'No, of course I didn't... It was a bit of a shock, that's all. I needed to think.'

'Sure, I can understand that.' Andreas sat back in his chair. 'It was a lot to take in. Do you want some of this?'

He gestured towards the flapjack, half covered in chocolate, on the plate.

'Fine thanks.'

Andreas broke off a large piece and scooped it into his mouth, hungrily.

'I'm starving,' he said, without waiting until he had fully chewed and swallowed the mouthful. 'I haven't eaten since lunchtime.'

He tore off another chunk and added it to the remains of the first, hardly breaking the rhythm of the chewing motion, then dabbed at the loose oat flakes on the plate with a plump index finger and brought the finger to his lips to suck the scraps into the mix.

'It's good.'

For a few moments, the only noise between them was the soft sound of the flapjack being devoured.

'How was the meeting?' asked Graham, needing to ease his own sense of awkwardness with small talk.

'Hmm, yeah.' Andreas chewed a little more and then was distracted by a bit of the confection stuck between his teeth, working at it animatedly with his tongue until he was satisfied it was loose.

'Just a normal meeting. We have a depot in Southampton and I go down there every week or so just to make sure everything is being done properly. You know, bang a few heads together, that sort of thing.'

'I see,' said Graham, not really seeing. He had been on the wrong end of heavy-handed management too often.

Clearly, the offending particle was still an issue. Andreas decided it was time to use his finger to deal with it.

'They're a decent lot really,' he added, checking his fingernail to see if he had managed to resolve the problem. 'But the depot manager's a bit of a soft touch. Give the drivers too much slack and they'll take advantage.'

He hesitated, reflecting on a sudden thought.

'Maybe I should sack him.'

Andreas took out his phone and scrolled down his contacts list. With his thumb hovering over the call button, he peered earnestly across the table.

'Do you think I should sack him? It's your decision. You decide.'

Graham stared back, not sure how he was meant to react. Was this a wind-up?

'I don't... I've never met the guy. No. No, you shouldn't. You can't just get rid of somebody like that.'

Andreas considered for a second and then put his phone back into his trouser pocket.

'Yeah, you're right,' he said and picked up his coffee cup.

Graham was confused. What was that about? Was it some sort of bizarre joke or a macho attempt to prove how big a deal he was? Am I meant to be impressed? There was no clue either way in the face of the man opposite as he sipped at his drink. He decided to move the conversation on.

'I looked you up on Google. Looks like a pretty big operation you're running.'

'We're one of the biggest independent freight companies in the country.' The assertive tone was intended to leave no doubt that the company was, indeed, a pretty big operation. 'We can run up to 64 artics in total across the two depots, operating in the UK and across Europe mainly, but wherever in the world you want cargo shipping to, basically, we can get it there. We've been in family hands since my grandfather – the original Harry Johnson – set it up as a coal business in the forties. His son, who was another Harry – my pappa – took it on in the late eighties and really built it to where it is today and then I took over when he passed. God rest his soul. We're always in the top 100 companies in the industry and I want to make us one of the top 20. I've got big plans.'

'I see.' Graham was truly impressed this time.

'So how did your mother end up being part of that family?'

'She met pappa when I was four. They fell in love, they married and pappa legally adopted me as his own son. He was a great man. What about you? You married? Kids?'

'I've been married to Janet for 28 years but we never had kids.' This was not the time to expand on that. 'Have you got someone, Andreas?'

'Nah!' He dismissed the notion with a shake of the head and not a hint of regret. 'I've no time for that. Relationships tie you down. I don't want that. I'm married to the business.'

That disturbed Graham. He hoped such lack of faith in the benefits of a long-term partner was not born of the uncertainty of the early years of his life and his origin.

'I know you said Lena told you about me being your natural father and such but I need to know. I've been thinking about this all week. What did she actually tell you about me?'

Andreas pushed the last large piece of flapjack into his mouth and eased back, almost to a full recline, chewing as he contemplated his response.

'She said you knew each other at university. She said you were on the same course and that she quite liked you, but that she never had the nerve to let you know. It's not really done for a Greek girl, you see. Wasn't then, anyway. She said you never appeared that interested, anyway, but then it came to the last night of the course and she saw you at a party and that you were really drunk.'

Graham smiled and blushed slightly at the memory.

'But she told me she had been drinking for most of the day too and that when she saw you she just decided "what the hell!" She said she realised she would probably never see you again anyway, so she decided it was time she found out what she had been missing. You see, she said you were the first man she had been with.'

'Really?' That made him feel worse.

'She said she heard you stumbling around in the morning trying to get into your jeans and that she watched you as you staggered towards the door and that you looked as if you were about to throw up everywhere, so she was glad that you were heading out of the room, but that you didn't come back and that was it. She didn't see you again.'

'And when she found out she was pregnant, what then?

Why didn't she try to find me?'

'She said she didn't think you were ready for that kind of responsibility and that she didn't want to get caught in a relationship with a boy she didn't really know just because there was a baby. She told me it was her mistake, her fault, and that it would not have been right to make someone else pay for that, so she moved in with my grandparents and they took care of each other.'

He leaned forward, wanting to stress his point.

'I was always loved. I never felt different or unwanted. That was just normal to me and then, when my pappa came along, it changed, but in a good way. I had a very happy childhood.'

'I'm very glad.' There was still an undeniable edge of regret in Graham's voice, as much as he tried to hide it. It was true that he would not have been ready for parenthood at 21, but he was hurt at not being offered the option, even more so after being told that Lena didn't think he was mature enough to handle it. There would have been big adjustments and sacrifices to make, but he had confidence in his younger self to think he would have been up to the challenges.

'I can see you must have been very close to your mother and I'm happy it worked out for all of you – with your other dad as well – but I can't really understand where I fit into all this now, Andreas. I mean, after the ...accident. After the accident, why did you want to come to find me? I'd never been part of your life, just a name in a story your mother told you. What do you want from me?'

It was the question that had most rattled around Graham's thoughts since that rainy night outside his home. He had, that night, dismissed Janet's suggestion that

Andreas could be looking for something other than to meet the man whose biological intervention was the reason for his existence but still it bothered him. However much he could understand, from his own research work, how irritating it can be to have to leave loose ends untied, he had not been able to work out why Andreas had gone to such lengths to find him after all this time.

What made you want to look for me?

What do you want me to be?

Andreas took a sip of coffee and his expression became serious, almost angry.

'That night, I lost the two most important people in my life. My grandparents on both sides had passed on, I have no aunts or uncles or siblings, so in one moment on one night everything I had was gone.'

He snapped his fingers with a sudden violence, filling the space between them. It made Graham flinch.

'I had nothing left. I felt emptiness in my life. I was alone but I also had a name. Your name. I had to find you.' Andreas drew up his right hand with the index finger pointing inches from the face opposite. Graham's focus was solely on the intense gaze he dared not break.

'You are the only family I have left.'

Graham swallowed hard. He got it now. The scale of this new responsibility loomed, intimidatingly, above him and made him feel as if he was a speck in its shadow. What Andreas needed from him was far more than the tying up of a loose end. He was needed to provide much more than a branch line on a family tree.

'So that's why I decided to look for you.' All the intensity in Andreas's expression evaporated in an instant. He sat back and picked up his coffee cup for another sip.

'It was not so difficult to find you. It's such an unusual name. By the way, is there any sort of connection with the actor fella?'

Graham shook his head with the usual air of feigned regret.

'No. No relation at all.'

Andreas's face sank a little in disappointment.

'Ah, pity. Anyway, the only Graham Hasselhoff I could find was in Derby and I found a link to an article in the local paper which said you worked in the library. It was something about the launch of a new service, from five or six years ago, maybe.'

'I remember the one.' The council PR people had insisted that he give them a full briefing about how the new service worked and had then sent out a press release which gave out false information. He had to deal with the after-effects of that one for months.

'So, on one of my trips back from Southampton, I decided to call in on Derby Library to try to find you. The people at the main library in the centre pointed me across the road to the other one – what was it? Local studies? Used to be a court building, by the look of it inside.'

'That's right. It's the former magistrates' courts.'

'The lady there was very helpful when I told her I was looking for you. She said to say hello but I can't remember her name. Mousy little lady. Funny teeth.'

'Nadeen.'

'That's the one. She said you didn't work there anymore and that she wasn't allowed to give out your details, so I thought I'd hit a dead end. But then she said I should look on the electoral register for an address and that she would show me how to do it. I had to join your library, though. I have a card and everything. I found your address and the rest was easy.'

Thanks, Nadeen. He hadn't been able to face going back to the library to say hello since he left. Maybe it was time he did.

'So when did you decide to leave the library?'

Graham shuffled in his seat. It was still a sore subject.

'I kind of had the decision made for me. I got made redundant. There was another round of cuts at the council and they decided I was expendable, I guess. I work at a DIY warehouse now.'

'OK. You're a manager?'

'A mere minion, I'm afraid.'

'OK.' The furrows on Andreas's brow became more pronounced as he appeared to struggle with the concept of why anyone would want to take on such a job.

'Is it ...good?'

'No. It's awful.' There was no point trying to pretend. 'It's tedious work and a little piece of me dies every time I walk through the doors to start my shift, but it's the only job I could get. I applied for all sorts of roles after the library let me go but nobody seemed to want to know. I knew I was comfortably capable of doing just about all the jobs I went for and I did go for quite a few interviews but, for whatever reason, it seemed to me that when employers saw my age it was the end of the story. I don't know if they assume you're just aiming to see out the rest of your days to retirement when you get to your mid-fifties but I got the impression nobody wanted to take me seriously and couldn't see what I have to give. I mean, doesn't life experience count for anything anymore? I'd tell them about what it entailed to effectively run the library operation myself – the organisational skills, the communication skills, budget management, dealing with the public – but I didn't seem able to get them past whatever pre-conceived ideas they had. Maybe they just saw me as a useless, unambitious older bloke who spent his days stamping cards and getting in a fluster whenever anybody put a book back on the shelf out of alphabetical order, but I got rejection after rejection until the redundancy money started to run out and I had to take whatever I could get. So that's what I do now. I do a dreary job in a vast, soul-destroying warehouse, but it pays the bills so I grit my teeth and get on with it.'

He had never vented his feelings like that to anyone, apart from Janet, and he had not even let her know just how unhappy working at the DIY store made him. That would not have been fair. He was glad to have vocalised what had been building up within him for months, but it made him feel self-indulgent. Andreas may be his child but he hardly knew the man. He shouldn't have been so forthright.

'Sorry for the rant.'

Andreas stared back at him, impassively. There was silence between them. Graham's discomfiture grew. It might be time to make an excuse and head home, but he was frozen in the scrutiny of that stare.

Andreas drew a deep sigh.

'You must come to work for me.' The tone left no room for discussion. It caught Graham totally off-guard.

'That's very kind but I wasn't trying to ...'

'No.' Andreas held up the palm of his hand to silence the dissent. 'You must come to work for me. I need a new transport administrator and you can do that role.'

'Transport administrator? I really don't know anything about your business. What would I have to do?' Graham's heart was thudding in his chest. He did not know whether to put that down to excitement or raw panic.

'You will organise the drivers' rotas, communicate with the customers to make sure the deliveries are made on time and to the right place, book driver cover through the agencies, keep the transport management system updated – we can teach you. It's basically a communication and organisation job. You will be good at it. And your wife ...' He paused for the necessary prompt.

'Janet.'

'Janet. She must come to work for me too. What can she do?'

Graham was caught in a whirlwind. It was irresistible.

'Err, office work – secretarial, office management, that sort of thing.'

Andreas clapped his hands, startling all four of the other customers on the upper level of the coffee shop.

'Perfect! I need someone I can rely on to work on the administration side. Janet can work with the finance manager and with me. The business is going to grow and soon we will need more assistance. It is done. I own several properties in the area and you can live in one of them, rent-free, of course. This is perfect!'

Graham was incapable of raising an objection, even if he had wanted to. It had escalated so quickly that it had swept him away like a storm surge.

'Andreas, really, this is ...I'll have to talk to Janet before I could ...'

'Of course, of course!' With an exaggerated flourish of his arm, Andreas took a stern look at his watch and gulped down another mouthful of coffee.

'Talk to her. Think it through and then get back to me to

let me know when you can both start. I will see to the rest. I have to go now.'

He shot to his feet.

'This is perfect. You and Janet will come to work for me and we will be a family business again.'

Graham stirred from his dazed state and rose, lifting his arm in anticipation of a handshake, but suddenly found himself grasped in a bear hug which squeezed the air from his lungs and knocked his glasses crooked.

Andreas released him, utterly unapologetic for the unannounced physical intervention, and beamed, holding the bemused figure in front of him with large paws clasping his upper arms.

'Perfect!' he said and spun on his heels to head for the stairs.

6

The yard was much more brightly lit than last time. No doubt about that. He spotted cameras where there hadn't been any last time too. At least he had caught their attention enough to make them feel the need to step up their security, but they hadn't heeded the warning.

That was stupid of them. They would have to pay for that. They will have to take us seriously sometime soon or they'll regret it.

They had a security guard on permanent watch now as well. That made it more of a challenge but he was not concerned. One fat security man was not going to stop him.

Even if the guard did happen to look up from his grubby porno magazine to the monitor at the precise moment the attack came, by the time the police were alerted it would be too late. He would have already disappeared into the night.

The security guard was out in the yard now. He had just completed a circuit of the perimeter fence, occasionally shining his torch in the direction of a rustle in the trees or a perceived movement in the shadows, and was rewarding himself for his vigilance by sneaking a cigarette.

He stood, nonchalantly blowing plumes of smoke up

towards the inky black of the night sky. The only light above them came from the pin-prick of stars and the pale slither of a crescent moon, so that looking out from where the security guard had chosen to have his cigarette he must have been able to see nothing beyond the artificial bright illumination of the arc lights. The perimeter fence might as well be marking the edge of the world.

There was no way he could detect the danger which lurked a few yards past the fence and into the void. No way.

The figure in black leaned against the thick trunk of a tree, patiently watching and waiting, as the security guard made the most of his last moments in the sultry summer night air, taking a final drag and tossing the stub to the ground before extinguishing it with a twist of his boot, then meandering slowly back towards the back door of the main block.

This is it. Time to move. At the pace that guy is moving, it will be all over by the time he reaches his screens.

The figure in black squatted to open the bag by his side and pulled out two bottles three-quarters full of pale yellow liquid. He unscrewed the caps on both and pushed in the rolled-up rags to soak up the liquid, placing them carefully on the ground as he took out the lighter from his coat pocket.

He picked up the first bottle and carefully held the ignited lighter underneath the exposed portion of rag still sticking out of the neck until it caught alight and wisps of black smoke snaked from the bright yellow-orange of the flame. He then hurled it over the fence towards the lone trailer closest to his corner of the yard.

The lit bottle flickered through the air and splintered

with a bright flash and a bang only a foot or so short of the trailer, the pool of flaming liquid instantly spreading underneath and over its target.

Quickly, he picked up and lit the rag of the second bottle and then cast it towards the other end of the trailer. It too exploded just where he wanted it to.

The fire was already catching and spreading up the fabric of the trailer side where the first bottle had landed. Soon, the tyres at the rear of the trailer were circles of flame.

Only one more thing to do.

He reached into the bag again and took out a large stone with a folded sheet of paper wrapped around it, fixed by thick grey tape. He threw that, too, over the perimeter fence but further than the blazing trailer; into the centre of the yard where it might be easily seen.

It was meant to be found.

They had better take us seriously now.

7

'What happened there, then?'

Graham shielded his eyes from the sun and was peering towards the charred skeleton of a trailer, the concrete ground blackened beneath it, in the corner of a depot yard on an industrial estate just off the main road connecting the M1 and the centre of Sheffield.

It had been just over a week since he had walked away from the coffee shop meeting with Andreas as disorientated as if he had been forced into an oil drum and rolled down an exceptionally steep hill.

The walk back to the bus stop was nowhere near long enough for him to process either the life-changing offer made, apparently on a moment of whim, or the decidedly erratic behaviour of the man he had, in part, been responsible for bringing into the world. If he had no idea what to make of either development, what chance was there of adequately explaining what went on to Janet?

Having almost missed his stop and dismissed a fleeting notion, when he reached the end of Seathwaite Street, to walk on and buy a little more time instead of heading straight home, Graham resolved to limit his report of the meeting to the life-changing offer and to save telling her about his son's strange foibles for another day.

He reckoned putting the notion that they might want to consider giving up their jobs and move to a different city on the promise of a man who was, only a few days earlier, completely unknown to either of them was enough for Janet to think about for now. It was.

Janet was less than enthusiastic. Initially, at least. Not unreasonably, Graham readily conceded, she was reluctant to consider leaving her home in the city where she had lived all her life, putting distance between herself, family and friends and giving up a job that, for all its occasional frustrations, was one that she was very good at and actually quite enjoyed, on the whole.

Sacrifice all that for what? Working at a truck company? What do either of us know about truck companies? What do either of us know about Andreas? These jobs might not even exist. I mean, I know he says he's your son, but what do we know about him really? Nothing. No, Graham, it's a ridiculous idea. I might have been more willing to take this kind of gamble 20 years ago, but not now. Not at our time of life.

He allowed her to say her piece without interruption. That was not difficult because she was merely vocalising the nagging doubts that had been rattling around his own mind for the last hour or so, but their view did differ on one important point.

Janet could not see beyond what she had to lose. Graham could already see the possibilities for gain. He had less to lose.

Sure, he loved their home, he was perfectly content in Derby, he got on fine with the in-laws and he quite liked most of their mutual friends.

But his job. He hated his job. He hated how it made him feel unvalued and unfulfilled. He hated how the balance of his life had been tipped uncomfortably closer to the realisation that he was stumbling towards its last phase without any great purpose. He hated the fear that he had been stripped of his usefulness.

He liked the prospect of taking on a new role that would challenge him again. Make him feel alive again.

So after readily accepting that Janet would be giving up the most, if the offer proved legitimate and if they decided to give it a go, he felt it not too overwhelmingly selfish to remind his wife that he had craved an opportunity such as this ever since the council made him redundant and that the apparent reluctance of employers to consider him worthy of such an opportunity elsewhere had led to a pretty bleak few months. For both of them.

Janet was well aware of that, of course. Her indignation abated. She fell quiet.

Graham suggested they take a little time to find out more. Think it over. She nodded.

As a first step, he suggested they both meet Andreas. Go for a meal, maybe. She thought that would be a good idea.

Graham was actually less convinced it was a good idea, though he knew it was absolutely the right thing to do, as a first step.

What if Andreas put on as eccentric a display as he had in the coffee shop? Janet would not like that. It would put her completely off the idea of working with him. Or having anything at all to do with him, for that matter. He knew what she was like. She didn't like volatility.

He needn't have worried.

They went out for a Thai meal. Andreas was charm personified. He told them about the business and the roles he had in mind for the two of them. He offered salaries that were better than either of them were currently on. He insisted on picking up the bill and would hear nothing of their protests that they should split it. Janet took to him straight away. What a lovely man, she said later.

Graham was bemused. Pleasantly so, but bemused. Andreas was nothing like as odd as he had been at the coffee place.

Perhaps that was a one-off. Perhaps they had both been a little on edge. Maybe, in his over-sensitive edgy state, he had read too much into Andreas's behaviour. Maybe.

Either way, Janet was sufficiently encouraged to suggest that Graham take up an offer to go and have a look around the depot when he next had a day off. So he did.

Andreas peered towards the burnt-out trailer and scowled. 'We were attacked.' Bitterness pierced his tone.

'It is the second time. Someone has a grudge against us.'

'Christ!' Graham stared at the wrecked trailer again, in a different light now. 'Do you know who did it?'

Andreas reached into his back pocket for his wallet. 'I have a good idea.' He took out a folded, crumpled piece of paper bearing a printed message in large bold type and handed it over.

YOU KNEW THERE WOULD BE CONSEQUENCES
STOP IMMEDIATELY
THIS IS A FINAL WARNING

Graham re-read it, though the message was plain enough

first time.

'Christ! What do they mean? What do they want you to stop doing?'

Andreas took back the sheet, refolded it and put it back into his wallet.

'There is another transport company operating not far from here. It is run by a bastard called Doug Bentley. He and my pappa were great competitors, though his company has never been anything like as successful as ours. He is a very jealous man and now he realises that I intend to take business away from him by expanding into the areas my pappa used to allow him to control. I don't intend to be as kind as my pappa and now this Bentley is trying to scare me but I do not scare easily. If he wants a fight, I will give him a fight.'

The menace in his words unnerved Graham. It was clearly already a serious situation and he did not like the thought that it might get worse.

'Surely this is a matter for the police to handle.'

Andreas's expression registered his disapproval at the suggestion.

'I don't trust the police. They interfere. The police are involved only to satisfy the insurance people but this is not a matter for them to resolve. You see, when you are confronted by a playground bully, what do you do? If you go running to tell the teacher you are only making it worse for the next time. No. The only way to deal with a playground bully is to stand up to him, face to face, make him back down and, if necessary, trade blows. Make him realise you cannot be intimidated. This is what I will do with Bentley.'

He read the alarm in the face opposite him.

'But do not worry.' He clapped his large hand on Graham's shoulder. 'I will not do anything foolish but I will settle this business, man to man, and Bentley will pay for the damage he has done. Enough of this! Let us continue with the tour. Have you ever been in the cab of one of these excellent trucks?'

Andreas was already pacing towards the red and yellow-painted tractor unit across the yard. A disquieted Graham followed closely behind.

In the cab sat a driver who appeared to be preparing for his next trip. Andreas opened the passenger side door and placed his foot on the lowest of five steps to raise himself above the level of the cab seats.

'Ray! How are you this morning?'

'Now then, boss. Good thanks. You?'

Andreas lowered himself to ground level again to speak to his escort.

'Ray is one of my best drivers. Go on! Climb in and take a look.'

Tentatively, Graham climbed the steps until he was inside the cab. A hand of greeting was waiting for him.

'Hi, I'm Ray.' It was impossible not to first notice the heavy black tattoo on the side of Ray's bald scalp, swirling like a tangled knot of thorns, but his long, wire-wool grey beard was also pretty eye-catching. His left arm was a colourful mass of tattoo ink and a pot belly stood way beyond the limits of his open high-viz vest, more than hinting at too much time spent sitting in a truck cab and too many fry-ups eaten in service stations. Though their appearances could hardly have contrasted more greatly, the two men were of similar age but Ray, for want of a better expression, looked as if he had more miles on the clock.

They shook hands.

'Graham. Pleased to meet you.'

'Graham is about to join us as the new transport administrator,' announced a voice from outside the cab.

'Really? I'd better start being nice to you then. Never know when I'll need a favour on the rota. Good to have you with us.' His accent marked him as distinctly local. Graham could note small but significant differences between it and the Leeds accent he had grown accustomed to at university.

He looked around the cab.

'The last time I was in one of these was when I was hitch-hiking back from a mate's in Bristol when I was about 19. I can't believe how uncomplicated it is on the dashboard. I expected it to be like the Starship Enterprise with all the technology these things must have these days.'

Ray gave him a proud, tolerant smile.

'I know how you mean. There aren't as many dials as there used to be when I started out. It's all controlled by the computer these days. This is one of the really new units and you've got all the switches within arm's reach – the safety features, the radio, the trailer brakes, the diff locks, everything. This one I like. It's the rear air suspension, so when you've released the trailer and you're ready to get moving again, you press that button and it automatically returns the vehicle to its standard ride height. It's a lot simpler than it used to be.'

Graham nodded, knowingly, attempting to hide the fact that he had not understood half of what had just been said to him.

Ray was just getting into his stride.

'This one's got a 12-speed automatic gearbox and cameras instead of the big wing mirrors, which is far more efficient and more economical as well because they don't create anything like as much drag. And see here between the two tool boxes underneath the bunk? Slide this out and you have a 25-litre fridge. You can control the temperature of that from the dashboard.'

'All the comforts of home,' said Graham, craning his neck to look to the back of the cab. 'Do you sleep in this as well?'

'Nah, mate. I've done my share of tramping. If you can't do a job there and back in a day, I ain't doing it any more. I like my own bed too much.'

Graham could understand that. He had never particularly liked the idea of sleeping in a caravan, never mind bedding down in the same space you've just spent almost the rest of your entire day.

'Do you still like the lifestyle, though? There's so much traffic these days it must get a bit frustrating at times.'

Ray stroked the steering wheel as he considered his answer.

'It's no fun when you're stuck in a tail-back on the M6 for three hours, let me tell you, but I wouldn't want to do anything else. When you're on a job, it's just you in your cab with nobody in your ear, you know what I mean, and nobody to tell you if you're playing your music too loud. I love it. It gives you time to think, if you want to, or just let the world go by, if you'd rather do that. You get to have a crack with the other drivers on the road and with the people at the other depots and you make some good mates. The biggest down-side really can be some of the other dickheads on the road, in their cars and their four-by-fours, who think you have no right to be driving at the same time as them.'

His expression became more serious as he turned to look directly at Graham.

'I tell you, everybody treats us like we're the lowest of the low. Not all the service stations are big enough for the artics and the lay-bys are often full before you get there. But what people don't ever think about is that all the food you eat, all the clothes on your back and all the electrical stuff you buy from the shops have all been on the back of one of these trucks at one time or another. This country couldn't function without companies like this and people like me.'

Graham felt a pang of guilt for the many times he had sworn under his breath at a truck driver for daring to overtake another truck travelling half a mile an hour slower on a dual carriageway. Ray's words hit home. He had never truly appreciated the value of the industry. Their presence on the road was not an inconvenience, it was essential. This is an important service.

'Good to meet you, Ray.' They shook hands again and Graham shuffled across the seat ready to climb down from the cab.

'You too. See you around maybe.'

Maybe. Yes, maybe.

Andreas was pressing commands into his phone as Graham lowered himself to ground level. He walked over to close the door of the truck without looking up before putting his phone back in his pocket and switching back to his tour guide duties.

'Good?' he asked.

'Very sleek.'

'This is one of our newest units. Top of the range. We could buy cheaper, but these are the best. Come, I'll show you the warehouse.'

Andreas set off at a pace again but stopped beside a large tank.

'This is for the additive we put into the exhaust fluid because it reduces emissions. All the companies use it these days. Effectively, it's pig piss.'

With that revelation and without explaining whether or not it was actually pig piss and, if so, how it was harvested, he shot off again.

'Tell me about how busy you usually are, Andreas. How many jobs do you handle?' asked Graham as he attempted to keep up.

The ploy worked. Andreas stopped.

'This depot does around 150 contract runs and 50 spot loads each week. Many of the contract jobs are fixed daily runs to places like Birmingham and Bristol with regular loads – like the sheet plastic on the pallets over there.' He pointed towards several stacks, a metre or so high, wrapped in clear film, beside the metal fence on the side of the yard they had been heading towards. A forklift truck was bringing another three wrapped pallets to add to the pile. 'We call these the milk runs.

'Spot loads are when companies contact us and ask us to make a particular delivery. These are one-way loads normally, so then it is important to try to organise a back haul from that area to make sure the vehicle is not running empty. An empty vehicle is losing money. Making sure that does not happen will be part of your job.'

Andreas held his stare to make sure that point had registered. Graham acknowledged it with a nod.

When he first arrived for his tour of the depot he found Andreas's certainty presumptuous. He was acting as if it was a done deal that the job offer would be taken up. At first, Graham wanted to point out that there were still important decisions to be made, but he did not any more.

He could picture himself a part of this. He felt like he belonged.

8

It had been a long day.

Graham was practically horizontal on the sofa, having quickly and effortlessly come to terms with his new surroundings. Janet lay with her head on his chest.

There were still two slices of pizza in the takeaway delivery box on the low lounge table in front of them and they appeared destined to remain uneaten. Ordering it had seemed a good idea to the point where it was almost a necessity but, when it arrived, they both found they were almost beyond hungry.

The remaining unpacked cases and boxes had been stacked and shut away in the dining room. Neither of them had the slightest inclination to put anything else away tonight. It would save for another day. All they wanted to do now was relax and allow a non-taxing TV show to drift before them.

Janet sighed. It seemed to Graham a contented sigh and that made him smile and pull her a little closer with the hand he held to her shoulder.

She had been preparing for the move for much of the previous week; listing, wrapping and bundling everything she deemed absolutely necessary to take with them right from the start of their occupation of their new home in Unstone, a former mining village between Sheffield and Chesterfield. It had been provided, rent-free, by the man they were increasingly accustomed to regarding as a new family member and who was also, the following day, to be employer to both of them.

Graham had only been required to give a week's notice to the DIY superstore. He had walked away vowing to himself never to set foot there again, even as a customer, and had completed his first week in his new role as transport administrator for the company of Harry Johnson Global Logistics. He had driven up each day and had found the 50-minute commute painless enough, though that and the heightened adrenal demands of taking on a new job had meant he had no trouble getting to sleep those nights.

Janet's notice period was shortened by the amount of unused holiday days she was owed and so most of the preparation for the move had fallen to her. She would probably have assumed charge of the task anyway. Graham would arrive back to their Derby home in the evening and be inwardly alarmed by how much more stuff had been processed into the first-weekend-of-the-move-essentials collection of cases, boxes and bags in his absence.

His reasoning that they could easily travel back to pick up more of their belongings the following weekend and the weekend after that, if necessary, was not seriously considered. His pointed observation, made only partly in jest, that if he had realised how much stuff she had wanted to take with them from the start he would have borrowed one of the artics to move it all, was ignored.

It had taken them two trips in the car, everything

jammed in with the skill of a world-class Tetris champion, and had seriously challenged the car suspension, but they had made it. They were in.

'It's a really nice place, isn't it?'

He knew Janet had taken to the house from the day they travelled up to be shown around for the first time by Andreas. It was an old Derbyshire stone cottage set back off the road and so instantly attractive, with trees and fields rising to frame the view as they climbed out of the car for a first look, that it was almost too quaint. Inside, it had been extensively modernised and had an en suite off the master bedroom. Janet had always wanted an en suite off the master bedroom.

That had certainly helped her overcome some of her misgivings about being talked into making such a radical change to their settled domestic life, which had been a huge relief for Graham. He nevertheless felt he had to keep monitoring her feelings, to reassure himself, as much as anything, and was conscious that he was bordering on overselling the potential benefits of taking on new jobs in a different part of the country. That had also been done partly to reassure himself.

This exciting new opportunities lark was certainly a scary business.

'It's a lovely house,' she confirmed again, partly for her own reassurance. 'I think we're going to be all right here.'

'Me too.' He rubbed his hand on her upper arm, comfortingly.

'I think you're really going to like the people at the depot as well.'

'Yeah, I hope so.'

Graham had told her a little about his new co-workers

through the week, but he sensed her lingering nervousness about the impending reality of them becoming her new co-workers too.

'I didn't say, did I? You know I told you about young Zoe on reception?'

'Uh-huh.'

'Well, she came into work on Friday on crutches. She broke a bone in her foot doing jujitsu.'

'Really?'

'Yeah. Honestly, to look at her you'd never think she was into something like that. She's tiny. She's really nice, though. I think you'll get on great with her.'

They fell into another contented silence, the type that only a couple totally at ease with each other can feel comfortable in. Another plot development of the TV show they were kind of watching was lost to them as their individual thoughts drifted in different directions again.

'Is that manager still being a cow to you?' Janet asked, casually, after a while.

He had regretted mentioning that to her. Rebecca the depot manager, his immediate boss, had been frosty with him, to say the least. Her initial run-through of his duties had been cursory and when he asked her for clarification on a point shortly after, she appeared irritated at having to repeat herself, as if she had spent the whole morning trying to teach a surly teenager how to start up the washing machine. It made him feel inadequate, compounding the sense of vulnerability he had anticipated as he set about tackling an unfamiliar system on the first day of a new job.

'She's been OK,' he responded, unconvincingly. 'Sort of.'

'Well, she'd better not be that way with me. I'll give her

what for.'

Graham was well aware of his wife's feistier side.

'Don't you think it's worth mentioning to Andreas?'

He flinched at the thought.

'I don't think that would be a good idea. I think the best way to win her over will be to show her how well I can do the job. She'll come around. You know the other lad who does the same job as me?'

'Dave?'

'Yeah, except everybody calls him Sparky.'

'Why?'

'What?'

'Why do they call him Sparky?'

'Oh. It's because his second name's Sparks.'

'Oh!' The explanation had clearly fallen some way short of her expectations.

'Anyway, he told me Rebecca's like that with everybody at first. He says she tends to regard everybody as useless until they prove otherwise.'

'How odd.'

'I know. He told me as well that he heard her complaining to Andreas because he'd brought in somebody who hasn't got any experience in the job, which I don't suppose has helped my cause. I wonder if she also feels a bit threatened, you know, with me being the boss's long-lost natural father and all that. I wonder if she's thinking I'm going to be moved up to take her place before long.'

'That would be a bit strange. Is she really that paranoid?'

'I don't know. I'm only guessing. I suppose in time she'll see that I can do the job and realise that I'm not trying to muscle her out of the building and we'll be fine after that. It'll just take a bit of time, that's all.'

'I guess so.'

Their wavering concentration was half-fixed on the TV again. A new character had drifted into the episode and neither of them had the slightest clue where he fitted into the plot.

'Gray?' Janet raised herself off his chest to look into his eyes. 'We are doing the right thing, aren't we?'

'Yeah, I'm sure we are, love.' He tried to inject as much certainty as he dared into the words. The effort worked well enough for Janet to settle her head onto his chest again.

'It's like we said, if we don't at least give it a go, we'll never know how good a move this could be for us both and even if, for whatever reason, it doesn't work out, it's not as if we're making a commitment we can't get out of. We can keep the house in Derby for as long as we like and, if we need to, we can just move back. But I'm sure we'll both be very happy here, once we get settled in, and all our old friends and your family are only 35 miles down the road, so we've no reason to lose touch with anybody. It'll work out just great, just you see.'

She sighed.

'Yeah. You're right.'

The noise jolted him out of his deep sleep with the violence of an explosion. Five mini-explosions. He sat upright with a shocked gasp and attempted to calibrate his addled senses in the unrevealing darkness of an unfamiliar bedroom but could not even be certain if he was suddenly awake or remained locked in the false reality of a panicked dream.

There were the noises again. Five loud bangs. They came from below and this time there was a voice, shouting, demanding.

'Open the door!'

Graham fumbled on the bedside cabinet for his glasses and tried to focus on the digital figures of the alarm clock. 3:58.

'Graham! What is it? What's that noise?' Janet was sitting up now and had grabbed his arm.

'I don't know. It's the middle of the night.'

What the hell could it be? It sounded like the noise was coming from the front door.

Five more bangs.

'Open the door! Last chance, open the door!'

'God, Gray – who is it?' She was almost hysterical, frantic, frightened.

'I don't ...Christ, what the ...Jeez.'

He shot to his feet and stumbled towards the bedroom light, switching it on and instinctively looking around for anything he could grab as a weapon to defend himself against whoever was announcing themselves with such undisguised threat. He stood blinking, in his baggy t-shirt and loose cotton shorts, moving only in sharp, jerky twitches and feeling like his heart was about to burst out of his throat, struggling to make any sense of this nightmarish awakening.

There was another noise, heavier and louder than the others, a thud against the door which shook the whole house. Two seconds later and there was another.

'Gray! They're breaking in! They're trying to break the door down! They're coming in for us!'

Janet was beyond comfort and he was incapable of offering any.

A third weighty thump rocked them and then a fourth,

this one followed by the splintering of the door as it was ripped from its frame.

'Police! Police! Police! Police!'

The yell seemed to come from five, six, seven different mouths, adding to the chaotic noise of a flow of heavy-booted bodies storming inside.

Graham grabbed his dressing gown off the suitcase at the bottom of the bed and dragged it on as he opened the bedroom door.

The house lights were on and three officers, in riot helmets and black stab vests, were stamping up the stairs towards him, yelling.

'Police! Stay where you are!'

He froze, as still as a statue, and feebly put up his hands in submission. The first officer up the stairs peeled off to the left towards where more boxes and bags had been put in temporary storage in a second bedroom. The next policeman closed in on Graham and barked at him, unnecessarily loudly.

'Anthony Verity!'

Graham had no idea how to respond. The words were delivered like an order but it was clearly a name.

'What? Who?' he stuttered.

'Anthony Verity. Where is he?' the officer demanded, the short peak of his helmet so close to Graham's forehead that it was almost touching. His expression was meant to intimidate and had served its purpose. His tone was so loud that, even if he had put the visor of his helmet down, he could still have been clearly heard several streets away.

Janet had put on her dressing gown and grasped hold of her husband for security in the same way as someone might take hold of a bridge support to avoid being swept away by a raging torrent. There was terror in her eyes.

'I've never heard of anybody called Anthony Verity.'

The officer turned his attention to two other officers at his shoulder.

'You, search the bedroom. You, that room at the end of the corridor.'

They bustled past to fulfil their assignments.

'I have a warrant to search this property and a warrant for the arrest of Anthony Verity. Do you know where he is?'

'I've no idea who he is. There's only me and my wife in the house. We've only just moved in.'

The officer took a short step back and bowed his head, then muttered 'shit'. He paused for a moment, contemplating his next move and turned to go back downstairs, turning briefly at the top step to stab a finger at the traumatised couple in dressing gowns and issue another order.

'Stay where you are. I'll be back.'

He stopped midway on the stairs to allow a dog, which was pulling its handler behind it so keenly that the leash was taut, to rush by. The dog stopped on the upper landing and looked back with absolute eagerness in awaiting direction. Its short tail wagged with unrestrained enthusiasm. The handler caught up and released the leash before pointing to the spare bedroom.

'Go on then, in you go.'

No second invitation was needed and the dog set off to nuzzle through, around and between the boxes and bags.

Janet pulled herself even closer.

'What the hell is going on, Gray?'

He glanced into their bedroom, where the policeman had

stripped off all the bedding and was lifting the mattress to look beneath it.

'I have no idea. Must be some sort of mistake.'

The officer was coming back up the stairs, this time behind someone in a fluorescent yellow jacket and the police cap of a senior officer. He was an older man, deeply into his forties, and wore the expression of someone who had just been told bad news.

'Do you live here?' he asked, as if it was a regular occurrence for him to come across a couple in their nightclothes who did not actually inhabit the house he had just broken into.

'Yes. Yes we do. We moved in today – well, yesterday. What is going on here? Why are all these policemen going through our things?'

The senior officer turned to his more junior colleague.

'Tell your men to go through everything but make it brief, Sergeant. We need to wrap this up quickly.'

'Sir.' He turned to go back downstairs, leaving the senior officer with the huddled suspects.

'We're acting on information that an Anthony Verity lives at these premises but you say you don't know who this man is.'

'That's right.'

The officer unzipped the inside pocket of his jacket and took out a notebook.

'Could you tell me your names please?'

The policeman who had been searching the master bedroom squeezed past on the landing, giving his superior the signal of a short shake of the head.

'Graham Hasselhoff.'

The officer peered at him by raising his eyes without

lifting his head.

'Hasselhoff.' He made no attempt to hide the scepticism of his tone.

'H, A, double S, E, L, H, O, double F,' added Graham, helpfully, he thought.

The officer wrote it down, reluctantly, it seemed, and then turned to Janet.

'And I suppose you must be Pamela Anderson.'

Janet let out a small sob. Graham looked down at her but could only see the top of her head as she bowed and burrowed it into his dressing gown. Normally, he would have expected her to stand up for herself but the situation was too much for her this time.

He had never been the type to carry unnecessary baggage into interactions with authority figures and had grown so used, over the years, to people making stupid, unoriginal remarks about his surname but he wasn't prepared to let it go this time. Once anyone dragged Janet into it, they had gone a step too far. No-one was allowed to upset his wife. It was time to take a stand.

'This is my wife Janet and I'll thank you to keep your sarcasm to yourself. Isn't it bad enough that you break into our home in the middle of the night like the bloody Gestapo, scare us both out of our wits and then riffle through our stuff without taking the piss as well? We don't know who Anthony Verity is and whoever the hell he is, it should be bloody obvious to you that he's not here, so I suggest you get all your men out of my house and start working on the apology you're going to have to make because, I promise you, I'm going to put in a complaint about this to your superiors and the bloody prime minister if I have to. This is not acceptable. I want everything put back where your men found it, I want a new front door and if there are any other breakages I want them paid for as well. So if you're done here, I suggest you leave. Now.'

Graham regretted the Gestapo reference as soon as it left his mouth but he felt better about getting that off his chest. It had cleared all feelings of confusion and alarm as effectively as a strong sudden gust of wind clears fallen leaves off a path. He had certainly caught the attention of the man in front of him, not to mention several of the other officers who had been momentarily distracted from their searches. The expression of the officer remained unflustered but the dynamic of the conversation had shifted significantly.

'I must ask you to calm down, sir. I apologise for the upset this must have caused you and your wife but we were acting on reliable information in attempting to apprehend a known criminal. It appears he is no longer here but we acted in good faith. I'm sure a formal apology will be issued to you both very soon and suitable compensation will be arranged. In the meantime, we still need to continue our investigation to find out where Verity now is, so could I ask, have you bought this property or are you renting?'

'Renting. Well, sort of. The house actually belongs to my son, Andreas Johnson, and he's letting us live here.'

The officer wrote down the name.

'In that case, we will need to talk to Mr Johnson. I need to tell my men to start getting ready to leave but, in the meantime, could you get me the contact details?'

'Yes. I can do that.'

The policeman gave a half-smile and turned to go downstairs.

Graham and Janet pulled each other closer in a

consoling hug.

'Soon be over now, love. Andreas will sort this out.' He kissed her forehead.

'This is just horrible, Gray.' She was plainly utterly unnerved by the whole experience. 'Did you see how all those policemen were dressed, like they were going into a war zone? Who's this man they were looking for? He must be a really nasty piece of work for them to do this because they don't break into houses at this time of night for people whose library books are overdue – and what if he comes back? We might be in danger here, Gray. I don't know if I can stay here anymore. And the neighbours – what will they be thinking? We've not been in 10 minutes and they'll be thinking the mafia's moved in. In a small village like this, they'll all be talking. I can't stop here another night, Gray. I want to go home.'

There was nothing he could do or say. He held her tight because that was what both of them needed right now, but there was nothing to be gained from offering a promise that it would all be all right or from fuelling her instinctive reaction of wanting to get back to the familiar sanctuary of home.

He didn't know what to do.

9

Graham had quickly learned to read the signs. When the sounds from the next office indicated that Rebecca was about to stomp into the main reception area, it was the signal that everyone should attempt to look like they were in the middle of concentrating on something important. The warnings were very easy to pick up. For a woman you would not describe as anything other than average height and weight, she was remarkably heavy-footed.

The reception was the hub of the depot. It was busily functional and certainly not a sleek space designed to impress new clientele. It was the place where drivers about to set out on jobs, just back from completing jobs or between jobs would file in and out in an almost constant stream to pick up delivery notes, drop off proof of delivery notes, check their schedules, download their tachograph records and attempt to out-banter young Zoe. They rarely got the better of those exchanges.

She was at her computer screen, making the most of a rare moment when her attention was not needed elsewhere, with her broken foot up on an improvised stool of catalogues with a cushion on top and her crutches propped against the desk. Graham was a few yards away, also behind the reception partition, with his back to Zoe and with two screens in front of him. Even though this was only day six in the job, the environment and his duties were already feeling less alien.

'Graham, I need you to arrange agency cover for the first week in September. We've got two drivers off.'

Rebecca was not one for small talk. She also had an irritating habit of cutting across conversations if she had something to say and always spoke with an edge of urgency in her delivery, which left the impression she felt her words were far more important than anyone else's could possibly be. You could tell the drivers didn't like her and it was obvious, too, that she didn't have a great deal of affection for the drivers. Graham picked up on that on his first morning.

'Don't take any shit from the drivers,' she told him. 'They'll try it on with you all the time if they think they can manipulate you. They'll complain that other drivers are getting the better trucks, they'll complain about the runs they have been allocated, they'll complain about everything. They're like children. They want their hands holding all the time. Just tell them to stop whingeing and if they've got an issue they're to take it up with me.'

That was an option very few were likely to exercise. All the exchanges between Rebecca and the drivers he had witnessed so far could be described as businesslike, at best. Curt would be a less generous but no less accurate description.

'Already sorted, Rebecca. I've been on to Bainbridge's and they've confirmed.'

'Oh!' The reply had a rare double impact, in that it both

stilled and silenced Rebecca. She clearly had not anticipated that Graham had the capacity for initiative.

'Good,' she responded at last. 'That's all right then.'

She turned quickly to stomp back to her office but then stopped and turned back, as if remembering there was something else a good manager should do in situations such as this, according to the manual.

'Well done, Graham. That's good work.'

She was away again without waiting for the potential embarrassment of a further positive inter-colleague interaction.

Graham spun round on his chair to look at Zoe, who was already pulling a face intended to portray mock amazement at what she had just witnessed. He responded by raising his eyebrows and smiling.

He and Janet had decided it would be better to go into work that day, as they reflected on and recovered from the shock of their early morning visit from the police.

Graham had called Andreas to tell him what had happened and, within the half-hour, Andreas was fully launching himself into berating the officer who had been left in charge after the rest returned to the station to reflect on an operation that had not gone to plan. They could hear his raised voice downstairs from the bedroom, happy to leave him to a role he clearly felt comfortable in while they re-made the bed together and felt their emotional state gradually return to normal.

After he had supplied relevant details to the policeman and vented some more, Andreas came upstairs to offer profuse apologies, though there was no question of them holding him personally responsible. He said someone was on their way to make the front door secure again, promised he would take up the issue of the intrusion further and offered them the chance to take the day off to recover.

It was Janet who declined the offer on behalf of them both and took the lead on reassuring Andreas that they were fine. That pleased Graham. It had unsettled him to hear Janet sound so vulnerable when she talked about wanting to pack up and go back to Derby because that was not like her. She was his rock. She was the rational one through the time they wrestled with the anguish of not being able to produce a baby. She made it easier for him to come to terms with his own sense of inadequacy. She helped him readjust his expectations and accept that their life together would not include raising a child. That was the way it was meant to be.

She didn't mention anything about being unable to spend a further night at the house again, as they got ready to go into work, and he didn't mention it either. He knew she regretted saying it. It wasn't like her to talk like that. She had just been spooked, that's all. They were both spooked.

He thought about her as he sat at his desk, plotting and updating the progress of the drivers out on the road on the transport management system, and wondered how she was getting along on her first morning of the new job.

The telephone on his desk rang; the continuous tone of an internal call.

'It's Andreas. Can you come through?' He hung up again without waiting for a reply.

'I've just got to pop in to see Andreas,' he told Zoe. She nodded an acknowledgement.

His office was down the corridor which also led to the back door of the warehouse. Graham hesitated at the closed door to the office, but then decided it was appropriate to knock and wait to be invited in. Son or not, he was still the boss.

'Have a seat, have a seat.'

Andreas gestured with a sweep of his arm to the chair on the other side of his desk while the thumb of his other hand glided furiously over the keypad of his phone.

The office was cluttered and badly overdue a repaint. A single, neglected pot plant on the sill of the sole small window seemed to be gazing out, longing for the companionship of other plants. It was the closest thing in the whole office to a token effort to make more homely a room which otherwise appeared reconciled to the gloom cast by an insufficient ceiling strip light. The walls were largely covered; with framed certificates, free calendars and a large year planner, all fixed randomly with no apparent concern over whether or not they were put up straight. The centrepiece of the most open wall space, opposite banks of battered filing cabinets, was a large framed black and white photograph which showed a grimy 1940s flatbed truck, heavily laden with sacks of coal, beside which three men with grimy faces, all wearing flat caps and heavy aprons, stood impassively, waiting for their image to be captured. Behind the truck was the entrance to a yard with the words 'H Johnson Coal Merchant' showing on a painted sign above it.

Andreas finished prodding at his phone and looked up to see Graham, still standing and studying the large photograph.

'Great picture, isn't it?'

Graham nodded. It was alive with a depth of character that only old black and white images of bygone eras were able to possess.

'The one in the middle is the company founder, Harry. He returned from fighting in the war in Europe to set up the business in 1946 and I believe that photo was taken around then.'

Graham studied the face of the figure at the centre of the picture. Whenever he came across old images of people who had gone to war, as he often had in his previous role as a librarian and family history researcher, he was always drawn to their faces, compelled by the thought that he might see and understand a little of what they must have gone through.

'And this is my pappa, Harry.'

Andreas had picked up a framed picture from his desk to show Graham, turning it from where it was set to face him.

It was a portrait of a smartly dressed and dignified man, his hair almost completely silver yet whose lightly lined and tanned face suggested he was no older than 60. The mouth carried the hint of an upward turn at the corners, just enough to depict the total confidence of a man who knew he was in control. He looked calm, trustworthy.

'And *this*, this is my beautiful mama.'

He turned around the picture, in an identical frame, which had been beside the other on the desk, and then handed it over.

Graham could recognise her features; her eyes, the broad unconditional smile on her full red lips which made her look so content. Her complexion had not yet recovered from the damage of teenage years when they were at university together but there was no sign of that now. Her hair, straight and still dark as varnished ebony, her olive skin firm and uncreased – she had, indeed, matured to become a beautiful woman. Looking at the picture, he was glad she had found happiness after the hardship he must have, unwittingly, made her go through and was also sad that her life had ended so suddenly and prematurely.

Lena Christopoulos. What might have been?

'That was taken only three years ago. It's how I will always remember her.'

The pain of separation was plain in Andreas's voice and his gaze drifted to the place elsewhere, where fond memories are still alive.

'She looks so different to how I had her in my mind's eye and yet I still think I would have recognised her. She looks like she had a very happy life,' Graham offered, still staring deeply at the picture. He passed it back to Andreas, breaking the spell.

'She was the heart of our family.' Andreas accepted the picture back and put it carefully in its place. 'Pappa adored her. I adored her. I take comfort from knowing that they were together right at the end.'

Graham remained reverently quiet as the words lingered in the air. It would not have been right to say anything more.

'Anyway, I owe you an explanation. Please sit down.' Andreas gestured towards the chair again, less extravagantly this time.

'I spoke to the letting agent about the man who had the Unstone property before you.'

Graham sat. He was keen to know what had been learned.

'Anthony Verity.' As he repeated the name Graham felt the shuddering impact of the words again - as they had been barked into his face earlier that morning by the policeman.

'I never met the man myself, but the lady who handles my properties says his credentials checked out fine, he paid on time and never caused an issue. He took out a one-year lease, which he decided not to renew, and left the property in the condition it was in when he first moved in. She said he was a model tenant. Now, whether or not his credentials were fake is up to our friends in the police to establish but I don't think we will be seeing Mr Verity again. It will be interesting to find out what sort of business he was involved in to justify breaking down the door to get him, but enough of that. How are you now?'

It was not the explanation Graham was hoping for. He imagined Andreas must have had some sort of personal contact with Verity and would have been able to offer more of an insight into who he was. His curiosity had not been satisfied, but that was the way it was sometimes. He knew that very well. The full picture is not always clear right at the start.

'We were both fine by the time we had a cup of tea and the chance to take a breath. It was just the initial shock, you know? We're fine now.'

'I've just been through to see Janet,' Andreas added. 'She's being shown around and told where everything is by Ken Arnold, our finance manager. He's a good guy, Ken. He's been with the company since before my pappa took over and he knows this business inside out but, actually, it looked as if Janet was showing *him* how everything was done!'

Graham laughed. That did sound like Janet.

'She's very efficient and she picks things up quickly. I didn't think it would take her long.'

'Marvellous!' Andreas clapped his hands joyfully and

with such a slap that the noise reverberated around the office.

'I told Janet that I insist both of you come for a meal with me on Friday night, so we can get to know each other a little better and so I can show you how grateful I am for being so understanding after the unfortunate business this morning.'

'That's very kind of you but ...'

'I insist!' There was no room for negotiation in the tone. 'I have to go to Southampton for a few days from tomorrow, but I will be back on Thursday. I will make the arrangements.'

'Thank you.' Further resistance would plainly have been wasted.

'But I have kept you from your duties for long enough. I will be getting you in trouble. Tell me, how are you finding my Rottweiler?'

Graham was confused for a moment but swiftly realised he must be referring to Rebecca. He thought it might not be a good idea to show that he had understood the reference too quickly so he held his tongue.

'That's what the drivers call her, you know. She can be a little formidable but, let me tell you, she is an excellent depot manager. I wish I had another like her in Southampton.'

'I'm sure we'll get along fine.' He judged that a reasonably neutral response.

'But the best of it is that she makes me look like I am the good guy!' Andreas threw himself back in his seat and clapped his hands together again, laughing far too enthusiastically at his own joke.

'I'll get back then. Have a good trip.'

Graham smiled and rose to go, leaving Andreas still marvelling at his own wit.

10

Janet flicked over another page. He wasn't keeping an accurate tally but that was probably the third or fourth occasion she had turned over a page of her crime novel in the time he had spent staring at the same page of his biography. It was no reflection on the merit or demerits of either book.

Graham had been bothered by it all afternoon, churning over the information in his mind and trying not to leap to conclusions, but it was hard to stay away from his darker assessment. Something was just not right. It was far from a fully formed theory and the evidence was much less than compelling but neither could the worst be dismissed. He was concerned. He had to talk it through with her.

'You know that thing with the police at work this morning?' he asked, tentatively.

She stopped reading and put the novel down on her lap, open but pages down to make sure she did not lose her place, then took off her reading glasses.

'Yes – what was all that about? They came to see me in the office and wanted to know where we were on Friday, who was there, what time we got there, what time we left –

I thought it was going to be about that business with the man who had the house before us, but they never even mentioned that.'

He nodded. The police had put the same questions to him and no doubt they left with the same answers from both he and Janet. The three of them went to a restaurant called the Bengal Tiger in the centre of Sheffield for the meal Andreas had insisted he would treat them to. They got there about 7.15 and Andreas turned up five minutes later. They had a very nice chat and a really good meal, popped next door to the Frog and Parrott for another pint afterwards, started to feel a bit full and irritated by how lary the gang of lads at the bar were getting, ordered taxis and left separately at around 10.15.

Why do you ask?

I'm afraid we cannot discuss that with you at the moment, sir, but thank you for your time.

But he had to know, so, half an hour after the police left, he found an excuse to go to see Andreas, to ask what it was about.

'Agh!' he responded with a dismissive wave of his hand and contempt in his tone. 'They have nothing better to do with their time and our money.'

'But what did they want?'

He pulled a face and tossed his pen down on the desk, making plain his irritation with their intrusion and his reluctance to discuss it further, but Graham stood his ground.

'It was about that bastard Bentley,' he said at last.

Graham had to think who Bentley was at first, but then he remembered. The rival Andreas blamed for the arson attack on the depot.

'Apparently, somebody assaulted him on Friday night and he told the police that I had been to see him and had threatened him.'

Graham hoped his eyes had not physically widened but, internally, he was certainly alarmed.

'And did you? Threaten him, I mean.'

'Noooo,' Andreas answered emphatically. 'Not really, anyway,' he added, a little less emphatically.

'I went to see him to see if he would be man enough to admit that he was behind the two fires at the depot and to demand that he pays for the damage. He denied all knowledge – of course he did – but I didn't expect any different with a snake like that. Then I might have suggested that this would not be the end of the matter. That's all. But how could I have assaulted him when I spent a delightful Friday in the company of you and Janet? It's ridiculous to suggest I would soil my hands on that maggot.'

Graham tried to appear as if he had accepted the explanation and made noises to support the supposed ridiculousness of any suggestion that Andreas had carried out the assault but something did not sit right. For sure, no-one can be in two places at once but still there was that nagging thought.

He told Janet about what Andreas had said to him and she listened intently.

'But he *was* with us all night. He couldn't possibly have beaten up this man.'

'I know, I know.'

'And if the police have been told that this Bentley might be behind the fires at the depot, shouldn't they be investigating him? Sounds to me like he got his comeuppance.'

Graham sighed and retrieved his bookmark from the bedside cabinet. He was not going to read any more tonight.

'I'm not certain Andreas has even told the police about who he thinks was behind the fires.'

He told her about the note in the wallet. Important evidence, surely, if the police were to be able to do their job properly.

'I get the impression he doesn't trust the police. I get a nasty feeling that Andreas is the type who would prefer to take the law into his own hands.'

'Oh!' Janet considered the point. 'But if this Bentley ...'

'And that's another thing. As far as I'm aware, Andreas hasn't got any evidence to suggest it *was* Bentley, apart from a hunch. There was nothing on the note to say who was responsible. Look, I don't know who Bentley is and I don't know if he's the type that would do such a thing as order an arson attack on a rival, but he says it wasn't him. I know you can argue that he's hardly likely to admit it, but if there is a dispute between them and it means that much to him why would he not want to confront Andreas about it when they are face to face? It just feels to me like Andreas is leaping to conclusions and I'm concerned that he's spoiling for some sort of war with Bentley when he can't be sure Bentley was behind the fires.'

'But he was with us on Friday night.'

'I know – but doesn't that strike you as a bit convenient? This may be an unfair thing to suggest, but did he ask us out for a meal so that he would have an alibi in place?'

'Oh, come on, Gray!'

'Just hear me out. It can't have been him who assaulted

Bentley but could he have fixed up somebody to do it for him? Think about the guy who lived here before us. As you said yourself, the police don't do dawn raids to nab traffic offenders, so lord knows what he was mixed up in. Andreas said he had no personal dealings with this Verity, but what if he did know him? At the end of the day, we know nothing about Andreas and the sort of company he keeps.'

Janet wore her best look of disapproval. He knew it well.

'How can you say such a thing about your own son? He's not like that. I don't know how you can say such a thing.'

He shrugged. 'You're right. I'm probably being really unfair because he's done so much for us in the short time we've known him and I don't want to sound ungrateful but I've got to get this off my chest. You've not really seen him as I've seen him. He always turns on the charm when he's with you, but some of the things he says and does disturb me sometimes. I couldn't say what it is. I can't put my finger on it but there's something about Andreas that's not right. It's like there's a side to his personality that he doesn't want anyone to see, but glimpses of it come to the surface every now and again and then he pushes it back into the shadows. I'd like to believe that he's not capable of something like ordering this assault but I can't be certain.'

There was doubt now in her mind. She knew her husband's instincts didn't often betray him.

'Was he badly hurt, Bentley – in the attack?'

'I went online this afternoon and it was in *The Star*. He was out walking his dog, apparently. The police are calling it an unprovoked attack and are appealing for witnesses, that sort of thing. They said nothing was taken but couldn't rule out robbery as the motive. But yes, it sounded like he took a bit of a beating. Enough to have to spend a night in hospital anyway.'

'Oh my god!'

'I know. Nasty.'

Janet pulled the duvet to her chest, as if feeling a sudden chill.

'So what is it that you've seen to make you say those things about Andreas?'

Graham contemplated for a moment, trying to compose his response properly.

'It's mostly little things,' he said. 'He can be a bit erratic, impetuous, in what he says and how he behaves, like he's a bit of a loose cannon. I get the impression he's capable of great generosity, like he's shown us since we first met, but I just feel like he's a man who experiences huge emotional swings and I wonder what he's capable of at the other end of the spectrum. I'm not saying he's a psychopath or anything but I do wonder if he's got it in him to be a little bit ...dangerous. That might be going too far.

'There are other bits I've picked up on. Zoe told me him and his dad used to have blazing rows, regularly, for a few months before the car accident. Well, she said it was only Andreas they could hear from down the corridor, yelling about how the old man was stuck in the past, holding the company back, couldn't see what needed to be done – that sort of thing – and then he would storm out of the depot with a face like thunder and not be seen for a few days. She said it could be quite frightening to see and hear him like that but then he'd come back and it'd be as if nothing had happened. She reckoned Lena was the one who always got him back on the straight and narrow. She was his calming influence. Zoe said they thought it would really hit him hard, the car accident, especially losing his mother, but she said he was in the office every day after it happened. He even came in later in the afternoon on the day of the funeral.

'This week as well.' Graham shuffled to sit more upright in the bed. It felt good to be getting this out into the open. 'Did you hear that he sacked Chris Yates?'

'Who's Chris Yates?'

'One of the drivers. Been with the company for years. I've not seen much of him myself because he's one of the trampers.'

'The what?'

'A tramper. It's what they call a driver who does the long-distance runs and more or less lives in the cab. I don't think it's a very complimentary term, but the drivers who do those runs seem to love it, for whatever reason. Chris Yates did some of the continentals, you know, going over to mainland Europe, and Sparky said he was very reliable – hardly ever missed a drop time, seemed very happy with the lifestyle. Anyway, word came through that Andreas had sacked him. Rebecca looked like she knew what was going on when she came in to tell us why we suddenly needed to fix up agency cover for his shifts, but it shocked everybody else. I don't know if he was on the fiddle or what but nobody saw it coming.'

'How odd. Is that going to leave you short of drivers?'

'Well, as it turns out, your boss might have come to the rescue there.'

'Ken Arnold?'

'Yeah. Apparently he knows somebody – friend of his son-in-law or something like that – who's got the full HGV class one and has been doing some freelance driving and is looking for something more secure. He's coming in to see Rebecca next week.'

'That sounds like a good solution.'

'Hope so – but getting rid of Chris Yates like that, it's strange. All these little signs start to add up.'

Janet picked up the book off her lap and marked her page with the bookmark to her side.

'I get what you're saying, Gray, but I think you might be looking into all this too deeply. Maybe Andreas is just a bit different. We can't all be the same and just because he's a bit more up and down than most it doesn't make him dangerous or the type of man who would hire a thug to beat someone up. We hardly know the guy yet. You'll get to know his ways and then you'll start to understand that how he acts might not be normal but it'll be normal for Andreas. We can't all be as sturdy and reliable as you, you know.'

She leaned over and kissed him on the cheek.

'I'm going to get some sleep, love. It'll be fine. You'll see.'

She turned over to switch off the bedside lamp and settled beneath the duvet.

Graham took off his glasses and rubbed his eyes.

Maybe she's right. She usually was.

He was glad he told her. Keeping his thoughts to himself had merely amplified them in his mind but their power now dissipated into the air like gases in a pressurised jar once the seal of the lid had been broken.

He set down the glasses on the bedside cabinet and turned off his light, staying upright in the darkness for a short while yet, as if to allow his rational brain to fully regain control.

She was probably right.

****

The rain had been pounding down all day but there was no more putting it off. Graham was needed out in the depot yard and that was that.

The wind bent his borrowed umbrella so fiercely, as soon as he stepped through the door, that it practically swallowed him like a carnivorous plant consuming an unwary fly and it lashed cold rain against his legs, wetting his trousers as suddenly as if a passing bus had splashed through a huge puddle.

He swore under his breath and leaned forward, driving himself into the gusts, short step by short step. The sound of the bullet drops of rain battering the overwhelmed umbrella canopy filled his ears, drowning out even the howl of the wind, but there was one other sound.

It was a voice.

'Hey!'

Graham was so consumed by the task of trying to keep his cover intact for long enough to get him to where he needed to be that the voice did not register in his consciousness at first but there it was again.

'Hey, you!'

He looked up, as much as he dare. The rain had managed to find a way under, over or through the umbrella enough to spatter against his glasses but he could make out a vague figure, standing beside the open gate which led out to the industrial estate.

About the last thing he wanted to do was to take a diversion in that direction but the figure was waving, beckoning him towards the gate.

As much as he wanted to ignore the invitation, he had to go. Surely only a lunatic would be out in this weather, loitering on the perimeter of a transport depot, but it might not be a madman. It might be a customer or a... This was not the time to speculate who it might be but Graham cursed again and accepted that he had to make an unwanted 15-yard detour to find out.

Whoever this person was, they had not been caught out by the weather. As he inched closer, Graham could tell it was a man but only his face was exposed. The rest of him was covered by a head-to-foot weatherproof outfit of canary yellow, broken by thick strips of black on the shoulders of his jacket and the length of the shins on his trousers, which made him look like he had just stepped off a trawler or an oil rig.

He stood unflinching, leaning casually against the gate post as if the weather was simply an irrelevance, while Graham, in his flimsy summer coat and sodden polyester cotton trousers, battled to try to keep his umbrella from tearing inside out.

Who was the madman now?

'You're Johnson's real dad, aren't you?'

It was about the last line of query he expected to be dealing with right now.

'What? What the hell is that...? Who the... Who wants to know?'

'Your wonderful son just sacked me.'

Graham squinted to try to get a clear view of the face beneath the yellow hood. His bulbous nose had been turned red raw by the driving rain, which streamed off the end of it onto his ill-kept grey-streaked beard. He had seen the man only once and briefly as he dropped off documentation at the end of another week-long run but he knew it had to be Chris Yates.

'Look, if you've got a grievance, you'll have to take it up with Andreas – or the union or whatever. There's nothing I can do to help you.'

He began the slow turn to resume his journey towards the depot yard but was made to stop again.

'It's more a matter of me helping you.'

Graham peered at the smug expression which now lit up Yates's face.

'What do you mean?'

The man paused, enjoying the spell of intrigue his words had cast.

'You need to be careful with that son of yours. You have no idea.'

'What?'

'I know things,' he added. 'I worked here for a long time and I know stuff about this company that people don't want others to know and I might just be the one to put the word out. I can bring this company and everybody within it down. People will go to jail.'

'Look, I don't know what you ...'

'Has he told you about the accident?'

There was a deliberately scathing edge to the way he spat out the last word.

'Did he tell you all about how his poor mummy and daddy died that night? Did he tell you about the motorbike? Oh, I bet he didn't tell you about the motorbike.'

Graham was no longer shivering in the face of the storm but had now been overtaken by a deeper chill, running the length of his spine.

'Ask him about the motorbike, but be careful to watch your back after that. Ask him why he gave up the motorbike just after his mummy and daddy were killed. You ask him that.'

Yates leered before spinning and sauntering away towards the main road.

Graham could not tear his eyes from the yellow figure as he wandered away, leaving the shards of the slow-motion grenade he had tossed to tear through his victim.

He stared until the wind changed direction and ripped the umbrella inside out.

11

Disgruntled former employee. They were the words he kept repeating to try to stop himself from becoming completely unsettled by the episode at the yard gates but the label was not robust enough to stop the poisonous allegations from seeping out from its edges.

What did Yates mean?

Could there actually be any truth in what he said?

He told Janet what had happened as they drove home, the steam off his still-damp clothes causing them to keep the windscreen demister turned on for the full trip, but she was not in the mood to encourage any more conspiracy theories.

'He's been sacked, Graham. He's not happy about it.'

'Yeah, but what if ...'

'What if, what? What if he feels like he wasn't the only one doing a bit of a fiddle on the side and he's bitter just because he got caught? And what was he even talking about with this motorbike thing? What has a motorbike got to do with those poor people dying in a road accident? I bet Andreas has never even had a motorbike. Can you really imagine Andreas on a motorbike?'

He couldn't, actually.

'This Yates sounds to me like a nasty piece of work. Fancy coming around just to try to make you believe his scurrilous lies. It's no wonder Andreas got rid of him.'

Only the sound of the wipers scraping across the constantly rain-smeared windscreen disturbed the awkward silence in the car for the next couple of miles.

The traffic was heavier than usual, but then it was a Friday evening. Janet occupied herself with paying close attention to the tail lights of the car immediately ahead and was getting increasingly exasperated by their lack of progress.

The driver of the car in front of them seemed in less of a hurry and Janet kept glancing over her right shoulder, looking for a gap in the unbroken line of traffic in the outside lane for the opportunity to overtake. When the car in front was slow setting away and then pulled up sharply instead of running a traffic light that had just turned amber, Janet jumped on the brakes and jammed the heel of her hand on the horn, accompanying the blast with an irate yell.

'Come on, you dickhead!'

Graham said nothing. It was usually better to allow her to calm herself down on the rare occasions when her anger boiled over. Then she would be back to normal. She was usually far more composed behind the wheel than he was, so something must be bothering her. In his state of preoccupation with the Yates encounter he had not picked up on the signs and he felt selfish.

The lights turned green and they edged away again.

'You all right?' he enquired.

'Sorry, Gray. Bit of a frustrating day.' She was calm again, though still flustered.

'What's up?'

'Oh, I'm just trying to get my head around everything that needs doing in this new job. Lots of it, like raising invoices and credit control, is like what I used to do at Royce's but there's other stuff like processing orders for tyres and oil and sorting accident repairs that I'm not used to yet and I had a list of jobs I wanted to get out of the way this afternoon, before the weekend, but I wasn't sure how they were done. So I had to wait around most of the morning for Mr Arnold to have the time to run through a few things with me and we'd no sooner sat down in his office when his phone went off and he said he had to pop out to take the call. Anyway, out he went, left me sitting there like a lemon for 20 minutes, and then when he came back he said something had cropped up and we'd have to do it another day. There's a pile of stuff on my desk that I couldn't clear and it'll still be waiting for me on Monday and I just hope it's not going to be like this all the time, working for him. I hate this feeling of not knowing what to do. I knew everything about the job at Royce's.'

The words spilled out in a stream of ire.

'It'll just take a little time, that's all, love,' Graham said. 'You've only been there two weeks. You're expecting too much of yourself. You'll get used to everything soon. Before long, all you'll need the boss for will be to sign the papers.'

She drew a deep breath and exhaled.

'I know. I'm just finding it harder than I thought to adjust after being at Royce's all those years and moving house and all that and then you're coming out with all this stuff about Andreas being this and that and I really don't want to hear it, Gray. I don't want you to think like that. I feel like I've got enough on and then you're telling me things that are doing my head in.'

The message was clear enough and was heard. He nodded. He had not considered Janet's feelings while he was spouting his wild theories.

'Sorry, love. I won't go on about it again.'

The traffic was flowing more freely now and, before long, they were home. They had planned to go back to Derby over the weekend, to see a few people and catch up on their news. It would do them good. It would do Janet good.

He tried to block out Yates and what he said. He tried to think more kindly about Andreas and his peculiar ways.

But there were too many loose ends, too much he didn't yet fully understand.

And Graham didn't like loose ends.

****

Almost there now. Chris Yates passed the Norfolk Arms and began to accelerate towards the stone circle that marked the boundary of the Peak District, out to where the bleak vastness of Burbage Moor stretched beyond the dry stone walls. He had driven out on this road many, many times before and whenever he reached that point in the road, past that marker, it always felt like he was making a break for freedom. An escape.

This road was his shortest escape route; the one from which all the rest spread like arteries across the National Park. Over the years, he had explored so much of the open ground between the farms and small communities that the terrain was impressed on his brain as clearly as any road route. Other people might need maps and compasses, but he could read every peak and undulation so well that he always knew where he was and which direction he had to go to get to wherever he wanted to be. He was in his element there. Out on the moors he could walk for miles and miles and not see another human being, yet he never felt lonely. He felt far more isolated in the city, surrounded by people. Out there, he was content. His was the only company he ever wanted to keep.

Whenever he set out, he liked to decide where he was heading by abandoning himself to whim instead of plotting his route in advance. That was real freedom. It was also the perfect antidote to the limitations of his working life, where he was confined to following motorways and A roads as rigidly as if the tyres on his truck had been removed and he was stuck on rails. Up and down, up and down. Same roads, same destinations, same tedious fools at the same stops trying to strike up the same conversations, like they expect they should share some sort of affinity just because they do the same work.

God, how he had come to hate that job. He'd been doing it for 23 years and had covered millions of miles and yet it had got him precisely nowhere. Now, just when he thought he had begun his real break for freedom, a proper escape rather than the temporary retreat of the Peak District, this happens.

But this was not the end of it. Not by a long way. They couldn't just drop him like that, discarded like damaged goods. He was entitled to compensation. He had been the one taking the big risks and he had taken the hit for them by keeping his mouth shut when their scheme was discovered. He'd been sacked but if he'd spoken out then, said who was really responsible, the whole conspiracy would have crumbled into the dirt. That meant they owed him – call it recompense for loss of earnings. That's only fair. And if they didn't do fair by him, then he might not be as willing to keep his mouth shut any more. He could make life very awkward for certain people. With what he knew, he could get them sent to prison for a very long time.

That was what he had told them. He had let them know they had better not fuck him about.

He had set the meeting place. They were going to do this on his terms. He was not going to let them tell him what to do. He told them – lay-by, three-quarters of a mile up the Ringinglow Road after the Norfolk Arms at 11.30. Be there. He told them he wanted cash. He told them he wanted no funny business or he would go to the police. He let them know they were not going to be able to just drop him like a dead weight.

He knew he was close now, even though he was not used to taking this route in the pitch dark of night. He spotted the lay-by ahead in his headlights, on the right, and pulled in, manoeuvring to complete a U-turn so that he was facing the way he had just come from. He wanted to see their car as it approached.

Often, when he had driven past this lay-by the spaces were taken up by the kind of people he loathed. They were the ones in their family saloons and their faux four-by-fours who would clog up the roads every time the sun shone, driving out with their pampered dogs and their despicable kids so they could take photos of themselves in front of the Ox Stones and prove to their friends they had experienced the wonders of the Peak District, like they were the last of the great explorers. Most of them would shit themselves if they wandered off more than 10 minutes away from their cars. He had nothing but contempt for those people. They had no place in his environment.

There was not a soul around now and that was the way he preferred it. It also meant there would be no-one snooping around to witness what was about to take place.

He climbed out of the car and strolled to the back to open the boot, taking out the hefty rusting wheel nut wrench he had decided to bring with him, as insurance. If they refused to give him what he wanted and thought they could try to bully him, the threat of a few blows with the wrench might make them think again. He closed the boot and placed the wrench under the car by the rear wheel – out of sight but close to hand, in case he needed it.

He had arrived deliberately early so that he could stay in charge. He reckoned that by already being there when they arrived he could show he was the one dictating the situation. And so he was happy to wait patiently by the side of the car, unperturbed by the emptiness all around him, his eyes fixed on the road back towards Sheffield.

Ten minutes later, he saw it, the full beam of its headlights becoming increasingly dazzling as it roared closer. Yates turned his head to shield his eyes and stepped back, deeper into the cloak of the night, so that he might not be seen, in case it was not them. The car slowed as it drew closer and pulled into the lay-by so that the front bumpers of the cars were facing. Yates stepped close to his own car again, touching the toe of his boot against the wheel wrench where he had left it, reassuringly.

He could not see who was in the other car because its headlights were still full on and neither could he see them when the lights and the engine were switched off. It was only when the passenger door opened and the internal light ignited that he could make out the figure which emerged from behind it.

The man rose slowly, as if his considerable bulk needed time to re-form from being compressed into such a compact vehicle. When it was free of the restraint, it rose to twice the height of the car and filled out to almost match its width. He was a large man and Yates stiffened. This was not who he was expecting to see.

The man spoke. 'You Yates?'

It was hard not to be menaced by the sheer size of him, but Yates had resolved he would not be intimidated, not under any circumstances.

'And who the fuck are you?' he challenged in reply.

As he spoke, the driver's door opened and another formidable shape began to unfurl to its full substantial expanse. The two men stood and stared, directing the extent of their seething aggression towards the older, smaller, unaccompanied figure in front of them. The one they had been sent to deal with.

Yates nodded, accepting and understanding his situation. They had sent their answer to his demands. His terms had been declined.

'So that's how you're going to play it, is it?' He bent to pick up the wrench. 'Come on then.'

The driver edged towards him as Yates tightened his grip on the wrench and lifted it to shoulder height, ready to strike. He waited until the man nudged closer, to a few feet away, and then he lunged, swinging the tool wildly, one way and then the other. It moved with a whoosh through the still night air but he had not judged the distance well enough in the gloom and the driver was able to sway comfortably out of harm's way.

Nevertheless, the act had been enough to deter the man from moving any nearer but then Yates noticed the passenger, his eyes fixed on his prey, approaching stealthily around the other side of the car. They were closing in on him from both sides and he stepped back, still crouched and alert with the wrench ready to strike, to keep both his assailants in his sight.

The passenger was closest now and Yates aimed a blow at him, with no great expectation of inflicting damage. His belligerence was quickly dissipating and all he had left was the forlorn hope of keeping them at bay as an increasing sense of helplessness started to overwhelm him. His fighting instinct would not allow him to abandon his defence but it could not mask the realisation that this was not going to end anything other than badly. He was cornered, outnumbered, with no chance of rescue. His breathing became shallow and desperate, his eyes wild, darting between the two imposing figures, waiting to see which of them would make the next move.

The slightest of movements from his right triggered another frantic swing of the wrench and the momentum of it exposed him. Yates felt the blow of a heavy boot as it sank into his ribs from the left. His knees dipped and he groaned, the air rushing from his lungs with the force of the kick. Then, from his right, a short, hefty cosh was brought down against the hand in which he held the wrench. He heard the crack of the bones and felt a searing pain shoot up the length of his arm. He was unable to hold on to the weapon and it dropped with a clang on to the hard surface.

Yates fell to his knees, defeated. There was no more fight left in him. He was at their mercy but he would not seek it. He would not give them that satisfaction. He raised his eyes.

The driver had snatched up the wrench. He held it to his chest and grinned, sadistically.

12

Just to be on the safe side, he decided to walk down to the warehouse himself to check. The warehouse manager was on annual leave and Graham wasn't completely confident his deputy had understood clearly how the 58 pallets of electrical components were to be distributed correctly between the five customers. The last thing he wanted on a Monday morning was a cock-up borne of confusion, but he need not have worried. It was better to make sure, though.

As he completed the check, he watched as Zoe hobbled by, wearing a grey plastic hard boot to stabilise her broken foot. It looked even more obtrusively ungainly attached to someone of such a slight physique. She dragged the boot through the wide warehouse doors and turned left, away from the main body of the depot yard, and, as she did, Graham noticed that she dropped one of the handful of sheets of paper she was carrying.

He scurried after it as it began to flutter away in the breeze, but before he could call after her, she had disappeared from view round the corner of the warehouse.

She was taking a first drag on a newly lit cigarette when he caught up with her and she shot him a guilty look as he rounded the corner. Her youthful appearance added to the feeling of a caught-behind-the-bike-sheds moment.

Zoe was, though, in her early twenties. Her momentary alarm at realising she had been rumbled quickly dissipated when she saw it was only Graham and she tipped her long mane of dyed cherry-red hair to release the lungful of smoke towards the clear skies.

'I know. I shouldn't,' she said, as if anticipating his disapproval.

He gave no judgement. 'You dropped this.' He recognised it as a proof of delivery note and offered it to her. The rest of the handful of sheets were folded over and tucked under her arm and she had to put the cigarette between her lips to accept the other back and put it with the pile.

'Thanks,' she said, the cigarette still in her mouth. She replaced the sheets under her arm, freeing her hand to pinch the cigarette between her fingers and take another drag.

'They're a prop. I always grab a handful of papers to make it look like I'm doing something. I don't know why. I suppose Rebecca makes us all jumpy.'

Graham had really taken a shine to Zoe. She had cultivated the veneer of a rebellious, not to be messed with, out to shock young woman, but there were no layers to break through with her. He found her to be a refreshingly open book from the first morning they met and it was clear, seeing her jousting with the drivers, that she was pin-sharp smart too. Other people – notably Rebecca – made more of a show of parading their presumed value to the smooth running of the company, but Zoe was the one who made sure all the small, important details were tended to. She was the glue.

'How are you enjoying the job so far then, Graham? You must have been here about a month now, haven't you?' She leaned casually against the warehouse wall and bent her left leg to take the weight off her injured foot.

'This is my fourth week,' he replied. 'Yeah, I'm enjoying it so far. It's never a dull moment here, is it?'

She blew out her latest intake of smoke with a laugh.

'We don't get surprise sackings and visits from the coppers all the time, you know. It's usually pretty uneventful.'

He too leaned against the warehouse and put his hands in his pockets.

'I got the impression everybody was a bit shocked when it came out that Chris Yates had been sacked.' Graham saw an opportunity to gain a little more perspective on the former driver and his unnerving visit a couple of days earlier, but was keen to dress his curiosity as offhand conversation.

'Yeah. Didn't see that coming. Mind you,' she lowered her voice. 'I can't say I was all that sorry to see him go.'

'Oh?' He turned his head to show she had caught his attention, inviting further explanation.

'I always found him a bit creepy. When you're a woman in a depot full of blokes, you get used to, you know, having them saying stuff to you, but you know they're mostly just larking about and you give them plenty back to keep them in their place but Yates was different. He'd look at you and you'd feel proper grossed out by him. Ugh!' She shuddered. 'Creepy.'

'I see.' In his very short experience of encounters with Yates, Graham could see how people would not choose to spend too much time in close proximity.

'He'd been here a few years, though, hadn't he? You too. How long have you been with the company now, Zoe?'

The end of the cigarette glowed again as she sucked on it. 'Five years,' she said. 'I came here when I left school. I love it here. Harry and Lena were great to work for.'

'So everybody says. I wish I'd have known them myself.'

She cast him a sideways glance. 'You knew Lena, though, right? I mean, I heard before you got here about how you and her ...you know.'

'That was a long time ago,' Graham explained, his cheeks reddening slightly. 'And we didn't really *know* each other all that well then, to be honest.'

Zoe chuckled to herself, enjoying his flush of embarrassment.

'I don't really know Andreas that well either, yet. He showed me the pictures of his mum and dad in his office and he's told me a little bit about them, but I haven't asked a great deal about them or the accident yet. It doesn't seem right. You can tell it's still raw for him. It must have been terrible for everybody when the news came through. Andreas must have been on his own when he found out and that must have been so hard for him.'

'He was at a do, as I remember,' Zoe recalled. 'Some sort of dinner for one of the customers. I remember getting a phone call from them the next morning and they were concerned for him. They said he was in a right state when he took the phone call.'

'I bet.'

'Yeah, poor Andreas, but it took a lot of character to keep the business going, as he did, after a shock like that. He must be made of strong stuff.'

Graham nodded. 'For sure. As I said, I'm still only just getting to know him and I'm finding out little bits to add to the picture every day. Somebody told me the other day he was a biker, for example. I didn't know if they were trying to have me on.'

'No, that's legit. He used to come in on it sometimes. Big, powerful thing it was. Don't know if he's still got it.'

Interesting. Graham still had no idea if that was a significant piece of information, but it was interesting all the same.

Zoe took a last puff at her cigarette and extinguished it on the ground with her foot, then picked up the stub.

'Don't want to leave any incriminating evidence,' she explained, holding it up.

That afternoon, the buzzer at the outer door sounded. All the personnel carried a security card to let them in. Unannounced visits were rare. Sparky went to the door to see who had buzzed and Graham's attention was drawn when he heard the crackly voice coming through on one of their radios.

He spun around in his chair. Two policemen, wearing flat hats and solemn expressions, were following Sparky through into the reception.

'It's just down there. Second door on the left.'

Sparky directed the officers to the corridor and they headed down, towards Andreas's office, leaving the hiss of another indistinct instruction over the radio behind them.

'This is becoming a bit of a regular occurrence,' said Sparky with raised eyebrows as the policemen disappeared out of earshot and he returned to his desk.

'What's *this* about?' asked Graham.

'Dunno, mate. They just said they needed to see Andreas.'

Sparky set about his warehouse admin again, but Graham stared towards the quiet corridor with concern. This was, indeed, becoming a regular occurrence.

Twenty minutes later, the sound of the two officers could be heard coming back up the corridor. As they walked past the partition, the second of them turned to the three on the other side of the divide, who were all trying their best not to stare.

'Thanks very much. We'll see ourselves out.'

Rebecca came to her door.

'What did they want?'

Graham shrugged. Zoe tapped at her keyboard. Sparky felt obliged to take the lead.

'They said they needed to see Andreas.'

'Oh!' Her eyes darted towards the corridor, as if she was considering heading straight down to ask for a more fulsome explanation but then she thought better of it and turned back inside, closing the door behind her.

The three of them settled into their regular work rhythms, disturbed only by two telephone calls, which Zoe dealt with. More than half an hour passed and Graham decided he could stand the suspense no longer.

He didn't feel brave enough to go straight through to Andreas this time. He decided to head out into the yard to see if any of the drivers were around. The drivers always seemed to know everything that was going on.

He slipped the high-viz vest over his shirt.

'Just popping out for a bit of air,' he said.

Outside, in the warm sunshine, he could see no-one at first but then he saw a group of four in a huddle by the mechanics' workshop. Two of them he recognised as drivers.

One of them saw him coming towards them and the others quickly picked up on the non-verbal warning of his approach. Quite a few of the drivers, warehousemen and mechanics still regarded him with an edge of suspicion. His genetic association with the boss made them wary of him.

'All right, fellas?' Graham did his usual best to sound as normal and non-confrontational as he could. 'How's it going?'

One of the drivers gave him a half-smile in response. The others were stony-faced, not prepared to make eye contact.

'Did you see the coppers just then? Any idea what they were after?'

He could tell that they knew something, but were reluctant to share. Graham stood, expectantly. He was about to abandon his attempt when one of them spoke.

'You haven't heard, then?'

Graham shook his head. Plainly not.

'It'll be about Chris Yates, I should guess. He's been murdered.'

13

'Murdered!'

Janet put her hands to her face in shock. He had led her from her office to a quiet spot in the warehouse to tell her. He had to tell her straight away, partly because he didn't want her to hear it from someone else first. He also needed the comfort of being with her to share his own sense of horror at the news.

'That's just horrible, Gray. The poor man.'

Tears welled in the corners of her widened eyes and she dabbed at them with her fingers.

Graham could not stand still. He paced, a couple of steps one way and a couple of steps the other, agitated. He was finding it difficult to absorb the information. His mind was already racing with its potential implications.

'One of the lads said he was found at the side of his car in a lay-by just off the road to Hathersage on Sunday morning and that he'd been hit over the back of the head. It's only three days ago since he was there at the gates, telling me those things, and I didn't want to hear them at the time but what now? He said he knew stuff that people here didn't want to get out and what if that was what got him killed?'

Janet took a step towards her husband and grabbed hold of his forearm, her expression filled with a new terror.

'Oh god, Gray! You don't think Andreas could have done this, do you?'

He stopped moving and pulled her towards him in a hug. It would have been a lie to say the thought had not already crossed his mind.

'I don't know what to think. I don't know what to do. This is just all too awful.'

They held the embrace. What are you meant to do? What are you meant to think?

'Do you think you should go to the police? Tell them what he said to you at the gates.'

He had been thinking about that all weekend. It was a dilemma he hadn't yet found a suitable resolution to.

'I'm really not comfortable with that,' he said. 'On one hand, I can see it's the responsible thing to do but, then again, what would I be telling them? What if, like we said the other day, Yates was just a bitter former employee who decided to get his own back? We have no proof to back it up. All we have are wild allegations aimed at Andreas – and not only suggesting there was some sort of criminal activity going on in the business but implicating him in the death of his parents as well. I can't tell that to the police because I'd be landing Andreas right in it and, for all we know, what Yates said could be completely unfounded. If we told the police what Yates said and then I get pressed by them to tell them anything else I think is relevant about Andreas am I supposed to tell them I've got a nasty feeling he might have organised a thug to beat up Bentley? He'd go right to the top of their list of suspects then and, for all we know, Andreas is completely innocent. Imagine if he got dragged over the coals by the police and then he worked out it was me who set them on to him. His reputation would be ruined and our relationship would be over. How could he ever trust me again if I did something like that to him with no good reason?

'No. I say we let the police do their job, do their forensics at the crime scene, gather their information. They know what they're doing. For all we know, they might already have a good idea who killed Yates.'

Janet was quiet, processing Graham's reasoning. She could see the sense in what he said.

'You could confront Andreas direct. I'm not saying you accuse him of anything, but you could quiz him – try to get a feeling for whether or not he's telling the truth.'

'Could do,' Graham conceded. 'The problem with that is how do I do it in a way that doesn't make him think I suspect him? Whether he's innocent or has got something to hide, it's hard to get that right. Besides, I'm not sure I could look him in the eye right now. I'm too confused by all this.'

'We could just leave.'

Janet pulled away from the embrace to look into his eyes.

'We could say we've made a mistake and can't settle up here. Blame me, if you like. Say I'm homesick. We go back to live in Derby, I see if I can get a job back at Royce's and we can look again at other jobs for you. Maybe there are trucking companies in Derby you could apply for jobs with, now that you've had this bit of experience. I'm sure Andreas would give you a good reference. Maybe Rebecca would as well.'

He scoffed, amused by that thought.

'But seriously, Gray, we could do that. I know we've not been here five minutes and we said we'd give it a while to make up our minds whether or not this move is right for us, but we didn't think we'd be letting ourselves in for this, with murder and beatings and people setting trucks on fire and suggestions of criminal goings-on. We didn't sign up for all that. It's frightening, Gray. It could get dangerous for us. I'm scared for us, Gray.'

He pulled her close again. He understood her fear. He felt it too. Running away from it would be the simplest solution but it didn't feel like the right thing to do. Not yet, anyway.

'I'm frightened as well, love, but I don't think we should just give up on it like that. The scariest part for me is that stuff is happening which is unexplained but I really don't think we're in danger. We've done nothing wrong. Besides...'

Graham let out a deep sigh.

'...whatever Andreas is and whatever he is or isn't mixed up in, he's family now. We've not known each other for long, I know, and we still don't really know each other, but he is my son and you don't just give up on family at the first sign of trouble. I couldn't just run out of his life again because I haven't got a handle on what kind of a person he really is yet. It obviously meant an awful lot to him to come and find me and for him to have me – us – as part of his life after everything he's been through and it would be so harsh to throw everything he's done for us back in his face – and for what? My half-baked theories about who he is and what he might be capable of? The ramblings of a sacked driver who must have been up to his neck in something nasty or he wouldn't have ended up dead in a lay-by? It doesn't add up yet.

'One of the things Andreas said to me that really stuck in my mind when we saw each other at the coffee place that time was that I'm the only family he has left and that really struck home with me because, do you know what, he's the only family I have too. I know I've got your family and they've always been very good about making me feel like I belong and I do feel like I belong but there's nobody really on my side. My parents are long gone and I'm not counting Auntie Rose.'

Janet smiled. 'Good old Auntie Rose!'

'I know. Mad as a fish. But take her out of the equation and Andreas is all I've got on my side and, like I used to find when I was researching my family history, you don't have to know someone to feel like they are part of you. As soon as you start to find little pieces of their stories – just a marriage certificate or an old photograph, whatever – they become part of who you are. That's why you see the subjects on *"Who Do You Think You Are"* break down in tears over sad stories of people in their family trees who died long before they were born. It's because they have awakened a part of themselves they never knew existed before but once you find out about Great-Uncle Fred or Great-Great-Grandmother Edith, they are with you forever. You can't let them go, even if you wanted to. I always got such huge pleasure from helping people discover their ancestries and one of the most rewarding aspects was seeing them understand that we are all part of something much bigger than ourselves. I only discovered Andreas a few weeks ago, but we're interwoven in each other's stories now and I can't just abandon him.'

They held each other in the quiet corner of the warehouse. Janet had never shared her husband's enthusiasm for digging up the past, but she could always see how much pleasure it gave him and how much it meant to him.

'You've got your answer then.' She released herself and smiled, taking hold of both Graham's hands. He looked back at her, quizzically.

'How many times have you said that the answer is always to research more thoroughly? Never assume you know what happened or you understand the cause of events in the past until you can back it up by gathering all the available information – that's what you've always told me. That's what you've got to do. You've got unanswered questions – well, find out what the answers are. Do your research, Gray. That's what you do best.'

He nodded. 'You're right. I can do that. I've always researched the past rather than the present, but the principles are the same. It should be easier, if anything.'

'Talk to people. Find whatever you can online. Try to get to the bottom of all this. It might make sense then.'

'Yeah. I always used to tell people they shouldn't be afraid of finding skeletons in the cupboard because it's all an important part of the full story, so I shouldn't hide from the truth now. I've just got to find out what the truth is.'

He hesitated.

'It's funny, you know. I've helped lots of people do their family histories and some of them are actually quite keen to find a bit of scandal among their ancestors. A proper black sheep. They get really disappointed when they can't find an adulterer or a conman or whatever in their pasts but here I am, hoping to discover that there aren't any skeletons in the cupboard. I suppose you could call that ironic.'

Janet laughed with him, glad that they were both looking ahead again.

'I'll find out whatever I can and then we'll be better placed to decide what we want to do next. Let's go back to Derby this weekend and we can look at what we know, add in what the police might disclose over the next few days and the picture will be a lot clearer. Let's do that.'

'Sounds like a good plan to me,' Janet replied with enthusiasm. 'Best case scenario, we establish that Andreas is not mixed up in any of this and we carry on working here and getting to know him properly. Worst case scenario – well, at least we'll know.'

'You're right. Thanks, love.'

He leaned in to kiss her, intending only an affectionate peck on the lips, but she took hold of him around the neck to commit him to something far more lingering.

'Love you,' she said as they broke the contact.

'Love you, too,' he responded.

'Do you want to know something else that came into my mind last weekend?'

She was intrigued. 'Go on.'

'You know when friends who have kids used to say things as if they were trying to make us feel better about not having kids ourselves – like we don't know how much trouble they can be and how they cause you a lot of stress and we don't realise how lucky we are, crap like that?'

'I know!' she laughed.

'Do you think this is what they had in mind?'

Graham fired up the laptop as soon as they got home.

There had been a sober, quietened atmosphere in the

building through the rest of the afternoon. There were no attempts at banter from the drivers. The news of the murder had shaken them all. Even the phones were respectfully silent. Neither Andreas nor Rebecca emerged from their offices.

There had been plenty for Graham to do as he tracked the drivers out on the road through the Trams traffic management system and fired off emails to customers but he had also found time to plan his strategy. He had to work out what he needed to find, where he had to look and in what order he wanted to search for it. In the end, he decided to begin with looking into the road accident that claimed the lives of Lena and her husband.

He knew nothing about the accident except for the little Andreas had told him and he hadn't thought it appropriate to ask for details. If he wanted to know more, he knew from past experience that the best starting point was to see if the local paper had reported the inquest. There was sure to have been an inquest and, because one of the victims was a prominent local businessman, Graham was confident the paper would have found it newsworthy.

Harry Johnson Lena Sheffield inquest.

He typed the keywords into Google and pressed return. There it was. A report from *The Star* dated February 7.

Haulage company owner and his wife died in unexplained road accident, inquest hears.

Graham clicked on the link and started reading.

The cause of a road accident which claimed the lives of the 'highly respected' owner of a Sheffield haulage company and his wife still cannot be explained, an inquest was told.

Harry Johnson, 59, of Aughton, and his 56-year-old

wife, Elena

Elena? He didn't know that was her full name.

Harry Johnson, 59, of Aughton, and his 56-year-old wife, Elena, died when the MG sports car they were travelling in swerved off the road close to the hamlet of Upper Whiston and hit a tree. The impact almost certainly killed them instantly, Sheffield Coroner's Court heard.

There was some comfort in that. At least they didn't suffer.

Graham scan-read through much of what followed. What he wanted to find was if there was any mention of a motorbike being involved. Here we go.

There were no witnesses to the crash but South Yorkshire Police put out an appeal shortly after the accident, which happened on September 13 last year, to try to find the rider of a motorbike which was seen heading in the opposite direction by the couple who arrived on the scene moments later.

The appeal failed to prompt the potential witness to come forward.

So that's where a motorbike came into the story.

The rest of the inquest report did not expand on why else the motorbike rider might be of significance, so he went back to Google. There might be a report from closer to the time of the accident about the appeal.

Mystery biker may hold the key to cause of death of Sheffield couple.

He clicked on the link.

South Yorkshire Police have appealed for information about a motorcycle rider who was seen heading away from the scene of a road accident which killed the owner of a Sheffield haulage company and his wife this month.

This must be the one. He skipped the next couple of paragraphs.

The Police Serious Collision Investigation team have been looking into the possibility that the motorcyclist may have drifted to the wrong side of the road as it approached the car driven by Mr Johnson, causing him to swerve and leave the road.

Oh really?

Graham eased back in his chair. That explained why they wanted to track down the motorcyclist but how did Yates think that tied in with Andreas? Was he suggesting Andreas was the mystery biker? More to the point, was he suggesting Andreas *deliberately* rode a motorbike on the wrong side of the road to make his dad swerve off the road?

How would that make any sense? Why on earth would anybody deliberately do such a thing, especially when you knew it might lead to the death or serious injury of your mum and dad?

He shook his head. No. The suggestion was ludicrous.

At least now he knew more about how Lena and Harry died.

He reflected for a moment. The terror they must have felt in those final moments. What a horrible way to go. Poor sods.

While he was in investigative mode, Graham decided to see if there was an update on *The Star* website about the Yates murder. He tapped the name of the paper into the search box and clicked to the home page.

The murder had taken second billing to a story about a 21-year-old man who had got his head stuck in a microwave oven trying to win a bet, but it was a headline just underneath the murder report which caught his eye.

Rother Valley Country Park dog snatcher suspect is arrested.

Rother Valley Country Park. Isn't that near where Bentley was beaten up?

He clicked on the link.

A man thought to be responsible for several dog snatchings and for terrifying their distraught owners has been arrested by South Yorkshire Police.

The man, believed to be behind a gang which steals valuable pet dogs on demand, is thought to have carried out five attacks in the area in the past month. Dogs were taken in four of the attacks while, in the other, a victim was left badly beaten and in need of hospital treatment.

Now that has got to be too much of a coincidence.

Graham cupped his hands behind his head. If the man in this report who was attacked was Bentley, that would mean there was no way Andreas was involved. Not unless he was involved in peddling stolen pooches.

He smiled. That's good.

The prospect of Andreas being implicated in the death of his mum and dad was ridiculous and he probably didn't order a hit on Bentley. That was a huge relief.

He felt bad about suspecting his son in the first place, but there was still the suggestion, also raised by Yates, that there was illegal activity going on at the firm. Could Andreas be behind that?

It would take a lot more detective work to find out the truth either way. That would have to wait for another day, but Graham felt he could face Andreas now.

He picked up his phone and scrolled through his contacts list.

'Graham, how are you? I'm sorry we didn't see much of

each other at work today. It was a bit of a nightmare.'

'No, that's OK, Andreas, I had plenty on myself and everybody was a bit distracted today after the news. It must have been a lot for you to handle. Are you OK?'

There was silence at the other end of the phone for a few moments.

'Fine, fine. It was a shock. Chris Yates was with the company for a long time and I know it ended badly for him here but...'

His voice tailed off again.

'It was just a shock and the police. I could do without having to deal with more police.'

Graham thought he sounded strained.

'I won't keep you tonight, Andreas, but I wondered, can I come to see you tomorrow for a word? It's important.'

'I've got to go to Southampton in the morning. I'm just packing a bag. Can it wait?'

'Not really.' That was only a small overstatement. He really did want to get answers sooner rather than later.

'OK then. There's a McDonald's at a leisure park just off the roundabout between the road to Derby and the dual carriageway heading to the M1 at Chesterfield. Do you know the one?'

'Yeah, I know it. The roundabout with the sculpture?'

'That's it. Meet me in the car park there at seven.'

'Sure. I'll see you there.'

They ended the conversation and hung up.

Graham started to plan the next part of his investigation.

14

Graham got there quarter of an hour early, parked up and went to buy a cup of tea. Even at that time, McDonald's was busy, with plenty of people at the tables eating over-processed breakfast meals from paper wrappings. He did not feel tempted to join them.

It was shaping up as a beautiful mid-August morning and he found a spot in the revitalising glow of the awakening sun to sit on a bollard and watch for when Andreas arrived for their liaison. Most of the rest of the previous evening, after he had arranged this morning meeting, had been spent on the laptop finding whatever information he could about Yates's murder and Andreas's business. The searches into Harry Johnson Global Logistics didn't tell him much that he did not already know. There was nothing obviously untoward on the Companies House or the *London Gazette* websites, which was where he usually searched for the sort of information that didn't always come to light in the mainstream media. Hardly any detail had been released about the murder as yet either.

That was not unexpected. Sometimes, you have to dig

deeper to find what you are looking for. It can be a matter of knowing where to search. His first step was to talk to Andreas.

The silver Jaguar pulled into the car park at just before seven. Graham walked slowly towards it as Andreas straightened up and turned off the ignition.

'Do you want a cuppa?' Graham held up his 100% recyclable beverage cup to illustrate what was on offer.

'No, no, I'm fine. Thanks. Come and sit in the car.' Andreas appeared edgy, distracted.

'I won't keep you long,' he said as he lowered himself into the passenger seat. 'It's this business with Chris Yates. I just wanted to know if there was anything I should be aware of in case the police come back to interview any of us at the depot. I don't really know anything about him and I wanted to, you know, present a united front.'

Andreas sighed and stared ahead, blankly, through the windscreen.

'There was not much I could tell them myself. I had to lose him and, less than a week later, he is murdered. I can understand why they came to see me but I have no idea why anyone would have wanted to kill him. It is a wretched thing to have happened.'

'But why did you have to let him go? Everybody I talked to said he could be a bit odd but he was completely reliable as a driver. Sacking him caught everybody by surprise.'

'Chris Yates was a good worker. He had been with the company for many years and hardly missed a day. He was as reliable as the day is long.' He spoke the words forcefully. This was no empty eulogy.

'Look, I do not want this to become common knowledge

around the company. It would be an insult to his memory but I had to tell the police the full story and so it may come out in time, but I don't want everyone to know until then.'

Andreas had turned to face Graham to spell out his message. It was understood.

'Anything you tell me is purely between me and you, Andreas, you know that.'

He nodded.

'Rebecca came to me a couple of weeks ago because she had noticed discrepancies and an unexplained pattern of behaviour in Chris Yates's data on one of his regular continental runs. We always use the Rotterdam to Hull route when we deliver to the northern continent from Sheffield and that's an easy run back to the depot at the end – two and a half hours max. Most drivers I know would want to come straight back after spending three, four, five days away but Rebecca noticed that Yates had taken a break at a spot off the M18 before Doncaster. He was well within his four and a half hours before he had to take a mandatory break and she could see no record of a reason for the stop – no reported hold-up or mechanical problem, anything like that. She checked back over his previous continentals and looked at his tacho records and he was making the same stop on the same run every four weeks coming back from Hull and no record of a problem. She became suspicious and brought it to me.

'I called on a favour from a customer I know very well in the Netherlands. His was the last drop-off and pick-up before Yates drove on to Rotterdam on his last run and I asked him to count how many pallets were on the load when Yates left his depot and checked that alongside how many were on the load when he arrived back in Sheffield.

He was carrying a couple of pallets more than he should when he left the Netherlands but arrived here with the correct number, so that indicated to us Yates was doing a bit on the side and dropping off the extra pallets somewhere between Hull and the depot.

'I called him to the office to ask him about these discrepancies and he became very aggressive. I asked him if he was doing a little sideline business and the odd part was that he didn't seem upset at the accusation of wrongdoing and started threatening me! He told me that if I interfered I would be creating huge trouble for myself and I would be better off if I turned a blind eye, but I could not tolerate that.

'He wouldn't tell me what he was mixed up in but, whatever it was, he was damaging the good name of this company and I won't have that. I had to sack him.'

Andreas leaned his head against the headrest and drew a deep breath.

'When I lost my mama and pappa on that terrible night, I thought I would die. I thought my world had ended, but I vowed that the best way I could honour their memories would be to devote myself to this company and make it a success beyond anything they ever planned. I was in the office the day after the accident and every day after that, even on the day of their funeral, so that I could fully prepare myself. My pappa had already taught me so much but I learned everything about the business and developed a strategy to make it grow. I want them to be so proud of me and I cannot allow anything which might compromise the integrity of the company. Yates had to go. Simple as that. Now that has cost him his life and I have to carry that burden.'

Graham took hold of the hand Andreas had kept on the gear lever all the way through his explanation and squeezed it, comfortingly.

'Whatever it was Yates was up to, it isn't your fault he was killed for it. That was his choice. If you thought he might be up to something that would rebound back on you, you had to sack him. You did the right thing.'

Andreas nodded slowly. He clearly had no doubts about the actions, only regrets at the consequences.

'Have you considered ...' Graham hesitated. A thought was forming. 'Have you considered that whatever it was Yates was caught up in might be connected to the arson attacks at the depot?'

The words jolted Andreas out of his contemplation.

'I mean, you just kind of assumed Doug Bentley was behind the fires but he flatly denied he was when you went to see him, didn't he?'

'He did but ...'

'What if he was telling the truth? What if the arson attacks were not aimed to hurt you at all but were some sort of misdirected attempt to put the frighteners on Chris Yates?'

Andreas attempted to digest the thought.

'I suppose it's possible.'

'There was something I found out last night,' Graham added. 'I think whoever assaulted Bentley the other week was targeting his dog rather than him.'

'His dog?'

'It was online on *The Star* site yesterday that somebody had been arrested for dog-snatching, stealing valuable dogs to sell on illegally, and that one of the people had been put in hospital when he tried to fight back.'

'That fucker accused me!' Andreas's temper quickly flared. 'He told the police I was responsible! I will have that bastard!'

Graham grabbed his arm and leaned closer, demanding eye contact.

'He told the police you threatened him – which you did.'

Andreas's silence was concession enough. His anger visibly cooled.

'Listen to me, Andreas. I know it's a bit late in the day for me to be playing the parental advice card but this thing with you and Bentley, it has to stop now. What I'm suggesting is that while you're down in Southampton I arrange to go to see Bentley, to talk to him. I'll patch up this spat between you and then you can both get on with running your businesses – and you and I can get on with finding out who really is behind the arson attacks and why they are doing it. That's the real issue here.'

The man in the driving seat was stony-faced, every inch the chastised child. Eventually, he gave in.

'OK,' he said.

'Good. Which day are you back?'

'Thursday. Late Thursday, probably.'

He nodded. He was beginning to see the sense in it.

'You are right, Graham. Go to see Bentley and make it good. We'll speak on Friday morning and you can tell me how it went.'

'Sure.' Graham released his grip on his son's forearm and gave it a rewarding 'well done' pat.

He moved to open the car door. He had what he wanted.

Their attention was caught by a loud roar as a motorbike turned into the car park. Its owner clearly enjoyed revving the engine as a way of getting noticed.

'Good lord! That looks a bit of a beast.'

It was sleek and black, like a drag racer, with three thick chrome tubes feeding from the engine to a chunky double exhaust, which seemed to serve mainly to amplify the roar generated by each flick of the rider's right wrist.

Andreas surveyed its magnificent curves appreciatively, the way some men pore over the sight of a glorious work of art or a beautiful woman.

'Triumph Rocket 3,' he said. 'The 2500cc engine is the largest in the world for a production bike and they reckon it has a top speed of 145 miles an hour. Very impressive but I still prefer the Ducati XDiavel S if you're going to go for a cruiser. They're both beasts but the Ducati is more of a sexy beast. Italian, you see.'

Graham watched as the bike chugged around the corner.

'You know your bikes. Do you have one?'

'Not anymore.' His tone was heavy with regret. 'I decided to sell mine soon after the accident. All part of becoming a more responsible adult, I suppose. Still.' He turned to Graham with a broad smile. 'The Jag has its consolations, I suppose.'

He tapped the steering wheel.

'I must let you get on your way,' said Graham, taking his cue. 'Safe journey and I'll see you on Friday.'

He watched as the silver Jaguar pulled away from the traffic lights and turned right to head towards the motorway.

Putting the last piece into the puzzle regarding the motorbike had been a bonus. He no longer considered it a serious possibility that Andreas had been the mystery biker who might have been involved in the fatal road accident anyway. It just made no sense on any level.

His main aims for the meeting had been achieved and he had also formed an ad hoc theory which potentially went a step closer to explaining the arson attacks. Making the effort to get out of bed earlier had definitely been worth it.

15

Graham made the call to the Rother Valley Transport depot, looking to set an appointment to see Doug Bentley, shortly after he arrived at work for the start of his shift. He was told the boss was not available but got the feeling he would not have been put through, as he had asked, whether Bentley was available right then or not. So he left his mobile number and asked to be rung back.

There was the sound of raucous laughter behind him as he hung up and he spun in his chair to see who the source of it was. It was Ray, the driver who had shown him around the cab of his lorry on the day Andreas gave him his first tour of the depot. He had nurtured a look that made it hard not to notice him and he had a laugh to match. Ray was attempting to wind Zoe up about her broken foot. She was threatening to kick him where he didn't want to be kicked to prove she still had full mobility.

Ray was still laughing as he picked up his delivery note and set off to do his pre-trip vehicle checks. Graham snatched the high-viz jacket off the back of his chair and set off after him.

'Ray!'

He stopped midway through pulling the door open on his way to the yard and held it open as Graham, scrambling to find the arm hole in his jacket, caught up.

'Now then, Darth. How's it going?'

Graham completed the challenge of pulling on the jacket.

'Darth?'

'That's what the mechanics are calling you.' Ray chuckled and stopped walking to face his puzzled co-worker.

'You know, Darth Vader. As in *Star Wars*. As in...'

He cupped his hands over his mouth to muffle the sound of his voice and spoke an octave or two lower than usual.

'...Luke, I am your real father.'

They set off walking again, Ray smiling to himself.

'I see. That's quite good. A damn sight more original than what I usually get, I must say.'

They turned the corner and headed towards the imposing flat front of the red and yellow tractor unit parked to their left.

'I bet. You must have loved it when *Baywatch* was at its peak.'

Ray pressed the keypad as they got closer, opening the cab doors.

'I had it before then as well. People used to think it was hilarious to put on a voice like that car computer and say things like: "May I suggest you engage the on/off switch, Graham?" It wore very thin after a while.'

'*Knight Rider!* I used to love that!'

Graham shook his head. 'I wasn't a fan.'

Ray turned to face him.

'You know, you should have done what my mate used

to do. His name was Michael Jackson and everybody knew him as Mick, but whenever he met people for the first time he'd introduce himself as Michael Jackson. If they came back at him with something stupid like "give us a moonwalk, then" he'd know they were a twat and he shouldn't have anything else to do with them. He used to say it was a very useful filter.'

'Ha! That's so true. I wish I'd thought of that.'

Ray continued his walk towards the driver's door.

Graham moved to intercept him.

'Before you get on with your checks, Ray, I wondered if I could just have a quick word. Just between me and you.'

He stopped.

'Sure. What is it?'

Graham moved two steps closer.

'It's about Chris Yates. I'm trying to make sense of this awful business and you must have worked with him for a long time. Do you know of anything he might have got himself mixed up in that landed him in such trouble?'

Ray's face turned serious. It was a look that, with his physical size, style and tattoos, made him appear quite menacing, though Graham already knew that was not in his nature.

'I worked with Chris for years but I can't say I ever really got to know him. I'm not sure anybody really knew him. He was definitely one who kept to himself, Chris, and, from what I'm told, he never really made much of an effort to be sociable when he was on the road either, but I never got the impression he might be on the fiddle. I certainly never heard anything. As I said, he wasn't the type who would give you a great many clues but, from what happened, he must have been caught up in something. He wouldn't have got sacked for nothing and he certainly wouldn't have got killed for nothing. I guess we'll find out before too long what it was.'

Graham nodded, solemnly. He was hoping to give the impression he was simply curious rather than conducting inquiries for a different purpose.

'Have you ever come across people at the company who might be doing a bit on the side? It must be tempting for some people to think that the odd flat screen TV wouldn't be missed if it disappeared off the load. There must have been some of that going on.'

'You hear about it at other companies,' Ray stroked his long beard. 'But, do you know what, I don't think I've once come across people doing that here. Old man Johnson was a really top bloke. Nobody had a bad word for him because he took care of his employees like we were all family and everybody who worked for him showed him that loyalty back. We were a really tight-knit bunch.

'When Andreas took over, he carried on in the same vein. I think everybody made an even bigger effort for him in light of what he must have gone through and I'm certain he recognised that. I know we all have a gripe or two with his Rottweiler and it's not unknown for him to chew your arse himself, if you've done something wrong, but you're never in his bad books for long. He'll never hold it against you. Andreas is rock solid, just like Harry always was, and people like working for him. He's a good man, your son. You should be proud of him.'

The words brought a smile to Graham's face. Parental pride. This was a new sensation for him.

'Thanks. I appreciate that.'

His mobile phone began to ring. He retrieved it from his

trouser pocket. It was an unrecognised mobile number.

'I'd better get this. Cheers, Ray. Hope the trip goes smoothly.'

Graham pressed the green answer button.

'Hello?'

There was a moment of silence from the other end, then a voice.

'Doug Bentley. I'm told you want to talk to me.'

'Oh hi, Doug, I'm...'

'I know who you are.'

The bluntness of the tone was off-putting but Graham pressed on with the approach he had rehearsed in his mind.

'OK. I wondered if we could meet up. There's been a fair bit of unpleasantness between you and Andreas recently and I wanted to try to clear the air.'

He allowed the proposition to hang for a while.

'You should get that lad of yours to watch his mouth then.' Bentley was clearly still not happy about his previous visit.

'Look, I'm sure things were said on both sides that shouldn't have been, but what I'm suggesting is me and you meet up and sort it out. I've talked to Andreas and he knows he went too far. He wants me to patch it up between you.'

Silence. Graham hoped Bentley was thinking it through.

'All right. I'll talk to you.'

'Great. Are you around later today? Or tomorrow?'

'I can't do today or tomorrow. I've got too much on. We can meet Thursday evening. I sometimes go for a pint after work at the Golden Ball in Whiston. Do you know it?'

'I don't, but I'm sure I can find it.'

'Meet me there at half six.'

He hung up. It wasn't the friendliest of exchanges, but the arrangement was made. At least it would be fresh in his mind for when he reported back to Andreas on the Friday morning.

Janet was keen for an update as they drove home to Unstone. Graham had told her about the morning meeting with Andreas as they were on their way into work but he was able to expand on his findings by explaining about the phone call with Doug Bentley and the brief word with Ray. He felt like it had been a very productive day.

'You've been busy,' said Janet, appreciatively.

He didn't feel like it had been an effort, though his attention levels dropped in the afternoon as the early start, as much as anything, took a toll. He was enjoying the buzz of the new research project and believed he was really making progress. He was, however, looking forward to switching off in front of the TV and sharing a bottle of wine with Janet.

There was little more he could think of to do before he went to see Bentley anyway.

'So you don't think Andreas is up to anything dodgy any more then?'

'I don't think so, no.' Graham conceded. 'I think his biggest fault – if it is a fault – is that he cares too passionately about steering the company to the next level. The intensity he shows in trying to live up to his own expectations and his desire to honour the memory of his parents is quite touching, really. He just needs to take it down a notch or two, for his own good, I think.'

Janet made it through the left turn at the Meadowhead roundabout without having to come to a halt, which was a rarity. They would be home in less than 10 minutes.

'Apart from making peace with Bentley, what else is on the agenda?' she asked.

'Well, it's the attacks on the depot. That's the biggie. If we're assuming they were nothing to do with Bentley – and I think we can, pretty safely, now – we still need to establish who carried them out. You know, the more I think about the possibility that it could be tied in with whatever Yates was mixed up in, like I suggested to Andreas this morning, the more that makes sense. I'd love to know what it was Yates was up to that drove somebody to want to kill him but Andreas didn't know and neither did Ray. He was sacked because Andreas said Yates got hostile about being accused of theft and painted himself into a corner and I got the impression from Andreas that if he'd owned up, shown a bit of contrition, he might have been given a second chance. I think it actually hurt Andreas to have to sack him. I suppose we'll have to wait to see what the police come up with. Until they can shed more light on who killed Yates and why, it looks like we're at a bit of a dead end, so to speak.'

Graham stretched and stifled a yawn as they turned off the next roundabout towards Dronfield. He was looking forward to that glass of wine.

16

The word soon got around. There had been a development in the murder case. A witness had come forward to say they had been driving on the road to Hathersage at around 11.30 on the Saturday night, past the lay-by where Chris Yates's body was found early on Sunday morning. They said they saw a man getting into the passenger seat of a dark car which was pulled in behind another car on the lay-by.

Graham called up the report on *The Star* website to read it for himself. There was not much more that was fresh about the information other than that. It was not a major breakthrough, but the police said they were releasing the witness account in the hope that it might spark memories from other motorists in the vicinity at a similar time and prompt them to come forward too.

If the police wanted to make sure they attracted maximum publicity, they could have done worse than to employ Smudge. He was a squat man who worked in the repair shop and he had made it his duty to ensure news of the development spread quickly around the depot. Having passed on the facts as he saw them in the reception leg of his tour, Smudge was moving on to giving Zoe the benefit of his opinion.

'I reckon they think the one who was getting into the car was the one who did it,' he declared. 'Either him or the driver. Maybe one of them got him talking while the other sneaked up behind him and smacked him over the head. I reckon they only meant to rob him but they botched it and hit him too hard, then they saw the car coming and panicked. They're still trying to work out what Yatesy was doing out there, in the middle of nowhere that late at night, but I heard it was because he was into dogging.'

Zoe squinted back at him, unable to disguise her faint disgust at the latter suggestion.

'How can you even...? Nobody has any idea what he was doing out there, so how can you...? I don't even want to think about that.'

Smudge held up his hands, suddenly eager to establish himself as the messenger and not the perpetrator of the theory.

'That's only what I've heard.'

Zoe returned to her work, making clear her distaste and signalling that the largely one-way conversation was over.

'Anybody who believes that bollocks should be ashamed of themselves,' she muttered, as Smudge skulked off to try to find someone more receptive to speculate with.

Graham shook his head. He shared her irritation and not only with the suggestion that Yates might have had seedy sexual habits. This was not the first wild theory that had done the rounds. They may now have a better idea of when the murder happened but they were no closer to finding out why and that lack of knowledge had left a void which some people felt compelled to fill with Chinese whisper-type insinuation. Perhaps that was a symptom of the social media age or maybe that was just how people always have been; only now their ill-formed speculation was able to spread to a wider audience much more rapidly. People certainly appeared more impatient for information than they used to be. The demand was for instant answers and he felt sympathy for the police because the truth still took as long to establish as it ever did.

Yet, for all his sympathy, Graham too felt impatient. Having made such good headway over the previous couple of days, he was at a bit of a loose end. The meeting with Doug Bentley was only a day away but the news update stirred guilty thoughts that he could be doing something useful in the meantime.

If there was a link between the murder and the fires, what was it? The reclusive Yates had left no clues – not at the depot, anyway.

It was such a pleasant day that Graham suggested to Janet that they take a walk by the golf course in their lunch break. It was good to escape the oppressive busyness of the industrial estate and follow the path through the woods, where birdsong masked the constant invasive hum of traffic from the Parkway and the only interruption to the brief secluded peace came in the occasional exasperated cry from the fairway of the eighth.

They walked hand-in-hand, as they habitually did, relishing how the sun cut through the canopy to pour beams of intense light on the wild flowers and dense greenery on either side of them. Janet was telling him, in more detail than was necessary, about a text conversation she had had with her sister midway through the morning and Graham was content just to listen.

'Oh, I got you that address you asked for,' she said, breaking the stream of her account just as she was about to tell him about an arrangement they had set to meet up on Saturday evening. She retrieved a piece of paper from her handbag and gave it to him.

'Why do you need to know where Chris Yates lived?'

'I was thinking I might go around there after work,' he replied casually in a way that suggested he still might not, even though he had decided, after coming up with the idea an hour earlier, that he definitely would.

'Nobody really knows much about him at work, even though he's been there for years. We don't even know if he lived alone or had a partner or what. I thought I might go around there to see if I can find anybody who knew him. Knock on a few doors maybe. He must have neighbours.'

'Do you think that'll get you get anywhere?' There was a hint of scepticism in the question.

'You never know. It's like I said to you last night, none of us understands anything about him but that might just be because he chose to keep his home life and his work separate. Some people are like that. I thought that by seeing where he lived I might just get a bit more insight as to who he was. It's worth a shot.'

Janet was not won over by his reckoning and neither did she understand his compulsion to find out but had prior experience of the lengths her husband was prepared to go to when he had the bit between his teeth like this.

'If you say so,' she replied and left it at that. They followed the path to where it led to the cemetery and neither of them raised the subject again.

Graham dropped Janet at home after work and set off

straight back towards the city centre. He knew that she thought he would be wasting his time and was aware of that possibility himself but he wanted to do this anyway, driven by the prospect, however slight, that he might find some small detail which could be the key to the big picture.

He parked part way up the steep road and eyed the climb ahead, hoping he had not underestimated how far up in front of him the house he was looking for actually was. He was aware of Sheffield's reputation for hills before they moved to the area but had not seen enough of the city yet to experience their challenges and wondered briefly if his creaking knee joints were up to the task.

Behind him, he could hear the faint baying of goats. The brown signs, as he approached the road he wanted, warned him there was a city farm close by but still the noise felt completely at odds in the urban setting.

The house closest to him was number 81. That meant he did not have far to go, which was a welcome bonus. Many of the buildings on either side of him were relatively modern but, as he trudged up the slope, the one he believed to be Yates's was among a block of narrow terraced houses. They looked as if they dated back to when similar buildings, on both sides and probably road-by-road for quite a way around them, must have stretched uniformly the full length of the street. He was glad some, at least, had survived town planning and the decay of time to serve as reminders of how the area would once have been.

Number 103 looked neglected. Stumps of iron railings, long since hacked down and taken away as scrap metal to be made into weapons in the 1940s, were embedded in a low wall in front of the house, leaving the much higher solid stone gate posts, standing beside the opening to a slender path, looking isolated and obsolete. Weeds poked from between the uneven paving slabs that covered the tiny patch of yard and the grimy blue paint of the large bay window was chipped and peeling.

Graham stood at the wooden front door and composed himself before knocking. He did not expect anyone to answer, but had a cover story prepared, just in case. There was no sound of activity from within but he was poised to try again when a voice called from behind him.

'You won't find anybody there, pal.'

A man was watching him from the path of a house opposite. Graham crossed the road towards him, keen to make the most of any opportunity to gather information. The man stood still, arms folded. He was in his forties and wore several days of stubble, a loose white t-shirt, baggy black shorts and flip-flops.

'Hi. I wonder if you could tell me if I'm at the right place. I'm looking for Chris Yates's house.'

The man eyed him with suspicion.

'Are you press?' he asked.

'No, I'm a work colleague. Well, former work colleague, I guess.'

'Only we've had one or two press around here.'

The man was clearly not in the mood to give anything away until he had been assured that the stranger was not looking for a fresh angle to a story. Graham reached into his trouser pocket and produced his work photo ID in the hope of appeasing him. The man inspected it warily.

'I worked with Chris at Johnson's,' explained Graham, taking back the ID. 'I've come to see if there was anyone at the house. The last time he updated his personal details at work he said he had no next of kin but that was a few years ago and I wanted to check if that was still the case. There's his company pension, you see. Do you know if he had a partner or any family?'

The man stroked his chin. 'Not that I know of. I've never seen anybody else coming or going from the house and I've lived here 13 years.'

That was less than promising. This man appeared to be the naturally vigilant type and if he hadn't noticed anything...

'So as far as you're aware, nobody has been to the house since he died?'

'Well,' the man shook his head, ruefully. 'Nobody that wasn't up to no good. He had a break-in on Sunday night, see. Later the same day after they found him dead.'

'Really?' Graham was shocked.

'There are some scumbags around. It must have only been a few hours after they announced the news. No respect, some people. The coppers were all over the house the next day, of course.'

'Was much taken, do you know?'

'I had a look through the front window before the coppers got there – just to check, like. It looked a mess. It looked as if stuff had been turned upside down and thrown around but it was funny because his telly was still there. You would have thought if somebody had broken in to do some thieving they would have nicked the telly, wouldn't you?'

That did strike Graham as odd. If they were not opportunist burglars, what were they after?

'Did you know Chris very well yourself? You say you lived opposite him for quite a long time.'

'Nah,' replied the man. 'We just exchanged nods and

hellos when we saw each other leave the house and that's it. He was never any trouble but he very much kept himself to himself, Chris. I'd see him in the Sheaf sometimes at weekends but he'd never socialise; just sit by himself with his pint and a paper. It's funny though ...'

The man suddenly sparked with a recollection.

'I had to tell my missus about this because it was so unusual. I was at the bar at the Sheaf, what would it be – three or four weeks ago? Anyway, I was waiting to be served and he came to the bar as well. I said "All right Chris?" and he said "Aye". That was about as much as you ever got out of him but then he just started telling me this bloody bullshit story.'

Graham was intrigued. 'What do you mean?'

'Well, he started telling me that he'd just bought a house out in Menorca and that he was going to sell up and move out there before long. Just came out with it like that. He looks like he never spent very much on himself but I wouldn't have thought your lot pays that much. Not so much that somebody could just pack up and go to live out in Spain at his age. He can't have been much older than me and I don't suppose there's much call for long-distance lorry drivers in Menorca. I thought he must be having me on but he kept a straight face and then as soon as he'd got his pint and told me his tale, he went off to sit by himself again. It was as if he just wanted to get it off his chest – you know, like he wanted to brag about it and had been busting to tell somebody. Weird – but that was Chris for you. I take it you're no wiser than I am about why somebody would kill him.'

The question snapped Graham out of his musings. The story of running away to a home in the sun was a revelation. It appeared to confirm the suspicions that Yates was mixed up in something other than – and far more lucrative than – being a humble lorry driver but what might that have been? Whatever it was, the timing of his sacking must have dealt a huge blow to his dreams, especially if it jeopardised his extra-curricular interests. It was no wonder he was full of threats and bitter recriminations in the exchange at the gates.

'No. None of us know why.'

The man sighed. 'We'll find out soon enough, I suppose,' he said, before being alerted by tapping from the inside of his own front window. A dark-haired woman in a low-cut pink top gestured for him to come back inside.

'It looks like my tea's ready,' he said, instantly lifted by the news as he began to edge back towards the door. 'I'm sorry I couldn't really help you.'

'Not at all. It's been good to talk to you,' Graham replied, raising his hand to confirm his gratitude to the retreating figure, who disappeared inside with a faint smile.

The conversation had been more informative than the man realised. It did not give any answers, but it had put flesh on the bones of the little he knew about Yates and that was worthwhile.

Graham thought about knocking on a couple more doors to see if further progress could be made. Could another neighbour be even more well-informed than the man in the flip-flops? Possibly.

He checked his watch. He had promised Janet he would not be long because it was his turn to cook their evening meal. He was almost at the outer limits of the time he had allocated himself. He thought again about knocking at maybe only one more door, just a quick call, but decided against. Another day, maybe. He shouldn't keep Janet waiting. That wouldn't be fair.

And so he set off back down the hill to the car.

17

It was a similar routine the following day. Graham was about to drop Janet back at home and head straight off but this time it was to meet Doug Bentley at the pub.

There had been no further official update on the Yates murder, though there had been plenty of continued speculation at the depot as to what degree of bad company he must have fallen into to have met such a grizzly end in a dark lay-by. The more cautious offered reminders that they didn't know he was up to no good and that he might have simply been the victim of a random attack. The only thing everyone was certain of was that they had no idea what the truth was.

Graham pulled up at the end of the drive outside their home and waited for his wife to make her move.

'Righto, duckie.' She released her seatbelt and leaned over to kiss him. 'Hope it goes well. How long do you think you'll be?'

'Hard to say.' He knew what he wanted to get from the meeting but didn't know how forthcoming Bentley would be. 'I shouldn't think it will take much more than half an hour.'

'OK. I'll cook for half seven. If you're going to be much later, give me a ring to let me know.'

'I tell you what, if I'm not back in time carry on without me and I can warm mine up in the microwave. You never know, we might find a lot to talk about, maybe some way our two companies can work together to benefit both of us in the future. I might be there all night.'

She cast him a sideways look.

'Yes, well, don't you have too much to drink.'

He responded with incredulity.

'You know I never have more than one pint when I'm driving.'

Janet would have been unable to come up with a single example of when that was not the case but it didn't stop her giving him a final doubting glance. He wondered if all women believed that inside even the most mild-mannered of men there was an inner Oliver Reed waiting to burst out.

'I'll see you later then.' She opened the door to get out and he watched her as she walked to the house. He had already programmed the location into the sat nav and had worked out that the trip would take half an hour. The clock on the dashboard said there were 42 minutes until the scheduled meeting time. He pressed the button for the sat nav to start dictating the best route and pulled away.

There was a large car park opposite the pub but few of the bays were filled. Graham steered the car into a space a third of the way down, well away from anyone else, and turned off the engine. He waited another moment to compose himself. The abruptness of Bentley on the phone had made him more nervous about the meeting than he might have been. He wanted to present himself as businesslike and not easily intimidated.

He drew a deep breath as he locked the car door and walked two steps before waiting for a large black BMW to pass by and turn into a space on the opposite side of the car park. Graham tucked his keys into his jacket pocket and strode towards the pub.

There were three steps leading up to the grey front door and a large golden orb was suspended ominously above the entrance. A pillar, unmistakably an old and crooked tree trunk, dominated the centre of the bar area and appeared barely capable of supporting the huge roughly carved beam of the low ceiling but, judging by its obvious age, it had clearly done the job perfectly well for a long time. Two groups of early diners were at tables to his right and he walked across the stone flags towards the bar on the left.

A young woman, her dark hair tied back in a ponytail, was consulting her notepad and pressing an order into the till.

'What can I get for you, love?'

He had a look at the hand pumps.

'Could I have a pint of the Thornbridge, please?'

'Of course you can.'

She finished with the till and went to pull the pint.

'I've come to meet a man called Doug Bentley. I don't suppose you know him?'

'Doug? Yeah, I know him. I'm sure he went through to the beer garden.'

She indicated the direction with a nod of her head and a flick of her ponytail.

He paid for the pint, gave his thanks and set off to find Bentley.

It was a warm, sunny evening and the beer garden,

sheltered from whatever cool breeze there was by tall conifers, was a fine spot. There was a young couple at one table and the man was sitting back with a pint of lager while the woman leaned forward to interact with a baby in a pushchair. The only other person in the garden was an older man, sitting alone and reading a newspaper.

Graham moved towards him.

'Hello. Doug?'

The man responded. He had a heavily lined, well-worn face the colour of old leather with grey hair combed back. There was a fading bruise and healing scar by his left eye. He was wearing a checked white shirt with the sleeves rolled up above the elbow and stood to a height of around six feet as he reached out a sinewy arm, well covered in thick grey hair, to offer a handshake.

'Aye,' was his simple confirmation that Graham had found his man.

He put down his beer on the table between them and took the handshake. Bentley gave the hand a strong squeeze and released it.

'Pleased to meet you,' said Graham.

Bentley lowered himself back into his chair.

'Sit yourself down, lad.'

The older man took a mouthful of his pint and surveyed the figure opposite.

'Now, what did you want to see me for?'

'It's as I said to you on the phone,' Graham replied. 'I wanted to draw a line under this fall-out between yourself and Andreas because it's no good for anybody. He asked me to apologise for coming on so aggressively when he came to see you but I wanted to explain to you what caused him to act like that. We've had a bit of trouble, as you've probably heard.'

Bentley raised an eyebrow. 'Aye. I heard.'

'I know you had a bad experience yourself recently.' Graham nodded towards the bruised eye. 'I hope you've fully recovered now. I saw they think it was this person who's been stealing dogs.'

He was glad to have the early chance to get that well-practised line into the open straight away. He judged that it made him sound concerned for Bentley's well-being while, at the same time, serving as a reminder that he had also done his bit to stoke the fire of mistrust between him and Andreas by indicating to the police that his rival might have been behind the attack.

Bentley stroked the area around the bruise.

'Back to normal now,' he said. 'I gave as good as I got but the bastard had some sort of bat and I took a few whacks from it. They made me spend a night in hospital.'

'What happened?' Graham took a sip of beer. He wanted to hear the full story.

'Well, I could see this bloke coming towards me with his hood up and then, when he got closer, I could see he had a scarf to cover his face as well, so I knew it was trouble. When I saw him take the bat from around his back I thought I had to get my retaliation in first, so I let go of the dog's lead and lunged at him, tried to take him by surprise.

'I don't know if he was expecting me to be just some doddery old bloke or what but I don't think he was expecting that. I smacked him a couple of times but then he swung and hit me on the arm. That went numb and useless, so I carried on going for him with the other hand but he caught me a few more times with the bat and I went down.

He ran away and left me there.

'If I'd known he was after the dog I'd have let him have the bloody thing. It's the wife's, one of those pugs. Ugly little bastard. Not even a proper dog, if you ask me. It ran away when the punches started flying and came back when it was all over. What kind of use is that for a dog, I ask you?'

Graham smiled back, amused by the end to the tale. It corroborated the version of events as he hoped it had been.

'I'm sorry that Andreas ended up getting a visit from the coppers but when they asked me if anybody had a grievance against me I ended up giving them his name. I was still a bit pissed off with him, to be honest, for coming around to my place and shouting the odds about me having petrol bombs thrown into his yard, telling me I was going to pay for it. Who the bloody hell does he think I am? Bloody Al Capone?

'I always got on very well with Harry. He was a proper gent and a good man. I never had a cross word with Harry and I always quite liked young Andreas but when he came over bloody ranting and raving and accusing me of all sorts he was lucky he didn't get my boot up his arse. There was no call for it.'

Bentley reached for his glass and a soothing gulp. Graham gave him a second to cool down.

'As I said, Andreas regrets what he did now but somebody caused the fires and we know it wasn't just vandals because there was a note.'

'A note?'

'It was a warning, saying the fires were a consequence of something that was clearly irritating someone. Andreas knew he'd been trying to move in on some of your customers, put two and two together and, well, made 58.'

'Look, lad.' Bentley sat forward. 'I've been in this business a long time. People try to steal your customers all the time. I've done it myself. You lose some and you win some, that's the way it goes. It's different if you sub-contract work to somebody and they go back to the customer trying to undercut you – you shouldn't do that – but us and Johnsons don't sub-contract to each other and so it's fair game. It's certainly not cause to start throwing petrol bombs at each other.'

Graham felt no reason to doubt his word. Bentley was not the man behind the attacks, he was sure of that now. He expected when they met that Bentley would be eliminated from suspicion and the picture was now apparently clearer.

Except that they still had no clue who was behind the fires and what they wanted Andreas to stop doing. That made it very difficult to bring the issue to a close.

'I believe you, Doug, and I'm sure Andreas will too. What I'd like to suggest is that the two of you also go for a pint sometime soon and put this thing to bed for good. How does that sound?'

Bentley took another mouthful of beer and nodded.

'Aye, I'll have a drink with him. I don't hold grudges. You tell him that.'

'I will.' Graham raised his glass. 'Cheers, Doug.'

Bentley looked at his watch and drained the rest of his drink.

'I'd best be off. Tell Andreas to get in touch. It's been good to meet you Graham.'

They shook hands again before Bentley picked up and folded his newspaper and took the path from the beer garden by the side of the pub.

Graham sat back. That went well.

He turned his face to the sun, which was getting lower in the blue sky, and felt pleased with himself. If he left now he could still be back home in time for the estimated 7.30 meal-time but he felt in no mood to rush. He still had more than half a pint left and was going to relish it.

If only they could work out who was behind the arson attacks. Why didn't they just show themselves? Make it clear what they wanted. The thought coincided with a small blob of cloud floating maliciously in front of the sun.

He nevertheless finished his drink in four more leisurely measures and rose to his feet. He checked the time. 7.12. Even if the meal was ready bang on time it would still be fine without reheating by the time he arrived back.

Graham crossed the narrow road from the pub to the car park and fished the keys from his jacket pocket. He could not see the car at first because a large black BMW had parked by the side of where he knew he had left it but, as he drew closer, he could see the back of the red hatchback and his fleeting concern dissipated.

18

He stood and he waited, sucking on a cigarette to pass the time. There were no nerves to settle. He knew what they had to do.

He was leaning against the rear of the car, the height of it shielding his compact, muscular frame from the small amount of activity there was on the road. He took another glance from around the car towards the road. Still no sign.

That's fine. They could wait all night if they needed to. The longer they waited, the more chance that they would have the cover of darkness for when they needed to make their move and that would be better. There were still probably a couple of hours of daylight yet.

Doing it in the daylight was riskier. More chance of being spotted by someone passing by or even by someone at the window of one of the houses on the opposite end from the road. The houses bothered him. From there, someone might see him leaning against the car and judge that he was acting suspiciously. Their attention would be caught. That would not be good. There should be no witnesses.

And so he was trying to look as casual as possible. Just

an ordinary bloke leaning against his car, having a fag, waiting to meet someone. Nothing suspicious about that.

In a short while, if the man still hadn't shown, he would go to sit in the driver's seat instead, just so nobody might see him still out there, still waiting, and start thinking he was up to no good. Some people don't know when to keep their noses out. He would still be able to keep watch from inside the car, but not as easily.

The other two were inside, both in the back, hidden from view by the concealing darkness of the tinted glass, waiting for his signal. Waiting to pounce.

This was not where they originally intended to do it. The plan was to take him outside the house, which meant they were going to have to take the woman as well. That would have been an added complication, but it would have been fine. Might even have given them extra leverage.

They didn't expect him to let her out and then drive off but you have to think on your feet sometimes. Things don't always go to plan. You have to be able to adapt. So they followed him, hanging back just far enough that he didn't think he might be being followed, until they saw him pull in again. When they were satisfied they hadn't been compromised and that he wasn't going to set straight off again, they also pulled in.

They watched him cross the road and go into the pub. Then they had a look around to check if this was a suitable place. No cameras, not a lot of activity in and out, not much traffic on the road. The houses at the opposite end from the road were a concern but, on the whole, they were OK with it. He made the final decision.

We'll do it here. We'll move the car across there to give us cover. If something crops up at the moment we need to move, we'll abort for now and follow him again to wherever he goes next. That will probably be the house. We'll follow him back there, if we need to, and do it then.

But it had to be done and it had to be done tonight.

He glanced around the car again, making the action appear as casual as he could. Still no sign. He took a last drag on the cigarette and stubbed it out on the floor. Then he reached into the inside pocket of his brown leather coat and took out the packet to smoke another.

Perhaps he was more nervous about this than he wanted to admit to himself. There was a lot riding on this. It had to go smoothly.

He lit the next cigarette and took another look.

From the path on the outside of the pub he could see the man. He must have come from around the back. It was definitely him.

He tapped three times with the middle knuckle of his index finger on the rear side window of the car and discarded the cigarette.

The rear door opened and one of his colleagues climbed out, closing the door behind him and moving, hunched, towards the front of the car to get into position.

He checked for unwanted activity. Nobody else coming back towards their cars or pulling off the road to park. No pedestrians or dog walkers. Nobody snooping from the windows of the houses. Good. He gave the signal of a sharp single nod to his colleague as confirmation.

It's on.

The man was getting his keys out of his pocket and craning to see where he had left his car, so he hid from view, satisfied the man was on his way. He would be here in no time.

He could hear the footsteps getting closer until they were almost level with him and then he stepped out from behind the car, trying to make it look as if he had just parked up.

The man paid him no attention as he walked past, ready to approach the driver's side of the red hatchback.

'Excuse me, buddy.'

The man stopped, no more than three steps away. Greying hair, glasses, doesn't look like he works out at all. This shouldn't be a problem, as long as they get it right.

He strolled the rest of the short distance towards the man as he spoke.

'Do you know if you have to pay at this car park?'

The man glimpsed around.

'I didn't see ...'

He pounced. Hand clamped over the man's mouth to stop him yelling out, other arm wrapped around his chest to drag him backwards behind the cover of the black car. As they got there, his colleague had opened the rear door and grabbed the man's legs to lift him. They bundled him into the back of the car, where the third of them was ready to drag him onto the seat.

The one who had grabbed the legs jumped in behind him and slapped his hand across the man's mouth before he could recover his senses and shout for help.

'Keep quiet and you won't get hurt,' he said, menacingly, jabbing a finger in the man's face.

The third tore off a strip of thick black tape and, as the hand was removed, the tape was fixed to make sure no sound would be possible. He then took a black hood from beside him on the seat and whipped it over the man's head.

The black car was already reversing out of the parking

bay. It squealed to a stop and jolted quickly forward, pulling out from the car park and away.

19

At first, Graham was too shocked to resist or shout for help. It all happened so quickly. By the time his brain had absorbed the scale of the trouble he was in it was too late.

He was now in full-blown panic mode. He breathed shallow and fast. His mouth had gone as parched as if a hot jet had been blown into the back of his throat and the restrictive tape left him unable to pull his lips apart. His efforts to draw in the air he needed through his nose was limited by the dense black cloth over his head, which was sucked with every hysterical breath to his nostrils like a valve clamping them shut.

He wanted to grab at the black veil which was suffocating him and had robbed him of the assimilating comfort of vision as well but his hands were immovably gripped around the wrist by the men on either side. The men who had swept him away and bundled him into the black car. The men who were taking him away God knows where to do God knows what.

The man on his right used his spare hand to grasp Graham's arm at the elbow and squeezed hard, administering a jarring jolt of pain.

'Keep still!' he commanded.

Graham wanted only to tell him that he could not breathe and that he felt as if he was having a heart attack but he could make no coherent sound. He was helpless, friendless, drowning in black cloth.

What is happening to me?

His distress was growing by the second. The beer he had savoured with such satisfaction such a short while ago churned in his stomach and made him feel as if he wanted to vomit but that really would drown him. There was no aid to be had from outside. He had to help himself.

Breathe more slowly. Breathe more slowly. Breathe more slowly.

Gradually, his agitation eased. The whirring light-headedness wound down. The air filled his lungs more generously. He stopped focusing on the black cloth and the tape over his mouth and the hands gripping his wrists and became more aware of the gentle up and down movement of the car and the way his body was made to sway to either side by curves in the road he could not see to anticipate.

The men said nothing, but his ears picked up the sound of the car's acceleration, sustained and increased now as if they had come to a stretch of faster road. He guessed maybe they had joined the M1. He had no idea which direction they were heading in but told himself it might be a good idea to try to estimate how long the journey was taking, so that he could give the police a clue as to where he had been taken.

Assuming he was later released, that is.

Realisation of the danger he was in came over him like a wave again. Deepening that dread was his absolute inability to even partially rationalise his situation with a possible reason. He was in the hands of unknown assailants who had come for him with an unknown motive and were taking him he had no idea where.

The whole scenario was beyond comprehension and that was truly terrifying.

The low drone of the car engine was broken only by the tick-tick-tick of the occasional signal as they pulled out to overtake. It didn't feel as if they were moving especially quickly. Apart from the small rhythmical bumps which marked their progress, it hardly felt as if they were moving at all. The driver must understand the wisdom of not attracting attention. The last thing they wanted was to be pulled over by the police for a traffic infringement. It was the thing Graham wanted most.

After around 10 minutes, the pitch of the engine changed. They were slowing down. The sound roared and died as they came down through the gears and then he lurched slightly forward as they came to a stop. He could hear traffic as it passed in front of them before their car moved away again, climbing the gears and slowing again into a turn, then accelerating again until they made another turn.

Graham tried to draw a map of their progress in his mind but it quickly became confused. Without the aid of vision, he could not keep pace with its changes. He abandoned the attempt. It was useless.

They wound through the streets for maybe 10 or 15 minutes more. He was past thinking about the journey and was full of what must soon lie at the end of it. He was really scared now. This nightmare might only be beginning.

The car made one final turn and the wheels scrunched to a halt over what sounded to be loose stone. The driver turned off the engine and Graham could hear the front door opening, then closing with a rush of warm air. The grip around his wrists was not yet released but then the rear door on his right creaked open and the man on that side let go to climb out.

He felt a grab and a pull on his upper arm, encouraging him to move, and heard a voice bark 'come on' as someone dragged him towards the open door. With his left arm also now free, he used it to help him shuffle across the seat, conscious that he needed to discourage any thought of violence in response to perceived resistance. He could hear the door to his left open and shut as the third of his assailants got out of the car.

Then he was on his feet and felt the sensation of rough loose stones under them as he was hurried, virtually carried, by two of the men holding him firmly on either side. He heard the click of a key turning in a lock and a door opening before he was bustled inside a building, feeling it suddenly cooler and quieter than it had been outside.

The three men's heavy footsteps echoed down what he perceived to be a corridor and then they were in a more open space. They travelled only a few yards further and the two holding him stopped. One of them pulled Graham's arm behind his back and then took hold of the other so his hands were together. He heard the tearing and snap of tape being pulled from a roll before it was wrapped around his wrists, securing them firmly.

His breathing was quickening again and his chest thumped with anxiety.

What are they going to do to me?

He was pulled backwards and felt the heel of his feet catch against something solid, then a hand pressed on his shoulder and a voice demanded 'sit!'

He sat.

There was silence around him again as footsteps trailed towards the far end of the room away from him, but he knew he was not alone.

What are they waiting for? Why can't they at least take off this hood so that I can see what's in store for me? So that it will be easier to breathe.

In his anger and frustration he shook his head and tried to scream words of defiance but the restraint of the tape across his mouth limited his protests to an inarticulate blur of sound.

He sat, wanting to spit out opposition, wanting to challenge the complete vulnerability of his situation, wanting just to know where he was, why he was there and what they wanted from him.

Tell me! Whatever it is, tell me!

Then he heard a voice. A female voice. And it stopped his dissent.

'Well, well, well. Graham Hasselhoff. Who would have thought it?'

As this new confusion scrambled his thoughts to even wider proportions, the hood was seized above his scalp by someone behind him and hauled off his head.

The light overwhelmed his pupils and made him squeeze his eyelids shut. He blinked and blinked again, encouraging his eyes to adjust and find their focus so he could take in his new surroundings. It felt good to be able to breathe without the stale filter of cloth, but he needed to see where he was.

Before he could become accustomed to the light, a hand reached down and tore the tape from his mouth. The relief of that release was tempered by a surge of pain which made him feel as if every nerve ending in his lips and around his mouth was throbbing and he yelled, both to celebrate being free from the tether of the tape and to express his sudden hurt.

The room was beginning to come into focus now but pulling off the hood had displaced his glasses down his nose and was preventing him from seeing properly. With his hands taped behind his back, he could not push them into place.

The man in the brown leather coat, the one who had approached him in the car park, came from behind him and stood at his side, glaring.

'Sorry, but I don't suppose you could just put my glasses on properly for me, could you?' Graham asked the man, aware that he had retained an astonishing level of politeness, in the circumstances.

'Fuck off,' replied the man, who was clearly less concerned with maintaining social graces.

'Now, now, Jason.' It was the woman again. She was leaning against a desk around five yards in front of him. He could not yet make her out properly but she appeared to be well dressed in a dark skirt and jacket.

'Remember that Mr Hasselhoff is our guest.'

The man bent over and took the glasses by the hinges at either side and hooked them back over Graham's ears, so that the frame rested back in the pressure grooves on the bridge of his nose.

The man leaned and sneered 'Better?'

Graham nodded. 'Thanks.'

The man had short-cropped hair which was beginning to recede at the temples and a curving scar, about three inches long, on his left cheekbone. He had a thick-set, powerful upper body, though he was not a young man – edging towards 40, maybe – and gave all the signs of having led a hard life. It had marked him with a disposition which was less than sunny.

Graham's eyes darted around the room. He was in an office. Not a cluttered, functional and haphazard office like Andreas's but a thoughtfully-conceived, out-to-make-a-favourable-first-impression office. It had healthy plants, a coffee machine and a carpet that hadn't been ruined beyond salvation by decades of muddy boots and spilled drinks. The walls were a light grey, with a large black cabinet dominating the far wall. A framed print of a snowy mountainside was hung to its left and, to the right, was a two-seat crimson sofa.

The woman rested her bottom on the curved front of a black desk with silver metal trim. She was in her fifties and stylish, making her appear almost as if she had been deliberately integrated into the design of her swish surroundings. She had her arms crossed and her legs crossed at the ankles and wore a lilac round-necked top with a heavy silver necklace beneath her tailored jacket. Her hair was shoulder-length, dark and elegantly cut and her expression was confident, challenging. In control.

'Could you leave us please, Jason? I'd like a few moments alone with Mr Hasselhoff,' she said.

Jason held his steely focus on Graham, calculating the risk of agreeing to the request without protest.

'Sure,' he replied at last and walked towards the door next to the snowy mountain print, turning back to stare at Graham again and adding, pointedly more for his benefit than the woman's, 'I'll be next door.'

After he left the room, the woman smiled.

'He's a good boy. He always looks after his mother.'

Without the intimidating presence beside him, Graham felt emboldened to speak up.

'Look, who the hell are you and why have you brought me here?'

He felt he was entitled to know.

She stood and strolled towards the coffee machine, which was on a table to his left. A tray with a jug of water was beside it and she poured herself a glass.

'Oh, I think you know why you're here.'

She brought the glass to her red lips and watched him as he attempted to process her reply.

'What the hell is that supposed to mean? I have no idea why your ...thugs grabbed me in a car park, blindfolded me, half-suffocated me, scared the living shit out of me and brought me here. I have no idea where I am or what you want, so I suggest you set me free right now because, I'm telling you, you've got the wrong man.'

She took another sip of water and replaced the glass on the tray.

'You are definitely the right man, Graham Hasselhoff,' she said as she ambled back to her position at the desk.

'That is not a name anybody could forget in a hurry but some of us have more reason than most for that name to stick in their minds. Some of us had their world turned upside down. Some of us were thrown out onto the streets with no money and a baby on the way. Some of us almost ended up dead in a grotty hovel at the hands of some smackhead. And now some of us have to take steps to protect their interests. Oh yes, you are most definitely the right man, Graham Hasselhoff.'

He was floundering, confused beyond words. Nothing of what she said made any sense to him. It was a tale of a personal nightmare that had no connection with his world. Yet she seemed sure she knew who he was.

'I don't understand. Who are you? What has any of what you said got to do with me?'

She shook her head, mournfully.

'How quickly they forget. Use you and move on. You never struck me as that sort of guy – a bit shy and quite nice, on the whole, but not really the love them and leave them type. I guess it's the quiet ones you have to watch.'

She stood and walked towards him. He watched her with unseeing eyes, too distracted by the utter bafflement occupying his brain as he attempted to find anything in her words that struck even the faintest chord in his recollection. His perplexity was leading him to the edge of panic as he desperately tried to unravel the puzzle.

'You really don't remember me, do you?' She stood no more than a foot in front of him now and leaned forward until her eyes burned into his, inches away.

'Let me give you a clue.'

She stooped to whisper in his ear.

'My bedroom in the house in Meanwood. The night of the Lindisfarne concert.'

She stood straight again, her gaze fixed on his face as the pieces began to fall into place.

He had only one sexual experience in his three years as a student at Leeds – besides the drunken encounter with Lena Christopoulos in the halls on the eve of final results day, that is. It happened at her house in Meanwood after they had been to see Lindisfarne in concert at the Queen's Hall and they went to a couple of pubs in town after the gig and she missed her last bus because they lost track of the time and he offered to walk her back to her digs and she invited him in for a coffee and all her housemates were already in bed, so they started kissing in the living room and then... oh god!

'Sarah?'

20

I was so naive back then. I honestly thought you liked me, you know? I remember when I first saw you at the History Society meeting in the union bar and I was really glad just because you sat next to me and talked to me. I was that pathetic. And then, when you asked me if I'd like to meet up for a coffee in the refectory the next day, you started blushing and I sat there grinning, looking like an idiot. God, it makes me want to vomit just thinking about it.

But I was actually happy. I'd never had a boyfriend. My parents sent me to a girls' school, I think mostly so that they could protect me from being exposed to boys, but I was so awkward and gawky-looking that none of them ever wanted to come near me anyway. You were the first and I thought you were really nice. You'd listen to what I was saying when we talked and we made each other laugh and I started to think *'This is what it must be like. This is how it feels to love somebody.'* I was properly loved up! After a couple of weeks! Can you believe that? What a stupid bitch.

And oh! That concert! I'd never been to a proper gig before and I couldn't get over the noise and the sway of the packed crowd and the joy! Everybody was having such a good time and singing along to all the songs and even though I didn't know the words to any of them, it was so fantastic just to be part of it and feel like I belonged to something so ...euphoric. It was liberating in a way I hadn't known before. Nobody could see you, nobody knew you, nobody cared who you were. You were one of them, part of the crowd, part of a shared experience and you could just let yourself go for an hour and a half or whatever it was and celebrate the freedom of being lost in the music.

I remember all those sweaty bodies coming out of the concert hall and it being bloody freezing outside because it was the middle of December. You could see the steam rising from them when they got out onto the streets and I could hardly hear you because your voice was so croaky from singing along, so you suggested going to the pub. I knew I was cutting it fine for my last bus back to Meanwood but I didn't want the night to end, so I didn't say anything. I honestly didn't expect you to walk me home because it was about an hour away and you were in a place near the centre, weren't you? You said you wouldn't let me go home alone because I think that was before the Yorkshire Ripper was arrested and the uni was very keen girls shouldn't be out on their own at night, so you said you'd walk back with me. Very gallant. I was impressed by that and so glad.

I couldn't have been more content than I was on that walk home. It was so cold but I moved up close to you for warmth with one of my hands inside that thick RAF greatcoat you used to wear. You had your arm around me and were still singing Lindisfarne songs and I felt like I wanted life to be like that forever. I know it probably didn't mean that much to you but I could tell you were happy as well, just perhaps not in the same way.

When we got back to the house I made us hot drinks and I put the electric fire on full so we could warm up. You were starting to get a bit frisky by then and were making a thing of trying to get me to kiss you. I was playing along, being coy and shy - I was very shy then – but then, when we were on the settee together and started kissing properly, well. I'd never known what it was like for someone to desire me like that and it just felt wonderful. Then you got all embarrassed when you said you had some johnnies, like you thought you were about to spoil it all by overstepping the mark, but ...well, you know the rest.

I did feel like I should say no because my parents used to tell me that men wouldn't respect me anymore if I gave in to them and that I should save myself for when I met the one true love of my life but I felt that night that I had found the love of my life. Going to bed with you was my way of expressing how I believed what we had was special. It felt so natural, like we were taking our relationship to the next level and that once we were there, we would keep going on and on and on forever, all the time making what we had stronger and stronger. It had only been a couple of weeks but I was infatuated. I could see myself with you for the rest of my life and I thought you felt that way too.

I got that one wrong, didn't I?

Those two and a half weeks over Christmas after that night were the longest of my life. We both went home in the term break and the days just dragged. I didn't want to eat, I couldn't sleep, I wanted to burst into tears all the time. I was pitiful. My parents kept asking me what was wrong and I had to tell them I was ill and that just about everybody on the course had gone down with it at some stage. What was it they called it – freshers' flu? I was sure my mum knew something else was going on but she didn't want to say it. All I needed was to see you again or just talk to you but I daren't let you have my parents' phone number because they would have disapproved, so I had to keep you a secret. I had to suffer in silence, all the time counting down the days until we went back for the start of spring term. Even when my parents drove me back to Leeds it wasn't over because I knew it would still be a couple of days until I'd get the chance to see you around. I kept hoping you might be there, waiting for me at the house, or that you might come round over the weekend before the start of term, but you didn't.

I knew something was wrong early on. You were still nice when it was just me and you. I suppose I expected you to be as smitten as I was and it disappointed me that you were just normal you but that was OK. It was when you were around those stupid mates of yours that was the problem. What dicks they were! They made me feel like I was shit on their shoes, looking down their oh-so-cool noses at me and cutting me dead every time I tried to join in their conversations and you just let them. I remember asking you why you were hanging around with such a bunch of tossers because I could see they didn't treat you like you were part of their group either. They kind of allowed you to hang around with them and you behaved like you were so grateful for that and I couldn't understand it.

You kept saying 'They're my mates, they're my mates. They're a good laugh. You'll come to like them as well soon. They're not being funny with you. That's just the way they are. They take the piss out of everybody. It's a way of showing they like you really.'

You couldn't see it, could you? I didn't want you to stop hanging around with other people – I wasn't that obsessive – but not them. Did you think I was trying to stop you from being with anyone other than me? Is that why you started avoiding me?

Don't suggest you weren't avoiding me because I knew you were. I even saw you change direction when you were walking across the quad one day and disappear into a building. You thought I hadn't spotted you, didn't you? Have you any idea how that made me feel?

I was properly heartbroken. I couldn't understand what I'd done wrong. I thought about packing in the course and going home but I couldn't face that either. I had no idea how to handle it all but that wasn't the worst of it. The worst of it came a couple of months later.

I knew I didn't feel well but I put that down to how I was about you. It must have been April, probably around the middle or late April, when I started with the strange feelings in my abdomen. It was a popping, rumbling sensation, a bit like trapped wind, and it happened more and more regularly. When I noticed the waistband on my jeans was feeling tighter and I could see that I was getting bigger I started imagining I had some sort of tumour or blockage, so I mustered some courage and decided I should go to see the doctor.

I had no idea. Even when he sent me for a pee sample and a blood test, I had no idea. When he told me I was pregnant and about 18 to 20 weeks on, I was completely floored. I mean, if I hadn't been sitting down they would have had to pick me off the ground. I couldn't get my head around it because I'd still been bleeding every month and I didn't know that could happen, so I'd never even considered it a possibility I could be carrying a baby. When you're pregnant, your periods stop, right? That's the first sign. Well, apparently not for everybody.

Plus, we'd only done it once and we used contraception. I could tell that night you didn't know much more about sex than I did but I didn't think there was much that could go wrong with putting a condom on. Maybe we were – I was – just unlucky or was it that you bought your johnnies, as well as your coats, from the Army Surplus shop?

Anyway, I was devastated. My world had ended. I didn't know what to do. I had nobody I could turn to. There was no point trying to find you because you'd made it obvious you didn't want anything else to do with me, so I packed a bag and caught a train home. I was dreading facing my parents but they were all I had. I thought they'd take care of me.

My parents were always strict and protective. They wanted to know where I was all the time when I was younger and didn't like me going out, even with friends, so they were dead set against me going to university. They wanted me to train to be a nurse or a teacher or something like that – so that I wouldn't need to leave home and they could shelter me from the big bad world for a little longer. At the very least, they wanted me to go to uni in Sheffield and carry on living at home but Sheffield rejected me. Leeds and Newcastle offered me a place, so they reckoned Leeds was fairly close and let me go there. I know they didn't want me to go at all but I really wanted to. I think it surprised them how much I stood up for myself and that made them realise I wasn't their little girl anymore. I had to put up with weeks of warnings about how I would have to stay away from men and drink and drugs and how I would have to be disciplined so I could put everything into my studies, to make sure I came out of the three years with a good degree, and I made all the right noises to reassure them.

The thing was, I meant every word. I'd never been a drinker, I wanted nothing to do with drugs and I didn't think boys would be interested in me. They never had been.

They looked so hurt when I told them. I felt like I'd betrayed their trust and I kept saying how sorry I was but they gave me nothing back. They just sat there with this awful disappointment written in their eyes and then they got angry. Really angry. They told me how much I'd let them down, reminded me how they'd warned me about these things, told me I had shamed them. Shamed myself and shamed the whole family. I begged them to forgive me but they wouldn't. They told me it would be best if I left. I told them I didn't have anywhere to go. They told me to go back to my boyfriend, that I was his responsibility now. I'd made my choice and I had to live with it. They told me to go – right then, that moment. They threw me out of the house. They told me it wasn't my home anymore. They actually told me they no longer had a daughter.

Can you believe that? How can parents be so cruel to their only child?

So I was 18, five months pregnant and on my own. I had to go back to Leeds because all I had with me was a few things in a bag. I shut myself away in my room mostly but then one of the other girls in the house, who I hardly knew really, knocked on my door to see if I was OK. I poured it all out. I think I needed to offload it and she copped for the lot. Everything. She was really good, actually. She told me I needed to go to see Student Services and offered to go with me, for support.

I decided I couldn't put her to that trouble but I did go myself. The man I spoke to was very helpful and told me I could take time out and rejoin the course later, if I liked. I wanted to quit, though. He mentioned that I might still have options if I wanted to consider an abortion, but I couldn't contemplate doing that. My upbringing, see. He also told me about what I could ask for from the council and I could see that was my only option. He tried to set me up with a meeting with the council there and then but I didn't want to stay in Leeds. Maybe I would have been better if I had stayed in Leeds but I had to get away – too many bad memories - and so I packed all my things in two suitcases and a rucksack and came back to Sheffield. I turned up at the council offices with all my stuff, having hauled it on and off the train on my own, and I felt so desperate that I broke down as soon as I walked into the reception. At least I got their attention! They interviewed me and said they could find me emergency accommodation so at least I had a roof over my head but, oh god, it was horrible!

It was in one of the roughest parts of the city and the room was basic, to say the least. There were three other women in the house but it seemed like anybody could come and go as they pleased – men and women. It really wasn't safe. There was a shared kitchen and the bathroom! I couldn't believe the bathroom. It turned my stomach to have to use the toilet and there was no way I was going to use the bath, so apart from going downstairs to warm up some food I hardly left the room. The only security was a lock which I couldn't get the key to turn in and a door chain which was practically hanging off the door frame. I had to manoeuvre one of my cases behind the door to barricade myself in and sat on my bed, trying to keep warm and getting more and more miserable.

I thought I had to have reached my lowest ebb but then, on my third night there, I was woken up by somebody pushing against my door, trying to get in. I started screaming the place down but the person just started pushing harder against the door. The case was being nudged further with every push and the chain looked like it was about to give way and I was screaming and screaming but nobody came. I was thinking 'How can they not hear me? Why doesn't anybody come to help?' but nobody did and then the chain burst free of the door frame and the case was pushed far enough and he was in.

He can't have been any older than I was. He had this filthy green jacket on and jeans but the light from the landing was behind him, so I didn't really get a good look at him until he moved closer to me. I was terrified and screaming and crying. I managed to say 'Please don't hurt me! Please don't hurt me!' but he kept coming towards me and I thought he was going to attack me or rape me or kill me. I was so frightened.

That's when I was able to make out his face. His hair was dirty brown and dank and even though it was a young face he had sores around his mouth but it was the eyes that got me. Heavy, like he hadn't slept for a week, and lifeless. No spark there at all. No humanity. Classic druggie look, as I now know.

He reached a hand towards me and I couldn't stand for him to touch me so I jumped off the other side of the bed and pressed myself into the corner of the room, still screaming for somebody to come and stop him.

Thankfully, he didn't try to get across the bed to me. He said: 'I just want money. Give me your money.'

I said: 'I haven't got any money', which I hadn't, but he said again: 'Give me your money' and his eyes were darting around the room, looking for whatever he could see to steal. I really believed he would attack me if he couldn't get what he wanted but then I became aware that there was somebody else pushing at the door to get through.

I saw this second man. He was taller and a bit older. I noticed his spiky bleached blond hair but that was pretty much all I noticed about him before he rushed at the other guy and pinned him to the wall by the throat.

The druggie didn't even try to fight back. His eyes were bulging and his hands were pawing at the blond guy's arm, trying to get him to release the grip. He started making this gurgling, choking noise and I actually started wondering if the blond guy was going to kill him but he held him there, long enough to get his undivided attention, and spoke. He didn't yell. He didn't have to.

'What have I told you about staying away from places you shouldn't go?' He was calm, measured, unambiguous.

'If I ever catch you anywhere near this building again I'll rip your fucking head off – do we understand each other?'

The druggie started nodding his head, frantically, desperate to be released.

'I said, do you understand?'

The nodding was even more panicky. He looked as if his eyes were about to pop out of his sallow skull.

The blond guy let go and the druggie scampered out of the room like a chastised puppy.

Once he could hear the stumbling footsteps on the stairs and the sound of the front door crashing shut, the blond guy looked over to where I was cowering in the corner.

I was still pretty terrified. Of course I was. I was shaking and sobbing and whimpering. I'd never gone through anything like that before and it was horrific but the guy started moving slowly towards me, around the bed, and everything about him was so reassuring.

'It's OK,' he said. 'He won't bother you anymore.'

I still didn't want him to come too close and he picked up on that. He kept his distance and did all he could to not appear intimidating but that wasn't easy, looking as he did, to be honest.

He wore a black biker jacket and skinny blue bondage trousers with a bold yellow check and as well as that wild hair he had more piercings – his ears, through his nostrils, one just below his bottom lip – than I'd ever seen on any person before. If you'd seen him coming towards you on a dark street you'd definitely move out and hold on to your handbag tightly but once you saw past all that, he was the most gentle of men. I saw it in his face for the first time then and I began to feel safe again. You can just tell sometimes, can't you?

He said: 'Everybody calls me Polecat. What's your name?'

I was still snivelling and I had tears and snot dribbling down my face but I managed to respond and he spoke again, ever so gently.

'It's OK now, Sarah. It's all over.' Then he started edging away, back towards the door, and said: 'I'll be straight back. Just stay calm. I'll be straight back.'

He left and I thought that might be the last I saw of him

but he did come straight back – with half a toilet roll. He tore off a length of it as he walked into the room and handed it to me, still staying as far from me as he could.

Gradually, I came down from my petrified state. He stayed with me for hours, until I was able to drift off to sleep, and then in the morning he was back with a screwdriver and some WD40 to get the lock working and fix the chain. We started seeing each other more and more and we fell in love.

He was the love of my life.

He saved me.

21

Graham listened to Sarah's story in silence.

He had to listen, of course, but even if he had not been bound and confined he would have been powerless to move. This time, running away to avoid the awkwardness he had created was not an option.

The story took him from surprise to shock to shame to the heartfelt sadness that only guilt, the exposed deep-seated individual guilt of a serious wrong committed in our own past, can carry a person. It did not matter at all that it was ignorance rather than malice that was behind committing the deed. The sin was his, all the same. Confronting that revealed to him a capacity for remorse more profound than he previously realised he was capable of.

He listened and each word diminished him drop by drop by drop until he was a quarter of his normal size, sitting perched on the edge of a now-oversized chair with his legs dangling, like an infant sent to the naughty step.

'You see,' Sarah added, content she had left her victim hanging in silent reflection long enough. 'We have had reason to keep a close watch on Johnson's for several months now and when we were informed that there was a newcomer in the organisation and that his name was Graham Hasselhoff, my attention was caught. When we looked into this arrival further and were told that this newcomer was, in fact, the long-lost natural father of Andreas Johnson – well, the irony!'

Graham raised his chin off his chest for the first time in several minutes to look towards his torturer, cringing in anticipation of the next slicing blow.

'What were the odds, eh? I knew it had to be you. Sure enough, here you are.'

She stood and meandered towards him, startling him as she raised a high-heeled foot to rest it against the edge of the chair, between his legs.

'You must have some dynamite in those bollocks of yours.'

She turned back towards the desk, all the way to the other side this time, and lowered herself into the high-backed executive chair.

Graham steeled himself to speak for the first time in what seemed an age, though he hardly dare ask the question.

'So, Jason?'

Sarah smiled broadly.

'That's right. Big strapping boy, isn't he? You must be so proud.'

Pride was not his overwhelming emotion. If pride was in there, it was having to battle against a torrent of more dominant, conflicting emotions for attention.

'I wouldn't really think about playing daddy with Jason, though, if I was you. He's not the sentimental type, our Jase. Not like Andreas. I thought it better not to mention the full extent of our connection from university to him earlier because I'm not certain he would take it that well. He knows that I was abandoned by his biological father before he was born and he's always sort of resented that. He is very protective towards his mother and prone to express himself, shall we say, a little more violently than some might find acceptable. Anyway, I'd not raise the subject, if I was you. Just to be on the safe side. I may tell him myself some day, if I need to.'

The implied threat caught his attention. Is that why he had been brought here?

'What do you want from me, Sarah? I can't undo any of the wrong decisions I made in the past and I can't make up for any of the trouble I put you through. If I could, I would, but it's too late for that. I don't know what else I can say. Sorry doesn't quite cover it, I know.'

She eased back in the chair.

'You're right. It doesn't come close but I didn't bring you here to apologise, Graham. What would be the point in that? We have more urgent issues to address in the present day, haven't we?'

He screwed up his eyes as he gazed towards her but there were no further clues. What could she mean?

'I don't understand.'

Sarah rose to her feet and folded her arms.

'Oh, I think you do. Don't play games with me, Graham. I'd prefer us to sort this out between the two of us but Jason and the two boys are in the next room, just the other side of that door, and they might not show the same levels of patience that I have.'

'I truly do not know what you are talking about, Sarah.' There was desperation in his voice. 'Please tell me what it is you want from me.'

She sighed and walked to the two-seat sofa, sitting to face him and crossing her legs.

'Why did he bring you to Johnson's, Graham?'

What did she want to know that for?

'He offered me a job. Me and my wife, Janet, he offered us both jobs. Andreas came around to my house in Derby one day, out of the blue, and told me his parents had died in a car accident and then asked me if I remembered Lena, which I did, from uni, and then he told me I was his natural father. We met up again and I told him that I'd been made redundant from a job I really enjoyed and that the only other job I'd been able to find was soul-destroying and he offered me a job. He offered us a fresh start and set us up with accommodation and everything. I think he felt the loss of his parents deeply and he saw nurturing a new relationship with Janet and myself as a way of filling the void in his life and we were grateful for that as well. I like him. He's a bit strange at times but I think he's a good guy and I want to get to know him better, so that's why I came to Johnson's. I'm a transport administrator. I allocate drivers and vehicles to the schedule, I liaise with customers, I arrange driver cover with the agencies, I operate the transport management system and I make sure the right orders are processed by the warehouse to get to the right customers at the right time. That's what I do.'

'And that's all you do?'

'Well, it's not *all* I do. There are other tasks which crop up along the way but that's basically it. I'm a transport administrator for a road haulage company – what else do you want me to say?'

Sarah watched him closely, assessing all the time.

'What about Andreas. Can you tell me what he does?'

'What? Andreas runs the company. He splits his time between the depots in Sheffield and Southampton and he's the man in charge. I don't get what you're driving at.'

There was an increasingly frantic edge to his tone.

'Do you know what else he does through the company? Apart from move crates of baked beans or whatever around the country, that is.'

Graham's chin dropped to his chest again, this time through a different form of confusion, a different kind of despair.

'I really do not understand. He runs a road haulage company. What else could he do?'

Sarah was on the move again. She stood a yard in front of him, her hands on her hips.

'Do you really expect me to believe you?'

'Yes! I'm telling you the truth. Just give me some sort of clue. Let me know what else it is you want me to tell you.'

She ambled towards the coffee machine and topped up the glass of water she had left there from the jug, then took a sip. Graham watched with his mouth and throat now parched dry but she did not offer him a drink.

'When things started getting serious between me and Paul – that was his name, by the way. Paul Catt. You can probably work out how the nickname came about. Anyway, when things started getting serious between me and Paul, I moved out of the council place to share his flat. It wasn't exactly luxurious but it was a damn sight better than the house and it was a better environment for when I had the baby. It worked out just fine.

'Paul was not what you might call ambitious, in the conventional sense. It didn't really fit with the whole punk rock ethos. What modest income he did bring into the flat came from supplying and distributing drugs. Strictly small-time but he also used occasionally, so it became a bit of a hobby that paid. Innocent little thing as I was, I was shocked at first but then I was a homeless teenage single mum, so it wasn't really my place to judge. Anyway, Paul's dealing put food on the table and he was careful; never kept his stash in the flat so that on the couple of occasions we did get a visit from Her Majesty's constabulary, they went away empty-handed.

'As I said, he was careful and he was a good father to Jason and he took care of me and we loved each other. In his later years, however, he began to enjoy using a little more than he should have and he got careless. That was what killed him in the end.'

'Overdose?'

Sarah took another sip.

'Sepsis. He left it too long before getting treated.'

Graham nodded sympathetically. 'I'm sorry.'

She ignored the gesture.

'Anyway, when Paul died around eight years ago we had a decision to make. The obvious answer was to take over his little distribution network but my thoughts had become bigger than that. Paul could never be bothered building his business but I could see potential for expansion. A gap in the market, you might say. At the same time, I thought it would be foolish to just wade in and start dealing larger quantities of drugs, extending the range and such like, because that could attract unwanted attention. I'd also taken on board the lessons of being careful at all times and keeping as low a profile as possible, so I decided to start up this business as well. My reckoning was that if I established a legitimate, mainstream business and started moving drugs in the background, as it were, we'd be less likely to arouse suspicion from the police and, I must say, the plan has worked out very nicely.

'I handle the running of this business and Jason takes care of the day-to-day running of the other. Quite a little family enterprise, don't you think?'

Graham did not think she was truly looking to see if he was impressed. That was just as well. He was appalled. The thought of dealing drugs and the misery that must cause was abhorrent to him. The idea of hiding the vile trade behind a veneer of respectability struck him as obscene.

How bad must her life have been since their brief time together at uni to make Sarah believe what she is doing is acceptable?

Then another thought occurred.

Am I responsible for that?

'I still don't see where I come into this – unless you're trying to make me feel worse about what I did 38 years ago. If that's what you wanted, you've succeeded.'

Sarah pulled a stern face and moved to the front of the desk again.

'Oh, Graham, Graham, Graham! Are you really so good a liar or can you be this innocent?'

She leaned against the desk again and folded her arms.

'I want you to very seriously consider your response to what I'm about to tell you next. Bear in mind that if I believe you are lying to me, it could turn out very badly for you. OK?'

He nodded timidly. He had no doubt she meant it.

'We're not the only business to hide our less-lawful activities behind a facade of legitimacy. A few months ago, at around the turn of the year, it came to our attention that there were drugs on the market in our territory which had not been supplied by us. Somebody was moving in on our patch. It wasn't a large quantity, but somebody was selling where they shouldn't and we didn't like it.

'After we tracked down a couple of the foot soldiers for our new rival, we encouraged them to tell us a little more about the source of this new supply and, after making a few inquiries with our sources in Belgium, we found out that it was coming into the country on the back of Harry Johnson Global Logistics trucks.'

She paused. Graham swallowed hard. He felt sick.

'This created a problem. As I said, we built our business on a foundation of discretion and we could have taken out the people involved in distribution, but turf wars are never discreet. The police tend to notice that sort of thing. That meant we had to cut off the supply.

'Now Jason, impetuous and forthright as he is, thought we should go straight to the top. He wanted us to snatch Andreas and persuade him that it would be in his best interests if he stuck to his business and kept out of ours, but I could see that might potentially create too many problems. Andreas is quite a high-profile person and, as I said, the quantity of drugs we were talking about was relatively small. I thought it might be using a sledgehammer to crack a walnut. I favoured getting his attention by hurting him in his back yard and that was why Jason carried out the two little demonstrations of our intent.'

'The fires.'

'Exactly. We hoped – rather, I hoped – it would show Andreas that what he was dabbling in was going to create more trouble than it was worth. I hoped he would take the hint.'

'Hang on a sec.' Graham's mind was racing now. 'Did you cause the accident that killed his parents?'

'Of course not.' Sarah was emphatic, indignant. 'That happened well before this new supply became an issue. It was only after Andreas took over that the new supply opened up. That's one of the reasons why we're sure he's behind this.'

'You can't be sure of that.'

'Oh, we're sure. It's not only the timing. Does he strike you as the kind of person who would allow something like this to go on within his business without his knowledge?'

Graham could not find a response to that.

'We even managed to find out the identity of his mule and were informed of the location where the drugs were loaded off the truck and on to the next stage of distribution. We planned to move in and put a stop to all this the next time there was a shipment but then we heard that the mule had met with an untimely end.'

'Chris Yates?'

'Maybe Yates demanded a larger share of the profits. Is that why Andreas had him killed?'

'Andreas didn't kill him. He sacked him. He worked out that something was going on with Yates and he sacked him to protect the reputation of the company.'

Graham tried all he could to put the force of commitment into the words, but even as he spoke them they sounded inadequate. All his former doubts over Andreas reopened like an unhealed wound. Had he been too willing to listen to Andreas's version of events because he wanted to believe his son was beyond suspicion? Had his new-found loyalty clouded his judgement and diverted his instincts? It still seemed impossible he had been duped so thoroughly, but there remained room for uncertainty to creep in. There were still unanswered questions over Yates's murder.

Sarah appeared to revel in the unease her words had created.

'Of course he did.'

A knowing smile spread across her face, deepening Graham's agitation.

'We did wonder if the death of the mule might spell the end of this little operation but our sources have told us otherwise. They've suggested to us that the next shipment will be considerably bigger and that it's due into the country sometime tomorrow. That's all we know for now and this creates a much graver situation for us. If Andreas is planning to release more of his merchandise on our market, then he's no longer a minor irritation. He becomes a major complication and we cannot tolerate that. This is where you come in.'

She stood and walked towards him. She circled the chair and came up close from behind him to speak softly into his right ear.

'If this shipment finds its way onto our streets, we will consider that an act of war and this time we will not be discreet. We will hold Andreas and we will hold you directly responsible and we will act. If Yates had not been taken out of the equation and we felt sure we knew the where and when we would've taken care of this ourselves, once and for all, without the need for further discussion but with a new mule and the potential of a new route we can no longer be sure.

'This is lucky for you. It creates an opportunity. If you tell us where and when, I give you my personal guarantee of your safety. For old times' sake.'

She leaned forward a few more inches and kissed his ear. The touch startled him. Her words chilled him.

She walked back to her position at the desk.

'I don't know what's happening. All this talk of drugs and smuggling and gang wars – these are things I've only ever seen on TV. I'm a librarian, for God's sake – or rather, I was a librarian and now I'm a transport administrator. I'm happily married and I've never broken the law in my life. I feel bad if I tell a lie to a cold caller on the telephone. There's no way I could become part of a drug trafficking ring. I swear to you, Sarah, I don't know anything about this.'

Tears filled his eyes. His desperation burned in his belly.

She stared impassively back.

'Why should I believe you, Graham? After what you did to me? Why shouldn't I turn you over to Jason and the boys so that they can find out what you really know?'

He broke down. The weight of a situation so alien and so out of his control was too much. The impending threat of escalation to levels too horrific to contemplate was too real. He had no bargaining chip to use in the effort to try to escape his ordeal unscathed and was powerless against a rising stack of accusations. He was pinned to the floor and incapable of doing anything to prevent the jagged rock which hung over his head from falling and obliterating him.

He slumped in the chair and sobbed.

'I swear.' The words choked in his throat. 'You have to believe me.'

He could not look at her but she did not take her eyes off

him. She was dispassionate. Unmoved.

The only sound was Graham's despair. The only movements were the convulsions of his shoulders. Then she spoke.

'OK,' she said. 'Maybe you don't have anything to do with this.'

He raised his head and saw, through watery eyes, the faint light of hope.

'I haven't.'

'But even if you don't, the issue remains the same. If the drugs are released on our streets, it's war, and you're still in the firing line. I may be willing to give you one last chance to save us all a lot of unpleasantness.'

Graham felt a surge through his body at the thought of a way out.

'What do you want me to do?'

'You've grown close to Andreas. He trusts you – yes?'

He nodded with enthusiasm.

'Then I'm going to give you the chance to talk to him. Persuade him to stop the shipment going into circulation and stay out of our business for good. If he listens this time and we never see sign of his merchandise again, we'll consider this the end of the matter. If he doesn't, then Jason will come looking for you both. Do I make myself clear?'

'Completely.'

'I understand that you cannot cancel a transaction without upsetting a great many people further up the supply chain who you really don't want to upset, not at this stage of the process, so I want you to put a further proposal to Andreas. After you talk to him and persuade him to stay out of our business, I need you to do something for me.'

Sarah went to the other side of the desk and opened a

drawer. She took out a mobile phone and held it up for him to see.

'You must take this. It has one number programmed into it and that puts you in touch with us. When Andreas has agreed to our demands, I want you to call us and tell us where the drop is. We will then meet the driver and he will hand over the merchandise to us. Call it a gesture of goodwill.'

She walked to him and slipped the phone into the breast pocket of his shirt.

'This is your one way out, Graham. Your lives depend on it. Don't even think about trying to pull a fast one.'

That was the last thing on his mind. He was clinging to the fraying thread of his only means of escape.

'I'll do it.'

'Good boy.' Sarah smiled.

She turned again, heading towards the door to their left, but then stopped and spun around.

'So Lena really was another one of your university conquests, was she?'

He nodded.

'Small world,' she added and continued her short journey.

'Jason, could you take Mr Hasselhoff back to his car please?' she asked after opening the door.

Graham's head dropped again.

This ordeal was over but he knew his troubles were not about to disappear. Far from it.

22

The car swung into the car park and came to a halt next to the red hatchback, as it had earlier. There were more cars there than there had been before but no people around. The cars belonged to customers for the pubs and restaurants, maybe. It was still a pleasant summer evening, though the sun had now set and the temperature had dropped a little.

The driver, in his brown leather coat, left the engine running and got out to open the rear door. Out jumped a man with a thick dark beard, who turned back towards the rear seat and reached in.

'Come on,' he ordered and dragged out a man with a dark hood over his head and his arms fastened behind his back, which made the act of getting out of the car more difficult than it should have been.

With brusque assistance from both sides, he was on his feet. The bearded man took out a knife from inside his jacket and sliced through the tape which held their victim's hands, while the driver whipped off the hood and tore off the strip of tape over his mouth. Without saying another word, they jumped back in the car. It was jammed into reverse and, in seconds, was heading away again, off towards the motorway.

Graham stood, alone, his eyes finding it easier to cope with the removal of the hood in the fading light than they had earlier. He flexed the muscles around his mouth to ease the tingling pain of the tape being ripped off and shook his arms from the elbow to encourage the blood to circulate back into his hands. He could hear the noise and see the lights from the pub opposite but all around appeared strangely oblivious to him. Of course they had no idea what he had just been through but he felt almost as if they should, like the world should have noticed him being beamed back to earth from a giant spaceship and have rushed to his aid. All this was too normal. He didn't feel normal anymore.

He looked at his watch. It was 8.55. The full ordeal had taken not much more than an hour and a half but it felt like a lifetime since he had strolled out of the pub to set off home.

To Janet. Oh, Christ – Janet! He had told her he expected to be home for 7.30, though he had mentioned he might be later. She might be worried that he hadn't been in touch, all the same.

He reached towards his inside jacket pocket for his phone but his hand brushed against the object in his shirt breast pocket.

He picked out the phone Sarah had given him and stared deeply at it. Such an unexceptional, everyday thing and yet this one appeared to him as deadly as a loaded gun, as ominous as the black spot.

What a mess. What a predicament. What am I going to do?

The harrowing trauma of the previous hour and a half

overwhelmed him again.

The strength drained from his legs. Graham slumped against the red hatchback and slid down its side until he sat, his useless legs stretched out in front of him, on the black asphalt and blubbered like a small child. He had been unable to hold back the tears when he feared Sarah was weighing up whether he should live or die and even if he had possessed the power to stop them this time he had no desire to. They had to flow. He had to release the tightly wound coil of anguish in his chest before he could maybe – just maybe – reignite the spark of reasoned thought in his brain which maybe – just maybe – would help him find a way out of the gaping chasm into which he had been dropped and abandoned.

When the tears stopped, he rested his head back against the car door, closed his eyes and drew deep breaths, feeling spent but cleansed. The rising of his chest was his only movement but, inside, the recalibration of his system was taking effect. Each deep lungful of air drove on the process until he stirred and took off his glasses to wipe his eyes on the sleeve of his jacket.

The phone – that phone – was still in his hand. He shoved it into the inside pocket of his jacket and took out his own. He would have to work out what to do with the other business later.

Sorry it's later than I said. Just about to set off x

Graham pressed 'send' and watched as the message box turned green.

God, what am I going to tell her?

Janet would be mortified if she knew what had just happened. Absolutely mortified. She was essential to his inner stability and he always felt there was nothing he couldn't tell her but this? This was like nothing they had dealt with before. Like nothing ordinary people ever encounter. Would it be the right thing to do – to burden her with this unthinkable, potentially deadly, load he found himself shackled to?

There was no way of telling what he might have to do next to escape this dire situation or how it might end. She would not allow him to take the risks he might have to face. Telling her could be to expose her to the dangers too.

He should say nothing. When it was all over, that's when he should try to figure out how to explain it all; including the relatively minor bombshell that it appears he fathered two children during his three years at university. All that would have to wait until another day. Not now.

Andreas. He was the key to all this. He's the one who could make it possible to get out of it unscathed. It's his mess and he has to clear it up. He has to. Both of their lives are at stake.

He scrolled down his contacts list to call Andreas but hesitated with his thumb over the 'call' button.

What should I say?

Graham stalled, his thumb poised, and thought.

Sarah had accused Andreas of smuggling in the drugs but she had offered no proof. It was all based on the assumption that Andreas, as the very hands-on owner of the business, simply *must* know what was going on – but was that necessarily true? Never assume or presume. Where is the evidence? How often had he preached that to customers setting out on their research projects? The principles held firm, even here.

The worst could not be dismissed but if he was to get to the truth, it had to be done face to face, not over the phone.

He would look into Andreas's eyes and he would know. He had to lay the full scale of this grave plight before Andreas and look into his eyes. Surely he could not attempt to lie. He must either confess and face up to his responsibilities or he would profess his innocence and they could work together to find a solution.

There had to be a solution. The consequences of not finding one were too awful.

Graham cancelled thoughts of the call and decided to send a message to the number instead.

I need to see you tomorrow morning as a matter of urgency. What's the earliest time we can meet?

The message was sent. Nothing to do now except wait. And think. Think it all through. Think how they might get out of this.

He pushed his glasses up onto his forehead with his hand and rubbed his eyes hard. This was an appalling, unreal position to be in but it had to be faced.

He roused himself to rise to his feet and fished in his pocket for the car keys.

It was time to go home.

As he pulled into the driveway, Graham's phone pinged. He hurriedly keyed in the security code to read the message.

On my way back to Sheffield now. I'll be in the office at 7am. Will that be ok?

That's fine. Early is good. The more time they could give themselves, the better, but he had to think first.

See you then

He gripped the steering wheel of the car and sat a minute longer, steeling himself for the act he had to put on. The one he had convinced himself was for Janet's benefit. It required him not to lie, as such, just not to tell the truth. There was a big difference, but that did not make him feel any better. He was dreading facing her and yet desperate to see her.

'Come on, you can't sit here all night,' he said to rally himself and opened the car door.

She was watching TV and already changed into her pyjamas and dressing gown – settled in, as she always called it, in an endearingly old-fashioned way – with her legs up on the sofa. She smiled as he entered the room.

'You're late, duckie. How did it go?'

Graham was knocked a little off guard by the question. Bentley. She means the meeting with Bentley.

'Oh, fine, fine. He's quite a nice bloke.'

'Did you come up with a master plan between you?'

'No, we just chatted, really. You know, getting to know each other. Just chatted.'

He became aware of how stilted his manner must be. He hoped he wasn't giving himself away. It was not easy to defy the habits of almost 30 years and be less than completely open with Janet. He imagined she must be able to see straight through him.

'Anyway, are you OK?'

She shrugged in a 'why wouldn't I be' kind of way.

'Sure. Just catching up on *Call the Midwife*. I put your tea in the microwave. Give it a couple of minutes and a stir and then see if it needs another minute.'

'Yeah, thanks. I will.'

He moved to go to the kitchen but she called him back.

'Gray.'

He stopped. 'Yeah?'

'You OK?' She looked concerned.

'Sure. I'm good.' He did his best to look and sound convincing.

'You just seem a bit off it.'

He shook his head. 'No, I'm fine. A bit tired, maybe. It's been an odd week. Bit hungry as well.'

Even he didn't find that very persuasive. Janet maintained her probing scan of her husband's face for giveaway signs for a few moments more before releasing him to go to warm up his meal.

'OK.'

In the tone of that one short word, Graham perceived that he had been given the benefit of the doubt rather than a full all-clear but that might have been his imagination. He was glad to retreat to the temporary sanctuary of the kitchen all the same.

He wasn't hungry at all but ate every scrap and said how much he enjoyed it, mostly so that he might not arouse more of Janet's instinctive suspicion. Having tidied away his plate and cutlery, he went to join her on the sofa.

She put her feet down and opened her arms, inviting him to lie on her bosom. He nestled into the soft cotton of her dressing gown with the soft flesh beneath and felt as soothed as a small ill child with its mother. She stroked his hair.

'It'll all work out, you know,' she whispered, reassuringly. 'We'll soon get to the bottom of all this and it'll be fine.'

Her words carried greater resonance than she intended, but they were all he needed to hear. He focused on the steady pace of her heartbeat and the clean smell of her nightclothes and basked in the warmth of her comforting and said nothing. The stresses of the night were draining from his body and he allowed himself to drift away to a simpler, safer place.

Graham did not go up to bed with Janet. He kissed her and told her he fancied watching a little TV to complete the unwinding process she had begun but that was another small untruth. He had thinking to do. His head felt clear again. He wanted to get his strategy straight before he saw Andreas in the morning.

The documentary on Victorian engineering would normally have held his attention but it played to itself this time.

Gradually, he came to what he believed to be two key conclusions.

Sarah had claimed that a larger drugs shipment was being brought in on a Johnson's truck, even though the man she had identified as the driver for previous shipments, Yates, was now dead. That must mean, Graham reasoned, that not only was there a new driver, there must be someone else within the Johnson organisation who had arranged the whole transaction. He or she would be the common link between Yates's involvement and the new driver. If there was substance to Sarah's claim that the smuggling operation was ongoing, that had to be the case.

The second key point, in Graham's mind, concerned Andreas. What it boiled down to was did he believe Andreas was the man behind the operation, as Sarah had said, or was he not? Sarah had assumed he was. He had no clue who it might be if it was not Andreas. It could be anyone. But first, Graham decided, he had to establish if he *believed* it could be Andreas.

His intuition told him it could not be. That was what he wanted to believe but was that wish clouding his judgement? He would be more certain of that when they met. He felt sure of that.

Their approach to resolving the issue would depend on whether or not Andreas was behind the smuggling operation, so he decided to leave that until the morning, but he was not in the slightest bit comfortable with the concept of turning the foul contraband and the driver over to the mercy of Sarah, Jason and their heavies. He could not trust them. God knows what they might do to the driver and whoever else was in their way. They would have to get the police involved. He could see no other way to escape this situation safely and safety – primarily his and Janet's – was uppermost in his concerns.

Graham hated the thought that he might be leaving Janet vulnerable to danger more than he was scared for himself. In a petrifying flash of speculative foreboding, a vision of how his wife might not be able to cope if he was suddenly ripped from her life came into his mind and he attempted to shake it from his consciousness before it could consume him. That was too much to contemplate.

Maybe they should run away. Go. Now. Get as far away from Andreas and Johnson's and Sarah and drug smuggling as they could and start again. They would have to change their names, for sure, but if they worked with the police to uncover Sarah and her vile trade that might be possible.

But if they took that course Graham knew he would be throwing Andreas to the wolves and he could not do that. If Andreas was innocent, they could be committing a crime more appalling than importing the drugs. Even if he was guilty, the retribution of Sarah's thugs was not a fate he deserved. If he was guilty, he should face lawful punishment but that was it.

Whether he liked it or not, Graham was involved now and he could not run away from his responsibilities. He had to see it through. Do the right thing.

There was one more thing he resolved he should do.

If the worst came to the worst, he had to set in place an insurance policy. He went to the cupboard where they kept their stationery and took out a notepad.

Graham wrote on it everything that had happened to him that evening, everything he could think of that might act as a clue to lead the authorities to Sarah and Jason and the rest, in case everything went horribly wrong. He included all the detail of the allegations against Andreas and his thoughts on the legitimacy of them. It would be wrong not to.

Then he wrote a separate note to Janet. He told her how much he loved her and explained why he felt he had to put himself in the way of danger and how he hated to deceive her and to leave her. As he wrote it, he became the junior infantry officer about to lead his men over the top into the face of an uncertain fate. Such historical letters left him humbled whenever he had the privilege to read them in the course of his research and now he felt a connection with them in a way he never imagined he could.

They were the hardest words he ever wrote.

He folded the letters into an envelope and sealed it before writing Janet's name on the front. It was important she should read it first.

With his heart now heavy as lead, he took the envelope and placed it, hidden but easily found, in the drawer where they kept their important documents.

When this was all over – when – he would retrieve it and he would destroy it.

23

The door was already open. He was expected.

'Here he is and he is...' Andreas checked his watch theatrically. '...two minutes early. Very impressive timekeeping. This is why I employed you.'

He rose and stretched out his arm to shake Graham's hand.

'Come in. Would you like a coffee?'

Graham took the hand but could muster only a thin, tense smile to go with it. He could have been in much earlier. Sleep had proved impossible.

'No, I'm fine thanks.'

They both sat down.

'So how was our friend Bentley? Full of contrition, I hope.'

Andreas was in one of his ebullient moods. It was a pity to drag him down but there really was no choice.

'Andreas, I have something incredibly important to ask you and I need you to be completely honest with me. Whatever your answer to my questions, it has to be the truth.'

The joviality drained from his face. Andreas sat back

and his brow knitted.

'What lies has he been telling you?'

Graham grew suddenly impatient. The spat with Bentley was utterly trivial and had no place in a discussion of such gravity.

'This has nothing to do with Bentley. He had nothing to do with the fires. Forget about him. We have much more serious issues to address here.'

The curtness shook Andreas. He was silenced.

'When I was going back to my car after seeing Bentley last night I was snatched.'

'Snatched? What do you mean snatched?'

'Abducted, seized, kidnapped. Three men in a four-by-four were waiting for me. They gagged me, put a bag over my head and drove me somewhere. I don't know where they took me but it was about 25 minutes, half an hour from where they grabbed me and I was bundled into an office, tied up and, basically, interrogated. They were part of a drug gang, Andreas, and they said there is a rival drug supply coming into the country on our trucks and they wanted to stop it. They were the ones behind the fires. The fires were their way of telling us that they knew our trucks were being used to smuggle in these drugs and that we should take steps to bring that to an end.'

'Drugs? Fuck!'

Andreas shot to his feet. His hands covered the look of complete incredulity which had steadily taken over his expression as Graham gave his outline explanation of the previous evening's events.

'I mean – fuck!'

He practically shouted the word. His hands parted in front of his face and he peered at Graham intensely.

'Did they say who was doing this smuggling?'

If Andreas was the mastermind, he was doing a fine job of disguising his guilt.

'They said Yates was the driver.'

'Yates! I fucking knew it! I fucking knew he was up to no good - but this? Drugs? On my trucks!'

'Andreas, that's not all.'

He was stilled, mid-rant. There was more?

'They said they believed you were the man behind the operation. They said you knew all about it and that you are planning to import an even bigger shipment next time. They also said they think I was brought here to somehow help with the smuggling and that if this next shipment gets through and is distributed, they will hold you and me responsible and they will come after us. Andreas, these people are not fucking about.'

Andreas turned to face the window. His hands were on top of his head now. Graham watched him closely.

'But this is preposterous,' he said at last. 'How can they think...? I would never... This is unreal. Just unreal.'

Graham allowed him to let the thoughts swirl around his consciousness for a few moments more before deciding it was time to put the question.

'Tell me truthfully, Andreas. Is it you? Did you know about this?'

Andreas spun to face his accuser. There was hurt and desperation in his eyes.

'No!' he yelled. 'No, no, no, no, no! You cannot... Drugs? I could never deal in drugs! It is an appalling trade, full of suffering and misery and... No! I swear to you, I know nothing.'

'You must tell me the truth, Andreas. If you lie to me

and we don't nip this in the bud now, these people will hurt us and they might even kill us. If you aren't telling the truth, you are putting both our lives at risk.'

'I swear! I swear! I know nothing! I would never do this. I would never put you in danger. I swear on my life. I swear on the lives of my mama and pappa.'

He was imploring Graham to believe him with every fibre of his soul, tears filling his eyes. Graham stared into those eyes and could not believe they were the eyes of a liar. He could not believe Andreas was the mastermind.

'I believe you,' he said, simply.

The relief of that reassurance made Andreas's shoulders and head sag. He leaned forward and rested his flat palms on the desk.

'But we have to find out who is behind this. Yates was not working alone. He was just the driver. Somebody in this organisation was making the connections, providing the capital and sorting the distribution and they're the ones planning to bring in the next, bigger shipment. We haven't got much time.'

Andreas raised his head.

'When did they say it was coming into the country?'

'Today.'

Andreas slumped again.

'Fuck!'

The enormity of their task hit him but Graham had had the head start of thinking time. He had thought of nothing else in the last 12 hours or so.

'We can work this out. We just have to approach it step by step and fill in the details. We start with what we know and what we know is that Yates used to be the driver who brought the drugs into the country.'

'Yates! Of course!' Andreas snapped back into focus. 'The unexplained stop-offs were all at the end of regular scheduled continental runs. It must have been the drugs he was dropping off. They must have been on the two missing pallets we discovered the last time before I sacked him.'

He jumped into his seat and stirred the computer into action by moving the mouse.

'It's all here on Trams. Come and have a look.'

Graham stood and walked to the other side of the desk to look over Andreas's shoulder. The transport management system was familiar to him now but he wanted to see how Yates's deceit had been uncovered.

'If I search for the records of Yates's trips we see that he did the same continental short run every four weeks, Wednesday to Friday, and see here.' He pointed to the time map which is part of the record of every journey the company organised for each of its drivers.

'This tells us when he drove off the ferry at Hull and we track him here – A63, M62 and then here, look. Just after he comes off the M62 at junction 35 for the M18 he pulls on to an old industrial estate. He did it here, look, and this time and this time – basically every time he did the run going back to February. He turns off the ignition for between 45 minutes to an hour each time and then he sets off again to complete the journey back to the depot.'

Andreas glanced towards Graham eagerly. There was a definite pattern to it. There could be no doubt about that.

'Lots of drivers use this industrial estate when they need to take their breaks because it's relatively quiet and they can get their heads down for a bit, if they want to, but there's no reason for Yates to stop. He's been on a ferry for 10 hours. He isn't due a break. Why doesn't he just want to drive home as soon as he can? It makes no sense. That was why Rebecca became suspicious.'

Graham could see that.

'So when was his last run?'

Andreas scrolled up the page.

'Here we go. He set out July the 17th and got back on the 19th.'

'Four weeks ago. I was told the next shipment is in today, which fits the pattern, so who did we send to do Yates's run?'

Andreas clicked back to another page.

'Oli Turnbull. The new guy. It's his first job for us.'

'And we've no other continentals arriving back today?'

They both checked.

'No,' Andreas confirmed.

'That's got to be it. Turnbull has to be bringing in the new shipment. When is the ferry due in?'

Andreas clicked for details of the particular trip.

'He's waiting to board at Rotterdam now. It sails at 8am, which means he's in at Hull at around six this evening and that means he should be back in Sheffield by around 9.30. If he makes the stop at Thorne, like Yates used to, he'll be there around 7.30 to eight and we could be there waiting for him.'

'Yeah, but we don't know they'll use the same meeting place. If it was you and you thought we might be on to you, wouldn't you want to arrange a different rendezvous point?'

Andreas considered this.

'You could be right. We'll have to track him and see where he leads us. I've got Trams on my laptop, so we could post ourselves somewhere along the route close enough to drive to wherever he pulls in so we can intercept him.'

'That should work,' Graham nodded.

'There's a service station on the M18...' Andreas called up the map on another page on his computer. '...here,' he pointed. 'That's a quarter of an hour from the industrial estate. If he doesn't stop there, we can jump in the car and follow his next move.'

The plan was forming. The two men were caught in its conception, ready to spin further thoughts off each other.

'Right, that's good, but don't forget we want to catch the main man here as well. Let's work out who it might be. What do we know about Turnbull?'

Andreas eased back in his chair.

'Very little. Rebecca interviewed him and checked out his references. She offered him the job and said he was experienced, available straight away and very keen. She had no qualms about assigning him this continental. I think she favours the sink or swim approach to finding out about new drivers.'

He smiled and Graham followed suit. Rebecca was not one to wrap a newcomer in cotton wool.

'How did he come to us?'

Andreas thought for a moment.

'It was Ken Arnold. Ken did the introduction and said his son-in-law knew him. Rebecca suggested the interview and Ken set it up.'

Graham recalled hearing the story just after Yates was sacked.

'That's right, I remember now.'

Andreas snatched up his phone and went to his directory.

'I'll call Ken. He must be able to tell us about Turnbull.'
He pulled a face and hung up.

'Straight to answerphone.'

'Is Ken in this morning?'

They shrugged at each other and Andreas rose. There was one way to find out.

Janet had decided she might as well come in with Graham for his early start and was already getting on with her day's duties. She hadn't expected a visit so soon from her husband, let alone Andreas too, and greeted them warmly.

Andreas was straight to the point.

'Good morning to you too, Janet. Is Ken with us today?'

'I'm sorry, Andreas, but he isn't. He told me he was taking a leave day today. Is there anything I can help you with?'

'Not really. Did he say where he might be?'

She shook her head. 'Not to me. Is it urgent? Have you phoned him?'

'Straight to answerphone,' said Graham. 'He must have it turned off.'

'What about his other phone?' Janet asked.

Both men looked perplexed.

'What other phone?'

'He's got two,' she explained. 'He keeps the other in his case. I presumed it must be his personal one and the other was for work.'

'In his case?' said Andreas.

'Yes.' Janet's cheeks reddened slightly, like she feared she might have said something wrong or stupid.

'You remember that night I was a bit snappy on the drive home, Graham, and I told you Ken had interrupted our meeting to take a call and when he came back he told me something had come up and left and I had to sit there twiddling my thumbs with a big pile of work waiting to be done? Well, the phone that rang was his other phone. The one in his case.'

'Have you got that number?' asked Graham.

She checked the desk diary, where she had dutifully recorded all the essential numbers for her new role.

'I've only got this one.' She turned the diary to them and Andreas checked the number with the one on his phone.

'That's the one I've got. I had no idea he possessed another phone. Why would anybody want to carry two phones? There are no restrictions on personal use for the ones we issue to management.'

Graham was thinking.

'Maybe he's just spending a day at home and doesn't want to be bothered by work, so he's turned his phone off. Do you know where he lives, Andreas?'

He shook his head.

'I've known Ken for a long time but only through work. The only times I've seen him outside work has been at functions – Christmas and so forth.'

'Could you pull his address from the records for us please, Janet, and see if there's a home number in there as well.'

'Sure.' She looked puzzled. She clearly could not see the need for all this urgency.

She found the address in the computer records and wrote it down.

'There's a number there as well,' she said, handing it to her husband. 'What's this about? Is Ken in trouble?'

Andreas attempted a reassuring smile.

'It's something we need to talk to him about. Nothing to worry about.'

Graham knew that would not be enough to placate Janet.

'I'll tell you all about it later, love. It's all OK. Thanks for this.'

He held up the Post-it note and the two men left.

They remained silent until they were out of earshot.

'What do you think?' asked Graham.

He knew they were both thinking the same thing.

'Ken's been with us for a long time, I can't believe...'

The sentence tailed off into nowhere. Graham finished it for him.

'And yet it all fits, doesn't it? Ken knows the business inside out and would know how to stay well below the radar. Ken was very quick to come forward and suggest Turnbull as a replacement more or less as soon as Yates was sacked - and you can understand his urgency if he's got another shipment he needs picking up days later. He's nowhere to be seen on the day the shipment is due in and then there's this business with a second phone. I didn't tell you this but I was confronted by Yates a few days after he was sacked. He told me he knew things that could bring the company down and put people in jail. He had to be referring to someone high up. That was the day Ken had his call on his second phone and left Janet suddenly because I remember telling her about Yates and what he said on the way home and she didn't want to talk about it because she was in a bad mood after Ken let her down. What if that call Ken took was from his accomplice, Yates? What if he had to leave in a hurry because Yates was threatening to expose him? That's what Yates suggested he was prepared to do.'

They came to a halt in the corridor. Graham took hold of

Andreas's forearm and they looked at each other. There was intensity in Graham's stare. This was painful for Andreas to hear but he could not shut it out. He feared he knew the words that were coming next.

'What if Ken had Yates murdered?'

Andreas pressed on the few more steps to his office and Graham followed him inside, closing the door behind him. The younger man slumped into his chair. This was a lot to take in.

He stared up to the grimy ceiling and was unable to formulate a contrary sequence of events. Not one that made any sense and yet the thought that faithful old Ken, the long-serving finance manager who must be coming up to retirement, was a murderer and drugs baron made no sense either. Everybody liked Ken. He was kind, efficient, perfectly pleasant in every way and had never given anyone a reason to offer a bad word about him. There must be another explanation but still there was so much in what Graham said that needed to be explained first.

'We must talk to him,' said Andreas emphatically.

'Do you want this home number?' suggested Graham.

He considered.

'No. I want to see him. Let's see if he's at home.'

24

Rebecca made no attempt to disguise the fact that she was not especially pleased to be told one of her transport administrators was wanted for other duties today. This was the kind of disruption she had feared would happen when the boss brought in his long-lost father, against her better judgement, to work in her team. She liked her authority to be absolute and felt undermined but knew there was nothing she could do about it. She decided she would find a way to make Graham suffer for this, to keep him in line.

Graham had much more pressing issues on his mind. He had decided not to tell Andreas that he knew the head of the drug gang from university because it struck him as over-complicating an already complicated situation. Telling him that they had a brief relationship which produced a child and that he had a half-brother who was a member of the drug gang would definitely have made the picture murkier.

So he decided to hold back that information for another day but there was another matter he had to raise.

'Just before they took me back to my car last night they gave me a phone,' he announced as Andreas drove a little too erratically, following the sat nav directions to Ken

Arnold's home address.

'A phone?' he answered, accelerating harder through traffic lights as they turned amber.

'Yeah. What do they call them – a burner?'

He had been a big fan of *The Wire* on TV.

'It has one number programmed into it and I'm supposed to call them when we know where the shipment is meant to be delivered so that they can intercept it. They told me they would confiscate the drugs – as a gesture of good will, they said.'

'They said what?' The conversation was not doing anything to calm Andreas's mood. 'I hope you told them they could go and fuck themselves.'

Graham gripped the edge of his seat a little more firmly as a line of static traffic became closer much more quickly than Andreas appeared to be reckoning for.

'I didn't think that would be a very smart thing to suggest in the circumstances,' he explained. 'Quite frankly, I was ready to agree to anything if it meant I could get away from that place in one piece.'

'Yes, of course, of course!' Andreas conceded as the Jaguar squealed to a halt a foot or so short of the bumper of the car in front of them.

'But there can be no question of us allowing them to get to the truck first, surely. They might decide to start another fire and, this time, while the trailer is fully laden.'

Graham hesitated for a moment but the second part of the sentence he expected to hear was not spoken.

'And we wouldn't want to put the driver or anyone else in danger either, would we?'

'Of course not! Of course not!' Andreas barked in a tone that made it sound so obvious a statement that it did not warrant saying.

'I won't hand over anybody to these gangsters and I won't allow them to seize the drugs. If we did that we would be leaving ourselves open to further trouble. They would have a hold on us. They could blackmail us into bringing more of their dirty business into the country on my trucks in the future and I cannot allow that. It would blacken the family name.'

Graham had not thought of that. It was a good point.

'In that case, we have to call in the police. Do it by the book.'

Andreas considered this. The traffic was heavy with other motorists wanting to get to work and being unable to go anywhere quickly had cooled his temper.

'In time,' he said. 'We go to them when we have established who is responsible and where the rendezvous point is. Otherwise, the police will just get in the way.'

The suggestion went against Graham's instincts but he reasoned that they would get to the right conclusion eventually following such a plan. Andreas seemed to have a real problem with authority figures. He might have to be prepared to put up with that.

'I'd go to the police straight away but OK, if that's the way you'd rather play it. As soon as we track down the truck and identify Turnbull, Ken or whoever else is mixed up in this, we call in the cops, OK?'

Andreas was satisfied with that. 'Agreed.'

They made the rest of the journey to Totley safely, wrapped in their silent thoughts.

The sat nav told them they had arrived and Andreas pulled up. They craned to identify numbers on the white doors of the creamy stone detached houses, with their uniform grey slate roofs, on either side of them.

'I can see number two,' said Graham. 'Which number are we after?'

Andreas checked the scrap of paper. 'Eight.'

'It must be that one there, up the driveway with the black car outside. Is that Ken's car?'

'I wouldn't know,' Andreas replied. 'Let's get out and see.'

They both climbed out of the car and walked towards the house they reckoned might be the one they wanted. It had a 'For Sale' sign posted on the front lawn.

'I'll handle this bit,' said Andreas. He rapped on the door.

Around 20 seconds later, a smartly-dressed older woman opened it. She clearly recognised the face immediately facing her but appeared surprised to see him.

'Hello, Jenny,' said Andreas, as if turning up unannounced on the front door so early in the morning was the most normal thing in the world.

She was confused. 'Goodness, Andreas! I haven't seen you since, well, the funeral. How have you been?'

'Good, thank you. I hope you are well too.'

Jenny glanced at her wrist and then noticed the other figure standing further back on the driveway. Andreas took the cue.

'Oh, I'm sorry. This is Graham, my colleague. Graham, this is Jenny Arnold.'

They exchanged awkward smiles of greeting.

'This isn't a good time, Andreas. I have to get to work and I'm running behind already.'

'Oh, I thought you'd retired.'

Her face went suddenly very stern and she let out a small 'hmphh!' noise. A nerve had been touched.

Andreas did not pursue the line.

'I don't want to make you late. We actually need to see Ken. He's not at work today – is he home?'

She stared at him, looking for anything other than innocence in the question. She saw no sign. He can't know.

'Ken hasn't lived here for six months. I threw him out. I'm divorcing him.'

The news stunned Andreas for a moment.

'Jenny, I had no idea. You and Ken seemed made for each other.'

Her features softened, the pain showing.

'I guess none of us really knows everything about a person, do we? In January, I discovered that Ken had taken out a huge loan without telling me and had used our home as collateral. I was under the impression that we were debt-free because we paid off the mortgage using a large part of my retirement lump sum but then I stumbled on a letter which suggested we owed over quarter of a million. I confronted him with it and he tried to fob me off with some story of it being sent by the building society in error and that he had sorted it out with them and that I should ignore it but I couldn't. I went in to the building society myself and they confirmed that Ken had taken out a loan for £270,000 last October.

'Of course, I was furious. I'd trusted Ken to take care of the financial side of things all our married life because that was his area of expertise, but we'd always made the big decisions jointly. I asked him why he'd done it and eventually he confessed to me that he was in big trouble. He was a gambler, Andreas. In all the time we'd known each other, I'd never seen him so much as go near a betting shop but it turned out he was hooked on the online casino sites and he'd lost everything. He told me he'd lost almost £300,000.'

Andreas's jaw was practically on the block paving of the driveway.

'That's why I had to go back to work. He ruined us. If it hadn't have been for financial help from our daughters, the house might have been repossessed. All I can do now is try to sell so that I can pay off some of what we owe. That's why I threw him out.'

He moved forward and took hold of Jenny's hand between his.

'I'm so sorry for you. I knew nothing about this. I only hope you are back on your feet soon but I really must talk to Ken. Do you know where he lives now?'

A tear came to her eye and she dabbed at it with the back of her other hand.

'The only communication we have now is through solicitors but I believe he has a rented flat in Handsworth or Darnall, somewhere around there. I'm sorry, Andreas, I really must go.'

'I understand. Just one more thing, though – who are your solicitors?'

She hesitated, unsure if it was wise to pass on the information, but relented.

'Tooms, Tonks and Taylor in town.'

He clasped her hand a little tighter for a moment and then released it.

'I'm sorry to have bothered you, Jenny. Goodbye.'

He backed away with a final sympathetic glance and the two men returned to the car.

Andreas slammed the car door behind him angrily.

'The lying, deceitful bastard! How could anyone do such a thing?'

He appeared ready to hit something or someone but contented himself with gripping the steering wheel with both hands as if he was throttling two chickens simultaneously.

Graham allowed the worst of the storm to pass before speaking.

'I understand you're angry but let's try to see past that. This is definitely pointing more and more towards Ken being our man. He's clearly desperate for money. If he's confessed to losing 300 grand to his wife it's not beyond the realms of possibility he could be even deeper over his head in debt. Maybe he devised a plan to sell drugs to generate the income he needs and now that he's getting bolder at it, he's looking to import larger quantities. I'm afraid it all makes sense.'

A further thought occurred.

'And could he have embezzled money from the company? Would he have the access to be able to do that?'

Andreas was almost grinding his teeth in fury. This new possibility made him stoop to lay his head against the steering wheel between his hands.

'I don't know,' he said despairingly. 'I would hope that a discrepancy like that would be picked up by the financial director above him but I don't know. I'll have to arrange for someone to go through the numbers.'

He stayed in his pose, locked in silent reflection.

'If he has cheated me as well, I will kill him myself.'

Graham was growing impatient with this self-indulgent show of rage.

'Come on, Andreas, we've got to get back on this. We need to find Ken and the only lead we've got for where he lives now is the name of the solicitors. How do we get the information from them?'

He snapped back into an upright position melodramatically.

'Yes. I know one of the partners. He owes me a favour.'

Andreas took out his phone.

'I'll try Ken's number again,' he said.

After only a couple of seconds with the phone to his ear, he brought it back down with a snort.

'Still turned off.'

He was looking for another number now and pressed the button to dial it.

'Hello, is Peter Tonks in this morning please?'

He waited for the query to be answered.

'He is. Good. Could you see if he can spare 10 minutes this morning for Andreas Johnson, please? It's urgent.'

Another delay. A longer one this time.

'Splendid! 11 will be fine. I look forward to seeing him.'

Andreas hung up and checked the time. It was almost nine. He turned the key in the ignition.

'Come on. We've time for breakfast.'

25

The rolling tide of disturbing developments had no apparent impact on Andreas's appetite. They called at a cafe on Ecclesall Road and Graham picked at a single slice of poached egg on toast while the man opposite devoured a generous plate of full English. It was probably wise of him to keep up his strength for whatever challenges lay ahead.

The first of them was to call at the offices of the law firm, Tooms, Tonks and Taylor, to try to persuade them to release the address Ken Arnold had moved to since he had been thrown out of the marital home. Andreas needed no prompting from the sat nav to drive straight to the public car park closest to the offices, just off Bridge Street.

'Peter and I have known each other for a long time,' he said as they walked towards the three-storey red-brick building with its triple-T logo set above a black-framed smoked glass revolving door. 'It'll be better if I see him alone. He'll be more likely to tell me what I want to know that way. You can wait in the reception, if you like.'

Graham nodded. He could see the sense in that.

Andreas strode ahead alone towards the silver-fronted reception desk in the large, pristine open floor area. Even the pale floor tiles looked as if a team of highly-motivated cleaners had only recently completed their task.

'Barbara, my darling, how are you today?'

His ability to slip effortlessly into full charm mode was impressive.

The older woman behind the reception desk smiled in recognition.

'Good morning, Mr Johnson. Very well, thank you. How are you?'

'Excellent, excellent. I have an appointment to see Peter at 11.'

The large black and silver wall clock to the left of the desk, a reminder maybe that this was a business where time really was money, indicated it was almost five to.

'I'll call through and let his PA know you're here. Would you like to take a seat for a minute?'

Andreas headed towards the purple chairs beyond the desk and Graham followed. They sank into either end of a soft sofa and stared towards a large, rectangular canvas with a very colourful abstract design on the wall opposite them. Its chaos was utterly at odds with everything around them. The two men studied it without comment.

Two minutes later, a young woman with blonde hair diverted their attention.

'Mr Johnson? I can take you through to see Mr Tonks now,' she said with an immaculate smile.

Andreas struggled to extricate himself from the sofa with all dignity intact before taking the cue to follow her towards the ground floor offices. Graham was drawn to look back towards the painting but then decided he had no idea what it was meant to represent and made a conscious effort to look at anything but the painting until Andreas re-emerged, unescorted, almost 15 minutes later.

Graham raised himself from the sofa at the third attempt as Andreas made for the exit without waiting. He increased his pace to catch up, eager to know how the mission had fared.

'Did you get it?' he asked as they stepped from the revolving door and back onto the street.

Andreas slowed and patted his inside jacket pocket.

'Peter is a good man,' he confirmed with a grin. 'Let's go and find him.'

They pulled into a space in front of a shuttered-up nail shop. To one side of them was a takeaway called The Peking Dragon, which looked as if no attention had been paid to its outward appearance since the time of the Ming dynasty, and to the other side was a convenience store whose main window was filled almost entirely with posters advertising offers on cheap lager.

'Is this it?' asked Graham.

If nothing else, the area certainly gave the appearance of a place where someone who was short of funds might end up.

'I guess so,' replied Andreas. 'We had better find out.'

They got out of the car and Andreas double-locked the doors. There were more shops to their left and, as they walked towards them, Andreas pointed out the number 398 above the door of a flower shop called Blooming Lovely, which had plainly been a long time closed and now looked more of a blooming eyesore.

'The number we want is 398a, so we can't be far away,' he suggested.

The next shop down was a cafe and the proprietor had

optimistically set out two metal tables with chairs on the area in front in case any customer felt inclined to sit and sip their coffee in the tepid sunshine and watch the traffic go by on the busy main road. No-one had taken up the opportunity but at least the cafe appeared to be open and so the two men headed towards it in hope of locating the flat.

The only person inside the cafe was an Asian man who was sitting cross-legged on a chair in front of the counter reading a newspaper. He seemed to not notice the two of them walking through the open door, even though he hardly gave the impression of having been particularly overwhelmed by custom.

'Hi,' said Graham and the man glanced at them over the top of his paper. Reluctantly, he folded the paper and put it down on the table as he rose to his feet.

'What can I get you fellas?' he asked, ambling towards the gap at the side of the counter.

'Actually, we're looking for someone who lives in one of the flats around here. It's number 398a.'

The cafe owner stopped, realising his culinary skills might not be required after all.

'This is 396. There are two flats above these shops which are rented out by a man called Kowalski but I don't know who lives in them. Are you the law?'

Graham shook his head.

'No, it's nothing like that. We're just trying to find someone. He's called Ken. Might he have ever come in for a coffee?'

The man gazed at them with suspicion, not persuaded by the assertion of innocent purpose.

'I don't know any Ken. The entrance to the flats is down the side, by the flower shop. There's a bell to ring for the flats.'

'OK,' Graham began to back away towards the door. Andreas had already retreated through it. 'Thanks very much for your help.'

Andreas strode down a gap about the width of a small car between the two buildings. Around two-thirds of the way down was a blue door with two bells fixed to the wall next to it. One had a label saying '396a' beneath it and the other said '398a'. Andreas pressed on the one they wanted and waited for a response, his head tilted to pick up any sign of a noise from within.

Ten seconds later, he rang it again, holding his finger on the button for longer this time. Still there was no reply.

He took out his phone.

'I'll try calling him again.'

Again, there was not so much as a ringing tone.

'Pah! Where the fuck is he?'

'Try ringing the other bell,' suggested Graham. 'Somebody might be in who could at least confirm that Ken lives here.'

Andreas pressed the second bell and then impatiently pressed it again a few seconds later.

'This is useless,' he snapped and pressed hard on the first bell again.

'It doesn't look like he's around but he must be somewhere,' said Graham, attempting to keep the conversation in a rational balance. 'There's not much else we can do, so how about we hang around here for an hour, just in case he comes back?'

Andreas gave the bell another frustrated push and then looked at his watch.

'It's nearly 12 o'clock. There are a million and one other

things I had to do today, so I don't really want to waste more time on this wild goose chase.'

He pressed the bell again, almost as if he wanted to punish it.

'Half an hour, then,' Graham reasoned. 'I can get us coffees from the cafe and bring them back to the car. He might just have nipped out somewhere. I'd hate to think we might have just missed him.'

Andreas drew a deep breath and exhaled pointedly.

'OK. 30 minutes. Do you think the man in the cafe could manage to cook a decent bacon butty as well?'

They sat in the Jag, sipping their drinks, and Andreas ate his comfort butty but still there was no sign of Ken. Graham disposed of their rubbish in a convenient wheelie bin at the side of the convenience store and they set off back to the depot.

Keeping tabs on Turnbull was considerably easier. They checked the Trams tracking together on the computer as soon as they got back to the depot and confirmed that he and his truck were around midway between Rotterdam and Hull on the North Sea.

All they could do was wait.

Andreas returned to his tasks and Graham picked up on his duties while attempting to avoid the further wrath of Rebecca. It was late afternoon until he felt he dare risk stepping outside for a short break.

It was time to make a call. Another chance he did not want to take was to give Sarah and her heavies any reason to suspect there was a deviation to their plan going on.

He stood against a wall in the yard, well away from anyone else, and stared at the phone for a while before he plucked up the courage to press call on the one programmed number.

It was answered after three rings.

'Yeah,' said a voice, tersely. Even with so little to go on, Graham felt sure it was Jason who had answered.

'It's Graham. I thought I'd let you know what the situation is.'

There was silence for a second, like a time delay, before the gruff voice responded.

'Have you got what we want?'

The question sent a shiver down his spine.

'I don't know the time or place yet but we've got a good idea who's behind this and we know roughly when the exchange should take place. We're expecting it to happen sometime between 7.30 and nine tonight.'

Again, there was a painful silence.

'Don't even fucking think about trying to put one over on us.' The threat in the tone could not have been clearer.

'Look, nobody's about to do anything stupid here.' Graham attempted to be as assertive as he was able. 'Andreas and myself have nothing to do with what's been going on without our knowledge and, believe me, we want nothing more than to bring this whole matter to an end. We're starting to put the pieces into place and when we figure out the exact details, I will let you know. You're going to have to trust me on this.'

It felt like a plea in vain. He did not imagine trust was a trait these people had much cause to exercise very often.

He waited for the response.

'You'd fucking better,' it came at last and then the line went dead.

He puffed his cheeks and tried to blow out the tension

which had quickly gripped every part of his body.

How did it come to this?

Not so long ago he was a humble librarian for whom gangsters and drug smugglers were merely categories in the fiction section but now... And the strangest part of it all was that the person he most feared might rip out his throat without a second thought was made partly of his own genetic material!

How bad a life would someone need to have to make him turn out so evil when his father was totally incapable of harming anyone? Jason must have had an awful childhood and been exposed to heaven only knows what at too young an age to have turned out like this.

Many families have their black sheep. He knew this full well. He had even sold the concept as exciting to researchers when they discovered theirs – a dash of colour in their ancestries they could tell stories about among their friends – but this was far too close to home to be a harmless thrill. This was downright terrifying.

Everybody would have been so much better off if he had simply kissed Sarah goodnight at the door of her digs and walked away back towards Leeds city centre, merrily whistling his Lindisfarne songs.

Better for her and definitely better for him.

26

Graham called in at Janet's office, taking the long route back to his desk. The door was open and he watched her busily leafing through the contents of a filing cabinet, with her back to him, for a few stolen moments before stepping through.

The phone call to Jason had stirred all the darkest terrors that held him in their clinch the previous evening and had deepened his sense of foreboding over what he and Andreas must face before this day was over. They could see no alternative to their plan to intercept the shipment at whatever handover point had been arranged, but the dangers of the unknown loomed ahead like a treacherous, gloomy threshold and the creeping shadow of the drug gang behind them made it impossible to turn back. The path they had to take was their only option.

Janet was unaware of his presence, just as she was unaware of so much that had happened to him in the last 24 hours. That was the way it had to stay. He hated shielding the truth from her but hated even more the thought of exposing her to harm. She would not like the deceit but she would understand once he explained everything, when it was all over.

'Hey, love.'

She turned and smiled.

'Oh, hiya, duckie, I didn't see you there. I'll only be a couple of minutes and we can get off.'

Out of her view, he grimaced and braced himself. More lies.

'Actually, I'm going to hang around here for a while yet. There's something else I need to do with Andreas.'

Janet stopped what she was doing and faced him again.

'I thought we were going back to Derby tonight.'

'I'm sorry, love, can we put that off until tomorrow morning? We're so close to getting to the bottom of all this now and I think we should have it all sorted tonight but there's something else we have to do first. I'm sorry.'

He regretted the second apology. He hoped it didn't betray how guilty he felt.

'Did you find him earlier?' she asked. His face must have turned momentarily blank because she felt the need to clarify.

'Mr Arnold. Did you find him?'

'Oh, right! No, he wasn't in and he's had his phone turned off all day. I don't suppose you've heard...'

She shook her head.

'What is this about, Gray? You and Andreas were very mysterious about it this morning. If Mr Arnold has done something wrong, I might be able to help.'

He walked over and embraced her.

'Thanks, love, it's all in hand. I can't really say if he has done anything wrong because we still don't know for sure but we should know by this evening. I'm sorry that it sounds as if I'm hiding something from you but until we really know what's going on, it's better that I say nothing. It could be nothing to do with Ken but once I know what the full picture is, I'll tell you all about it, I promise.'

He kept her in his arms, glad not to have to extend his pretence to his expression as well.

'You get off. There's no point you hanging around for me. You take the car and Andreas will give me a lift home later.'

'OK,' she replied, more in resignation than reassurance.

'You're not in any trouble, are you?'

He closed his eyes. This was unbearable.

'Me? No! You know me, I never do anything that could land me in trouble. It's not like that.'

'But a man was murdered, Gray.'

This was doing little to alleviate the fear she had felt since he first told her Yates had been killed. His next words had to be well chosen if he was to avoid adding to her anxiety.

'I know, love, I know, but that's not connected to what we're doing tonight. We're not trying to solve the murder here. No doubt the police have got all that in hand but what we're hoping to get to the bottom of is who was behind those fires they had in the depot yard earlier in the year. We think Ken knows something that might explain it and that's why we've been trying to find him and we think we know where we might be able to speak to him tonight. That's all. Nothing to worry about.'

More lies. He just hoped they came across as believable.

'I'll get something to eat with Andreas and I'll send you a text when I'm on my way home. I'm not sure when that'll be but it won't be too late. If you could pack us a few things tonight we can get straight off to Derby in the morning. Is that OK?'

She did not answer straight away.

'Yeah, OK.' She broke away from their hug. 'Just let me know what's happening and be careful. I don't like this, Gray.'

'I know.' His heart was as heavy as a stone. 'It'll be fine, love. I promise.'

They kissed.

'Love you,' he said.

'Love you,' she replied and kissed him again.

The unguarded concern in her face troubled him even more. He should go now, while he still could.

'See you later,' he said, trying to sound as casual as he was able, and then he left the small office.

Graham sat quietly at his desk, occupying his mind with the comforting distraction of routine tasks. Zoe, Sparky and then Rebecca all completed their shifts and went home, leaving him on his own.

He looked at the clock. It was 10 past six. It was time to check Trams to get an update on Oli Turnbull's journey from Rotterdam.

The system refreshed and showed that he had arrived in Hull. The truck engine was running. He must be waiting to disembark the ferry.

Graham jumped from his seat and stepped quickly down the corridor towards Andreas's office. He was at his desk, looking at his computer screen, but stopped what he was doing.

'He's landed,' said Graham.

Andreas nodded. 'I've just seen. Everything is on time for now. I think we should make a move.'

'OK.' Graham's stomach churned with a surge of nervousness but he tried not to show it.

'I've been thinking about this,' added Andreas. 'We have to assume that the old industrial estate is still a possibility for the rendezvous point, but we can't assume that it will definitely happen there, so I suggest we drive to the services on the M18, as I said earlier, get on to their WiFi and monitor his progress on my laptop. If he stops at the industrial estate, we're 15 minutes away, but if he drives past, we have to anticipate his next move. I don't think they would use the services we're going to because it's not really geared up for artics and there will be too many people about. I can't believe that he will divert too far off the motorway because they must know that their route will be traced on Trams and on the tacho and it will look too suspicious if he pulls off the most direct route for no good reason. That's why I think this is their only realistic alternative.' He gestured for Graham to come round the desk to look at the computer screen. 'Here, look.'

He waited until Graham was at his shoulder before clicking to bring up a map.

'See, there is a large truck stop at this end of the M18, close to the junction with the M1. It's usually very popular with the truckers and the parking area is normally just about full because they pull in for the night, get some food, have a couple of pints and get some sleep, then it's up in the morning for breakfast and away again.'

Graham looked at the satellite image of the map. It did look like a big place.

'But if it's so popular, surely it'd be hard to do something as obvious as take goods off the back of the trailer and load it onto another without attracting suspicion?

With so many truckers about, somebody would be bound to realise what was going on.'

Andreas almost anticipated the objection.

'I said *usually* very popular,' he added, with a flourish. 'Most trampers finish their runs on a Friday and head home, so the truck stop is quiet on Friday nights. The parking area is big enough to pull in well away from anyone else and then do what you need to do unnoticed. They will know that. They serve food until nine, so it's easy to explain away a stop there, even though it's so close to the depot, by saying you wanted to call in for a meal before it got too late. See?'

Graham nodded. It sounded plausible.

'And there's nowhere else you know of where he might pull in?'

'Not unless he stops right on the motorway and that's far too risky. It has to be here if it's not the industrial estate.'

It was a guess but it was as good a guess as they had. With the advantage of Trams, they could always react and head elsewhere if they needed to.

'Right. Let's set off for the services, then.'

It was around 10 to seven when they pulled off the motorway and parked at the services. Andreas opened the rear door to retrieve his laptop bag from where he had cast it onto the back seat and set off towards the glass-fronted main building.

There were plenty of people about. The two children of a family were skipping eagerly towards the promise of a fast-food treat while their parents stretched out the fatigue of their journey, walking slowly behind them. A group of five men in their twenties at an outdoor table, all in shorts and sunglasses, were laughing loudly as one of their number cursed the ill-fitting plastic top on his large cup which had leaked his soft drink down the front of his t-shirt.

Graham followed Andreas reluctantly, his trepidation growing, into the main food court. The centre of the court was dominated by a large tree, replanted, presumably, in a valiant attempt to temper the ugliness of its surroundings with the simple beauty of nature. Chairs scraped across the tiled flooring as diners rose from their tables and other people milled around the outside of the dining area, trying to pin down their best options from the usual big-name food outlets circled around the outside of the building.

A big screen behind them was booming out the build-up to the night's big match as Andreas led them to one of the booths where a listless staff member was about to clear away a tray left by the last occupant.

'We'll set up here. I'll make sure I can get on their WiFi.'

Andreas took out his laptop and started it up. Two minutes later, he had connected and was waiting for Trams to load.

'Now let's see where our man has got to,' he said, clicking impatiently and waiting with a puff of the cheeks as the links took him to the information he wanted to see.

'Ah ha!' he pronounced at last and Graham gathered closer to look.

'We have him on the A63 around North Ferriby. That's at least another half-hour or 40 minutes out. Do you want something to eat?'

Food was low on Graham's wanted list.

'Just a coffee, thanks. I've no appetite right now.'

'Really?' Andreas appeared bemused by the suggestion. 'Thinking makes me hungry. I need to feed my brain. Keep an eye on this, will you?'

He rose and headed towards the food outlets.

Graham watched the progress of Turnbull's truck as the system automatically refreshed every 12 seconds. As he followed the red blob of the signal on his screens at work, it always seemed so satisfyingly positive – the sign of a job on its way to being well done – but this was different. This time, it felt like watching the advance of a predator closing on its prey and they were about to put themselves in the way of its widening jaws.

He had to turn away and look for a distraction. An old couple at a table close by were watching a small child in a high chair at the next table push long, thin chips into its mouth and chew contentedly. One of the cleaning staff, with a long-handled brush in one hand and long-handled dustpan in the other, watched the child too and anticipated the mess that she would inevitably have to attend to soon.

Graham moved his hand to touch the outside of his jacket, where he could feel the shape of a phone in the inside breast pocket. Sarah's phone. In his heart, he knew that handing the drug shipment and the fate of the driver over to the gang was wrong but his terse conversation with Jason in the afternoon had raised misgivings. He was concerned that not going along with their plan to the letter could have implications. Not allowing them to take the drugs would surely piss them off greatly. They could get nasty. He did not share Andreas's confidence that they would accept the decision to hand the smugglers over to the police just because they had been given no choice. They still had the choice to seek retribution.

His hand traced the outline of the phone in his pocket and he considered again – are we doing the right thing? But what is the right thing to do? It was an impossible predicament.

Andreas bustled back holding a plastic tray and set it down on the table next to the laptop. He handed over a red disposable cup to Graham and settled down to empty a large brown paper bag of its contents. He flipped open a cardboard box to reveal a pungent burger, then poured straggly chips from a cardboard sleeve into the empty top of the burger box and ripped open a sachet of tomato sauce with his teeth to smother it over the chips.

'Want some?' he offered.

'No thanks,' said Graham, feeling queasy from the aroma and resisting the temptation to wonder out loud where his son found the room, never mind the will, to eat so much.

'When was the last time you tried Ken's phone?'

Andreas attempted to tear open another sachet of tomato sauce with his fingers but quickly abandoned the effort and cast it into the empty brown bag.

'I've tried it a hundred times. He's not going to turn it on now. He must be using the second phone to communicate with the driver. There's no point trying again.'

He took a large bite out of the burger.

'Where is he now?' he asked through a full mouth, looking to the laptop screen.

Graham waited for the dot to edge along with its next refresh.

'On the M62 now, coming towards Howden. Maybe another quarter of an hour, 20 minutes.'

Andreas nodded and scooped up a large pinch of chips.

'Are you sure you don't want any of these? You should eat.'

Graham's stomach was curdling.

'Actually, I think I'll just go and get some air for 10 minutes.'

He got up and headed towards the exit. Tracking the truck was doing nothing to soothe his apprehension. He envied Andreas's apparent composure because his own lingering doubt was overwhelming him. There was so much at stake.

It wasn't just a matter of anticipating the smugglers' next move and then calling the police. If only it was that straightforward.

What if there was no handover? Could they be certain Turnbull was the new carrier? Might Ken Arnold – if, indeed, Ken Arnold was the man at the heart of all this – have made other arrangements? Where had he been all day?

What if the handover had already taken place? There might have been another liaison point closer to the ferry port they were not aware of and it might have already happened, undetected.

What if it was still to happen but they and the police didn't get there in time?

If any one of those scenarios played out – and the more he turned them over in his mind, the more likely all of them appeared to be – he and Andreas would be in serious trouble. They had taken matters into their own hands by deciding that calling in the police, rather than the drug gang, was the best way to deal with bringing a close to this wretched business and if they failed... If they failed... The consequences did not bear thinking about.

The group of young men had headed on their way, leaving only a moderate amount of mess in their wake, and he ambled back and forth by the back of the empty tables, attempting to calm himself. The hum of the motorway traffic hung over the car park as more people came and went, carrying on with their ordinary lives, oblivious to the inner turmoil of the inconspicuous man in his fifties who was loitering by the food court entrance.

He watched them, looking over the top of his glasses as he attempted not to be noticed, and the more he watched, the calmer he became.

The rest of the world had not changed significantly in the last 24 hours. It was still turning on the same axis at the same speed and it would still be turning tomorrow. Who knows what all these people have had to go through at some stage in their lives but they came through the challenges to be able to get on with everything as they had before, tempered by their experiences but intrinsically the same.

Why should it not be the same for him and Andreas? This was their big test. It might go wrong but they might also get it right. They had thought it through. They were as sure as they could be that they were still in control and so, in no more than an hour or two, it will be over. Tomorrow, life will resume. He will wake up beside Janet and they will go back to Derby for the weekend and catch up with family and the balance of normality will be restored. All that needs to be done is to get through these next couple of hours, see it through.

'We can do this,' he said, aloud.

He watched as the old couple whose attention had been taken by the small child feasting on chips tottered by, arm in arm, and ambled towards the nearby blue badge parking spots.

He wasn't in this alone and they would get through it, intact. They had to be focused, measured, in control. They have a plan. They need to see it through.

Graham felt his resolve growing.

We can do this.

The automatic door to the food hall opened and Andreas burst through with his laptop bag over his shoulder.

'He's driven past the industrial estate. Let's go.'

27

'I'm glad we found each other.'

Andreas turned and smiled as he said the words and then leaned to slap his large hand twice on Graham's thigh.

Graham snapped out of his spell. He had been mesmerised by the motorway traffic, rushing by on both carriageways, as he locked himself away in his thoughts. Neither of them had said a word since they left the service station and set off back towards Sheffield. An affectionate declaration like this was about the last thing he expected to hear.

He looked towards his son, a quizzical expression on his face like he expected a further explanation of why he chose to say those words at this time, rather than why he said them at all, but Andreas didn't offer one. He stared ahead, grinning broadly, like he was driving them on a long-anticipated excursion or on an adventure.

Was he actually enjoying this?

That could not be possible, surely, but he appeared to be thriving on, rather than being daunted by, their desperate and dangerous situation. All Graham could hope was that this was down to strength of character and not because he did not appreciate the full gravity of the position they were in. He still had so much to learn about Andreas. They were so different.

'You found me, strictly speaking,' he said. 'Until you turned up at my house that night I had no idea you even existed.'

This was factually correct but Graham immediately chastised himself for his mean-spiritedness. His reply hardly matched the generosity of the original statement.

'Did I?' Andreas focused straight ahead and the smile did not move from his lips, as if he was pleased with himself for having set a riddle.

His companion was certainly puzzled.

'What do you mean?'

'I mean of course it was me who did the legwork and initiated the contact but I think it was fate that led us to each other, just as it was fate that brought you and my mama together that night. If that had not happened, I wouldn't have existed and so many lives would have been so different. You and I were also meant to find each other.'

Graham fell silent. He hadn't thought of it that way.

'Do you not believe that too?'

This was not a direction he expected to be taken but he knew it would be churlish to respond to it with a flat yes, no or don't know.

'I suppose I don't really see things that way. I'm used to drawing up the tracks of people's origins in lines and plotting where those lines intersect with other families to form new branches and I find it interesting to establish where and when they came together but I never really think of it in terms of a greater force bringing them together. Most times in the past, people lived in the same region for generations and it was practically inevitable that they would meet someone whose family had also lived in the same region for generations. If they did move to new places it was usually to look for work or to escape difficulties – very practical reasons like that. Is destiny guided by fate? I don't know about that. It's a nice thought but I guess I'm just a bit too pragmatic to believe that. Sorry.'

Andreas laughed heartily.

'Who knows where the answer lies, eh? What I do know is that I am glad we found each other. We make a great team, you and I.'

He clapped his great hand down on Graham's shoulder this time, shaking his slighter frame.

'When this is over, I would like us to work more closely. I would like you to take on a bigger role in the company.'

This was unexpected. Graham thought of how he had been aware that Rebecca might see him as a threat and how he had determined he should prove to her that he was not.

'Do you mean depot manager? I don't think that would be fair...'

'I don't want you to be my new Rottweiler,' Andreas interjected. 'You could not replace Rebecca. I want you to help me drive the company forward, not do the day-to-day stuff. I need you to be my right-hand man.'

'But I've only been in the business five minutes. I barely know anything. I'm not ready.'

His protests ran deeper than self-effacement. It had been four weeks. His feet had barely hit the ground.

'I do not need you for your experience in the business. I understand the business. I know it inside and out. What I need is someone beside me I can trust absolutely and discuss ideas with. I thought I could trust Ken Arnold but this has shown me I have very few people around me I can truly count on. You are not afraid to tell me what I need to hear and I need that. I know I can be a little hot-headed but you make me see sense again and I lost that influence in my life when my mama and pappa passed on. I respect your honesty and I trust your judgement. Besides...'

He released his hand from the steering wheel and brought it down heavily on Graham's thigh again.

'...you are family! We are family!'

Graham laid his hand on Andreas's. He was moved.

'That's very kind of you to say, Andreas, and I feel flattered. Of course I'll help in any way you want me to. I'll do whatever I can and yes – I'm also glad we found each other.'

Andreas shook Graham's knee and withdrew his hand.

'Good, good,' he said, with an air of perfect contentment.

They drove in silence for the rest of the way. There was so much he did not know about Andreas and they were so different but, in these few short weeks, they had begun the process of bridging a gap of 35 lost years and the adversity they now faced together was driving them closer still. Maybe they really could go on to achieve great things together.

They pulled off the motorway and followed the broad sweep of the road past a mass of barely distinguishable low-level industrial units, many now closed for the night. The light was also closing fast. As the Jaguar turned off the road, at the sign directing them to the truck stop, Graham checked his watch. It was just after 10 to eight.

A wide expanse of parking space stretched to their right

and very little of it was taken by stationary trucks. It was a huge area, just right for conducting clandestine business well away from prying eyes.

In front of them, they could see moving trucks on the motorway, setting a suitable backdrop for the red-tile-roofed building they were now approaching. It appeared to be more like the kind of pub families would go to for Sunday lunch than the archetypal truckers' haven he had in his mind's eye.

'It's not what I expected,' he said.

Andreas steered the Jaguar towards an area marked out for car-sized spaces close to the building.

'They've moved on a long way from the greasy spoons, thank god!' he replied as he pulled up and turned off the engine.

Inside was also like a pub – the type that tries to attract diners rather than drinkers – but most pubs would hope for a few more customers on a Friday night. A group of three drivers, each eking out the remains of a pint in front of them, were almost lost among the lines of tables as they crouched forward wearily in quiet conversation; talking over the last dregs of another busy week on the roads.

Andreas headed for a table at the opposite end of the dining area and quickly set up his laptop.

'Shall I go and get us a drink?' Graham suggested, as Andreas fidgeted impatiently, waiting for the WiFi to kick in and the page to load.

'I could kill for a beer, thanks,' Andreas answered, his finger poised over the mouse, ready to progress to the next stage of finding out how far the truck was behind them.

Graham thought his terminology unfortunate but he understood the sentiment. Since they had arrived at the truck stop, the adrenaline had really begun to kick in and his mouth felt dry.

'Hi.' Graham mustered an edgy smile as he approached the bar. 'Two pints of Pedigree please.'

The barman, a prominent pot belly straining behind his apron, picked up a straight glass and began to fill it from one of the hand pumps.

'Will you gents be wanting food? We stop serving at nine.'

Graham turned to look towards Andreas, who was staring intently at his laptop screen and tapping on the keyboard. He didn't feel entirely confident that the chance to eat again would be turned down but decided not to put the option to him. It might only be another quarter of an hour until they found out whether their truck would be heading for this truck stop. If not, they might have to track it to a new destination. Either way, they didn't have the time to order and eat a meal.

'No, just the drinks please.'

He carried the pints back to the table. 'Have you picked him up yet?'

Andreas snatched up the glass almost as soon as it was placed in front of him and took a large swig.

'I've got him past the junction for the A1(M),' he replied. 'Not far away now. Seven or eight miles.'

So close! Graham swallowed two mouthfuls of his beer before moving near enough to watch the menacing red dot pulsing its way across the map towards them.

Their task would be much more complicated if the dot cruised straight past junction one and away towards the convergence with the M1. They watched together, united in their desperation for it to be drawn into the trap of the next left turning. The page auto-refreshed again and it edged another few millimetres their way.

'Should we make the call now, do you think?' Graham asked.

'The police?' Andreas's gaze remained fixed on the screen. 'Not yet. We have to be certain.'

'But they could be on their way.' The response left Graham feeling uneasy. He did not want them to be left open to any risk of their prey slipping through the net.

'We wait.' Andreas was adamant. 'If there is police activity and Turnbull does not turn off here, we might scare them away. We have to be sure.'

'But the truck isn't going to disappear. The police can still apprehend it and if the drugs are in the load...'

'We wait.' His tone allowed no room for compromise and silenced Graham's objections, though it did not ease his concerns. Andreas reflected on his abruptness and realised he needed to explain himself more fully.

'I want us to catch them both. It's not enough to stop the truck and seize the drugs. Arnold cannot get away. We have to be sure where the transaction is happening before we bring in the police. We have to get this right, so we wait.'

'But if they're too late because we should have called sooner...'

'There will be time. Patience.'

Ordinarily, in his past life, it was Graham who had to urge patience in others but, in these new circumstances, he found his own stretched to breaking point. Andreas wanted to see the whites of their eyes. He was more aware, after all, how long it might take to offload the shipment and transfer it. Perhaps he was right in his judgement that they should hold their nerve.

'Almost on top of us now,' said Andreas.

The red dot had moved beyond the point on the motorway where they might have been able to stand out in the large lorry park outside and watch it speed by. If it was going to turn off, the truck must be slowing down.

They waited for the system to refresh again and simultaneously reached for another gulp of their beers.

It was on the slip road. It was turning off.

'That's it. Come to daddy.' Andreas was staring at the screen with eager anticipation. The next refresh showed the dot past the junction and heading towards the road leading to the truck stop. Andreas's confidence over the rendezvous point appeared well founded.

Graham sucked in a long breath. This is it. Taking away the doubt over the destination was a huge relief. Now for the next stage.

'Once we definitely know he's heading for this lorry park I call it in to the police,' he said decisively. 'Once we get eyes on him we turn it over to them, like we agreed, right?'

Andreas continued to glare intently at the screen, like the dot was a bug he was poised to swat.

'Right, Andreas?'

'Yeah, yeah,' he finally acknowledged, irritation in his tone.

Graham pulled his phone from his jacket pocket, poised.

Andreas craned to look out of the window towards the lorry park entrance.

'He should be coming round that corner any ...minute ...now.'

Seconds later, the front of a truck in red and yellow

livery came into view and swung between the wide posts that marked the entrance. As it cleared the posts and drew forward, turning towards the far end of the large swathe of asphalt, away from where they were watching, a white van with the markings of a hire company turned in too and followed the lorry.

'And I bet that's our treacherous dog Arnold.' Andreas virtually spat out the words, making no attempt to disguise the venom in them.

'OK. I'm going to go outside and watch where they park up and call for the police. You stay here.' Graham stood and moved quickly for the exit, keying the three nines into his keypad before he reached the door.

It rang four times and was answered.

'Police please.'

He waited to be connected and stole a look towards where the two vehicles were pulling in at the furthest end of the parking area.

'Yeah, I'm at the truck stop just off junction one of the M18 and I have very good reason to believe a large drug transaction is just about to take place. Drugs, that's right. They are on a red and yellow truck owned by the Harry Johnson Global Logistics company and I can see it parking up now at the far end of the lorry park and I can see a white hire van with it which I believe is being driven by the person who is going to take the shipment away once it's offloaded.

'Sure. My name's Graham Hasselhoff. Hasselhoff, that's right. H, A, double S, E, L, H, O, double F. Yes, that's it. I'm at the main diner part of the truck stop about 400 yards away. Yes, of course I'll stay out of the way until you get here. How long do you think they will be? Good. Hang on just a sec...'

A large shape in a suit bustled past Graham with a laptop bag over his shoulder. He was heading purposefully towards the far end of the lorry park.

'Andreas! What the hell are you... Sorry, I've got to go. Please get here as soon as you can.'

He hung up and sprinted towards the rotund figure, its arms swinging as it marched into the evening gloom to confront whatever lay ahead. Graham grabbed hold of an arm and swung in front of him, blocking his way.

'Are you mad? The police are on their way. We said we'd let them handle this. We agreed, Andreas.'

The younger man stared furiously ahead, fire in his eyes, hatred burning in his heart.

'I have to talk to him. I have to make him look me in the face and tell me why he betrayed me – why he betrayed my mama and my pappa. I have to know.'

He tried to sidestep his obstacle but the move was countered. Graham strained to hold him back.

'Don't do this, Andreas. We have to let the police take over, remember? It doesn't matter why he did it. All that matters is that we stop him. You might scare them off. They might get away.'

'Get out of my way!' With a swipe of his powerful arm, Andreas broke free and strode away again; his rage unquenchable, his purpose irresistible.

'Andreas!' Graham was helpless. He watched the figure eat up the shortening distance between themselves and the red and yellow truck and panic filled his soul.

What should I do?

He should stay back. They should stay back. What the hell is he thinking?

I can't let him do this alone.

Graham broke into a half-trot to catch up with the disappearing figure ahead of him.

28

They marched beyond the last of the parked trucks; Andreas, undaunted, still setting a furious pace and Graham, warily, two steps back. The parking area narrowed to the point of an elongated triangle and the tip of it was capped by loose gravel, which crunched under their footsteps. If the noise of their approach was noticed, it was not yet acknowledged. Maybe the motorway masked the sound.

The Johnson's truck was parked on their right, against the grain of the marked bays to ensure that whatever was being done on the other side of it was completely shielded from view, should anyone peer across from the main building.

It was not until they were within 20 yards that the front of the white van became visible to them. Andreas did not slow at all until he caught sight of the slender man with his back to them at the back of the van.

'How fucking dare you! You back-stabbing bastard! How fucking dare you!' he boomed.

The slender man was operating an automated tail lift, lowering a compact forklift from the back of the hire van, but he stopped the process and turned, startled, when he heard the voice.

He was under-average short and wirily thin, his sallow face made to look momentarily longer by the shocked bemusement that overcame his expression as he recognised the source of the sudden rebuke. He was dressed all in black, grey hair peeking below a black beanie hat, giving him the look of a cat burglar who had ventured out of a long retirement.

'Jesus, Andreas! What are you...' he stammered.

Andreas barely broke stride, charging towards the object of his indignation as if he was intent on tearing Ken's frail frame apart.

'After everything my family has done for you. This is how you repay us?'

Graham was too far behind to stop him but a tall and muscular man emerged from the shadow of the trailer to bar his way. Andreas attempted to barge past, but there was no sweeping this obstacle aside.

He was powerfully built beneath a close-fitting blue t-shirt and had black hair combed back. This had to be Turnbull. He held his arms wide to cover much of the space between trailer and van and hardly appeared to register the impact at all as the shorter, more rounded man in front of him bumped against the barrier of his body.

'OK, let's all just calm down here, shall we,' he reasoned, like a nightclub bouncer trying to defuse a squabble.

Andreas was not so easily placated. 'Don't fucking "calm down" me! I want to teach that duplicitous bastard what it means to betray my family.'

Turnbull's interception gave Graham time to catch up

and he attempted to wrestle Andreas away from the confrontation. Finally, the younger man gave up his attempt to burst free and turned, holding his head in the frustration of his unfulfilled anger.

Ken stayed safely behind the protection of his co-conspirator.

'Look, I'm sorry, Andreas, I had no choice. You have to understand. I never meant to disrespect you or your family but I had to do this. Look, we can work this out. I can give you a cut...'

The offer only served to fuel the smouldering embers of Andreas's wrath.

'I don't want any of your filthy money,' he raged as he jostled again towards Ken with renewed vigour, only this time to find his son, as well as the sturdy Turnbull, in his way. He quickly gave up the attempt and turned again, swinging a kick at the ground.

'Why did you do this, Ken?' asked Graham, his tone calm and reasonable. 'This is just wrong. How could you get mixed up in this terrible business?'

Ken was quaking, desperate. The weight of torment stooped his slight body even lower.

'I lost money, lots of money. When all the cash ran out from the loan I took out against the house I had nowhere to go but to borrow from people who don't take it well when you can't pay them back. The people I owed found out where I worked and told me I had to work off the debt by smuggling drugs for them. There was nothing else I could do.'

'But the risks you were taking. You must have realised it would catch up with you in the end.'

'It was all going so well!' he pleaded. 'Using the

Johnson's line and one of the regular drivers was perfect. We were hiding in plain sight. Nobody suspected a thing. It was going so well until that bitch Rebecca got Chris sacked.'

Andreas pointed a thick finger of his shaking hand accusingly. 'Don't blame her for this and don't blame me!'

'Did you kill Chris Yates?' asked Graham, surprising himself at how dispassionately he was able to put the question.

'Of course I didn't,' protested Ken. 'It was them,' he said with a flicked nod of the head. 'Chris was stupid. He threatened to go to the police and tell them all about me and the operation after he was sacked. He wanted to be paid off but these people aren't to be messed with. He should have known that. Stupid. Such a waste.'

His voice tailed off in regret and suddenly sparked again as he attempted to bargain directly with Graham.

'But look, this doesn't involve you two. You can just walk away now, turn a blind eye. What we're doing here doesn't have to cause you any trouble. Two more runs – three max – and I'll have settled my debt to these people. I'll leave the company and not say a word. You needn't ever hear from me again.'

Andreas released an anguished cry into the night, causing all three of them to stare at him as he circled, unable to vent the heat of the cauldron blazing within him.

'You're wrong, Ken,' said Graham. 'We're in this up to our necks. What you are doing has upset some people who don't like it that someone else is selling drugs on their patch and they hold me and Andreas responsible. They've threatened us that if we don't bring an end to this straight away we...' He turned and gestured towards the pacing figure behind him, then back to himself, '...are going to feel their retribution. They were the ones who carried out the arson attacks on the yard. Those were warnings – didn't you think they could be connected with what you were doing? So you see we can't just walk away. We are very much involved here. This is our lives at stake. That's why this has to stop now. It's over, Ken.'

The man in black sagged, resting his hands on his knees to stop him bending pathetically double. He was overwhelmed and, as he watched, Graham felt for him. He had been dragged into a pit of suffering from which there was no release through the weakness of his own compulsions and the more he struggled to break free, the deeper he was dragged into its suffocating hold.

'It's not over.' Turnbull's steady voice stole their attention.

Turnbull reached to where he had drawn back the curtain of the trailer and pulled out a metal bar, holding it menacingly.

'Ken needs this. We both need this. We've both got debts to pay and you're not going to stop us. I'm sorry it's brought trouble down on your heads but that's just tough. It seems to me that if you're being held responsible, not us, then that's your problem. We'll carry on and find somewhere else to sell, find another way of bringing the merchandise into the country as well if we need to. As far as I can see, that problem's solved.'

Graham backed away, eyes on the metal bar in Turnbull's hand. The callous simplicity of the argument left him dumbfounded.

'How can you... This is your responsibility! You can't just...'

The sound of a vehicle, advancing at speed, from the direction of the diner made his heart leap. It must be the police. Just in time.

Graham could not see round the truck to confirm his hopes but he looked towards Andreas, who was in a position to see it and was peering towards the sound as it rapidly closed on them. The sight of it did not appear to be giving him comfort.

Seconds later, it was there. A large car. A black BMW. It wasn't the police. Graham knew who it was.

Barely had it skidded to a halt when a man with a thick dark beard bounded out from the rear door, a handgun raised. The driver was soon also out of the car. He too had a gun. Jason. Around the car, from the front passenger door, emerged a third man, also armed.

Instinctively, Graham crouched low to the ground, arms in front of his face in a painfully inadequate attempt to protect himself, and he squeezed his eyes shut, as if expecting but unable to face the force of whatever was to happen next.

Turnbull, stunned into stillness at first, rallied and charged towards the car, the bar raised above his head. It was a defensive, intuitive, foolish and fatal reaction. The man with the black beard saw it and fired, once. Turnbull was knocked off his feet by the impact of the bullet on his chest. He fell backwards, lifeless.

Ken Arnold had watched the men jump out of the car and recognised the danger straight away. Too much exposure lately to too many men who had scant regard for the value of human life had opened his eyes. He saw no way this situation could end well for him and decided to run. He scampered beyond the cover of the van and towards the point of the parking area, lured by the potential salvation of a gap in the trees 30 yards away, but his days of making a quick getaway were long since behind him.

Jason watched his laboured dash coldly. His lifted his arm, aimed and released a single shot. Ken tumbled and lay in a motionless tangled heap.

The violent crack of the two shots hung in the air and reverberated in Graham's ears as he cowered, not allowing himself to breathe, anticipating the force of a third shot ripping through his body.

It did not come and slowly, timidly, he opened his eyes and lowered his arms.

By the side of the trailer he could see the soles of Turnbull's heavy boots and could tell that one of the shots, at least, had done its shattering worst.

He looked to where he had last seen Andreas, dreading what he might find. Andreas had also thrown himself low to the ground but was raising himself to his knees, his arms above his head in supplication and terror in his widened eyes.

Where was Ken? He was no longer at the rear of the van. Graham could not see him but then noticed the man from the passenger seat ambling towards a low shape, like a crumpled pile of black rags, 20 or so yards from them. The man kicked at the bundle and gave Jason a single nod to confirm that his aim had been true.

Jason moved three slow paces closer to where Graham still crouched, the gun in his hand but now down by his side.

'You didn't call,' he growled.

'I'm sorry, I'm sorry.' His body was trembling. In the blink of an eye, two lives had been taken and as he began to absorb the horror of that he felt sick to his core.

'How did you...?'

Jason surveyed the scene around him, assessing his handiwork.

'Tracking device,' he said. 'In the phone.'

They must have been following the movements of the pair of them in the Jaguar all day in just the same way as he and Andreas had tracked Turnbull on Trams.

Jason looked at both of them in turn, disdainfully.

'I knew you two were behind this.'

'No, you don't understand...'

Jason silenced Andreas's protest by spinning quickly and angling the gun towards him.

'Shut the fuck up, you!' he bellowed.

Andreas bowed his head and said no more. Jason lowered the gun.

'See now, the problem is because you didn't do what we told you to do, you've left us with a mess to clean up.'

The man with the thick black beard had wandered towards the trailer and was poking at the stacked pallets inside.

'What are you going to do with them?' asked Graham, fighting to stop himself shaking.

Thick black beard walked back towards his associate and gave a shrug, as if to say it was not obvious what part of the shipment was the one they were interested in.

'Not them,' snarled Jason, his lip curling with bitter hatred. He pointed the gun at Graham.

'You!' he said, turning sharply to aim at Andreas. 'And him!'

'No, no, no! Please don't do that!' Andreas begged, curling his stout body into a ball.

'And leave two witnesses free to pin all this on us? Do you think we're thick or something?'

He kept his arm at full stretch, the weapon pointed at the pitiful figure to his side. Graham stared, helplessly, and saw the glint in Jason's narrowing eye. He was the executioner, relishing his moment of perverse control; the absolute power of life and death in his hands and the knowledge that there was nothing his victim could do except wait until he chose to squeeze the trigger slowly beyond its point of no return. There was no scrap of compassion battling for control behind that eye. It was the eye of a man used to killing.

'Wait! You can't!' Graham rose to his feet. Jason's two accomplices raised their guns to cover whatever move he may be about to make but he remained still.

'Don't do it. We're your family.'

The sheer absurdity of the objection disturbed Jason enough to make him tilt his head towards where Graham now stood, five yards away, though his arm remained outstretched and poised. Andreas lifted his gaze from the ground, no longer simply waiting for the inescapable finality of his last conscious moment, and also looked over.

'Your mother, Sarah, was my girlfriend when we were at uni together in Leeds and we only slept together once but ...well, we stopped seeing each other shortly after and that was my fault but I never knew she was, you know, until you snatched me from the car park yesterday and she told me what happened to her. I had no idea why she left uni so suddenly until then but she told me I was your father and so you can't do this. I'm your father and Andreas is ...your half-brother.'

'What?' said Jason, incredulously.

'What?' said Andreas, equally incredulously.

'We're all made, partly at least, from the same genetic material. We have the same blood. We share the same ancestral lineage. We're spurs off the same family line which can be traced back centuries and centuries through generations and generations and that means that we may be different people but, essentially, we are the same. We're part of the same story.'

'What the fuck are you talking about?' said Jason, scornfully. 'This is bollocks.'

He turned again to face Andreas and his finger tightened on the trigger.

'No, it's true! You ask your mother. She was Sarah Collins when I knew her and she was about a month younger than me, so her 57th birthday was in February. I took her to her first real gig, I bought her a book of Philip Larkin poetry and I got her into watching *Coronation Street* on the telly. She said her parents never allowed her to watch soap operas when she lived at home. She had a dog called Bruce, which stuck in my mind because I was a huge fan of Springsteen at the time, and has a scar on her forearm from falling off her bike when she was a little girl. She never used to wear short sleeves because she was so self-conscious about it.'

Graham held his breath, desperate for evidence that one of his burbled random Sarah facts had penetrated Jason's hardened mind and registered a spark of recognition.

The eyes widened. The finger eased. The gun was lowered.

'So you're saying you were the one who got my mum pregnant, then ran off and left her and ruined her life?'

It was not the interpretation of the new information

Graham was hoping for.

'Well, not exactly. I didn't intend to cause her trouble. I didn't know she was pregnant. If she'd told me, I would have done the right thing but I didn't know. It was the same with Andreas and his mother.'

He instantly regretted adding the last part.

Jason spun to face Andreas again. 'He got your mum pregnant and left her as well?'

Andreas nodded, meekly.

'I only meant it was the same in that I had no idea I'd fathered one child, never mind two, and that if I'd known about either of you I would have tried to be a proper father to you. I regret what happened but I can't change the past. None of us can change the past; we can only influence the future. Please don't do anything hasty now that you might regret later.'

Jason hung his head. He was wrestling with his thoughts. Graham had given him a dilemma. There was the faintest chink of hope for them.

'All my life I've dreamed about being able to get my hands on the bastard who ruined my mother's life,' he reflected, sullenly. 'She could have been dead in a ditch, as far as you were concerned, and that's where she might have ended up if it wasn't for Polecat. He was my real dad. We made it through despite what you did and now you expect me to give you a great big hug and call you daddy?'

He pointed the gun at Andreas again.

'And him. You have the nerve to say he's my brother? What have I got in common with this bloated, privileged fat fucker who's never had to fight and graft for anything in his life? He's not my brother. These two...' He gestured with a flashing dart of his simmering eyes towards the two gunmen on either side of him. 'These two are my brothers because we've killed for each other and we'd die for each other if we had to. They're my family.

'You two are nothing to me. You're the kind of people who've never done anything other than look down on the likes of me for my whole life and you want me to let you go? Let you go so you can run straight to the coppers? No way. You don't deserve to live. You deserve to die.'

With a defiant roar and in one last vain attempt to escape the seeming inevitability now closing in on them, Andreas hurled himself towards Jason but he could not close the ground between them quickly enough. A gunshot stopped his attempt and silenced his cry, the bullet striking his skull above the right eye and exiting in an explosive plume of blood as his body was propelled backwards to skid across the loose gravel before stopping close to the spot he had begun his final, useless attempt to grapple life from the teeth of death.

Graham watched the despairing move and its gruesome outcome in paralysed silence. He felt the shockwave of the impact of Andreas's limp corpse as it rose momentarily and slumped to the ground with an empty thud. He stared, transfixed, as the first oozing trickle of dark liquid seeped from the back of his son's skull to soak into the dirty ground.

He turned his gaze to face Jason again, unable to comprehend what his eyes had just shown him, only to see the gun now pointing at him and to feel the tear of the small pellet as it cracked into his ribcage and lodged in his spine, the force of it knocking him off his feet. He crumpled, his head rebounding as it struck the stony floor before coming to rest, leaving his unblinking eyes peering sightlessly towards the darkening skies.

From the distance, the sound of sirens penetrated the echoes of gunfire.

'Jase, come on! Let's go!'

The three gunmen jumped in their car and sped away.

As the spray of dust from their tyres settled in the still late summer air, it fell on the body, lying flat on the ground, of a man in his late-fifties whose thin greying hair was now flecked with dirt, his metal-rimmed glasses displaced and by his side. His chest rose slowly, fractionally, as the final laboured beats of his punctured heart pumped blood through a compact wound, disguising the point of entry with a spreading dark patch on his light shirt.

In those last, fading moments of his life he had no thoughts for those who had gone before him, their names saved from being lost in time by the diligence of his research. He had no thoughts for those yet to come or whether his name would one day be recalled and immortalised too. He had only one thought.

He thought of Janet.

Acknowledgements

It felt like a considerable personal achievement to see my first novel, *Sunbeam*, through to publication. The whole experience taught me a lot about myself as a writer and I learned many new skills through the stages of self-publishing, publicity and marketing.

But it was far from a lonely process and I am again hugely grateful to everyone who has helped in the production of *Family Business*.

Good research is always important and I received excellent guidance from Mark Lewis, Shaun Howe, Andy Summerfield and Alun Smith. Alun and the rest of the team at Meachers Global Logistics in Derby were especially invaluable. His patience in explaining how their business works allowed me to form a template for the haulage company in *Family Business*, though I'm certain no such shady goings-on ever happened at Meachers!

I must also give belated thanks to Helen Balfour for her advice on *Sunbeam*. Sorry for the oversight.

Family and friends have been exceptionally supportive throughout and I appreciate every kind and constructively critical word that has been offered. One of the real bonuses of this venture has been the opportunity to make new friends, whose input has proved so useful, but I must also offer thanks to those new friends I have not yet met.

I said before releasing *Sunbeam* that I would regard it a triumph if only one person I did not know read my book and enjoyed it and I have since confirmed that this is, indeed, the biggest compliment of all. To everyone who took the time to get in touch or write a review, I can only say that your efforts mean so much.

Nicky Lovick's editing skills and Andrew Rainnie's cover design helped see this through to the finished product. You've both been great to work with.

Writing a second novel has been less of a discovery but every bit as much of a joy. To everyone who has contributed to that, thank you very much for arming me with the confidence to complete this and other projects to come.

Also by Mark Eklid

Sunbeam
Published November 2019

John Baldwin has been on a downward spiral to self-destruction since the day he witnessed the murder of his best friend, Stef. It has cost him his marriage, his business and his dignity.

One year on from the day that turned his world upside down, he sees Stef again. John fears he has finally lost his mind but Stef is there to pull his friend back from the brink, not tip him over it. He offers John a fresh start; a new destiny.

John rebuilds his life. He has everything again but there is a price to pay. The killer is still on the loose and Stef wants revenge.

Reviews for Sunbeam

A plot that is so full of unexpected twists and turns that the reader is left guessing until the final page.
Derbyshire Life magazine

This was a cracking read.
Andy Angel, book blog review

Eklid tells a good tale and the smooth writing had me racing to see what was going to happen next.
Colman Keane, Reedsy Discovery review

A massive five stars from me, loved it.
Anita Waller, author

Don't worry about what genre it is, it sits across many. Just read it and enjoy.
Marilyn Pemberton, author

Sunbeam is an excellent first novel. The writing was superb; wordsmithery at its best.
Ralph Jones, author

Sunbeam had me from page one right through to the ending, which left me wondering... for days.
Moira Hodgkinson, author

More twists and turns than a Scalextric race track and couldn't wait to get to the end to find out what happens.
Clare Naylor, Amazon review

This is not just a novel that provides a great read, but one that will make you think beyond the last page.
Tracy Holmes, Amazon review

What a fantastic book - up there as mainstream and could easily compete with Linwood Barclay and the like.
V G Wilcox, Amazon review

One of the best books I've read in a very long time.
Harris, Amazon review

To find out where to buy Sunbeam and for news of all of the author's works, visit his website, markeklid.com

Printed in Poland
by Amazon Fulfillment
Poland Sp. z o.o., Wrocław